Archie.

a rock n roll
romance

Archie®

a rock n roll romance

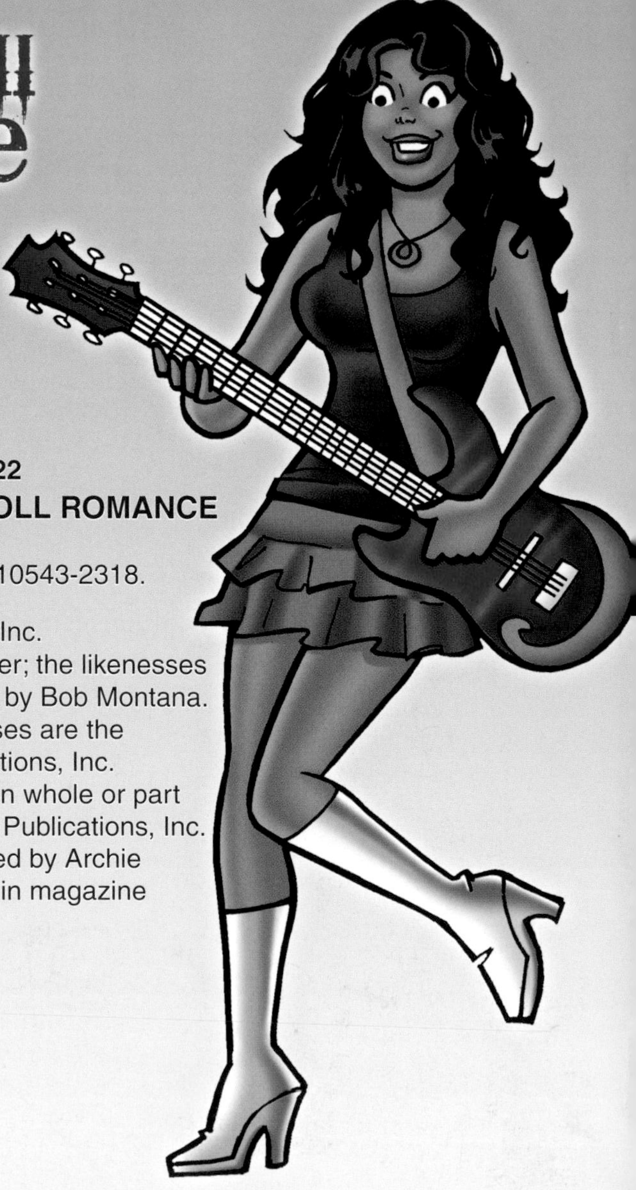

Archie & Friends All-Stars Series: Volume 22
ARCHIE'S VALENTINE: A ROCK 'N' ROLL ROMANCE
Published by Archie Comic Publications, Inc.
325 Fayette Avenue, Mamaroneck, New York 10543-2318.

ISBN: 978-1-936975-33-4

FIRST PRINTING.

Printed in Canada.

Archie

a rock n roll romance

Story & Art by:
Dan Parent

Inking by:
Rich Koslowski

Letters by:
Jack Morelli

Coloring by:
Digikore Studios

Publisher/Co-CEO: Jon Goldwater
Co-CEO: Nancy Silberkleit
President: Mike Pellerito
Co-President/Editor-In-Chief: Victor Gorelick
Senior Vice President - Sales & Business Development: Jim Sokolowski
Senior Vice President - Publishing & Operations: Harold Buchholz
Executive Director of Editorial: Paul Kaminski
Director of Marketing & Publicity: Steven Scott
Production Manager: Stephen Oswald
Project Coordinator & Book Design: Joe Morciglio
Editorial Assistant / Proofreader: Carly Inglis

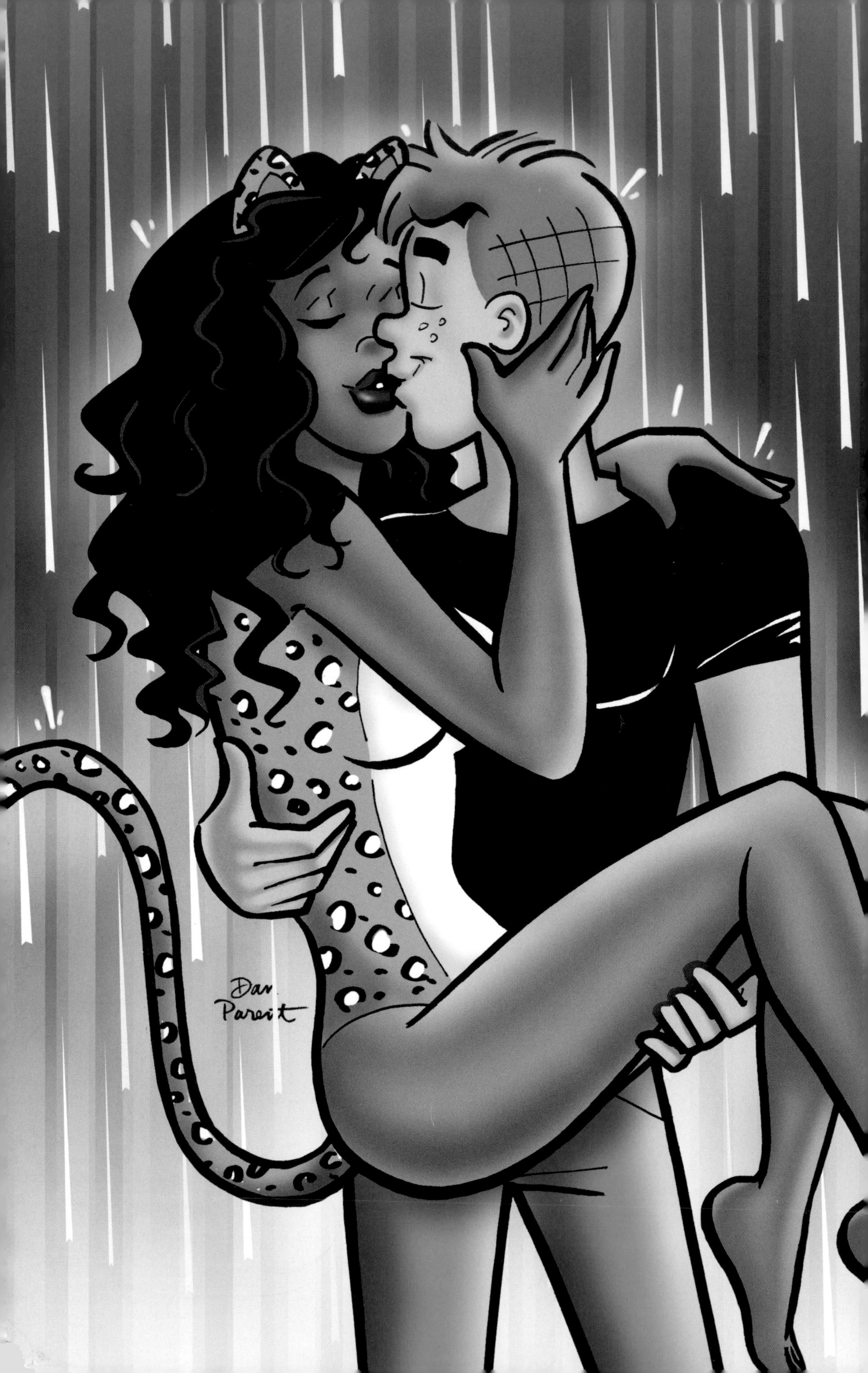
Dan Parent

Chapter One:
Another
Love Song

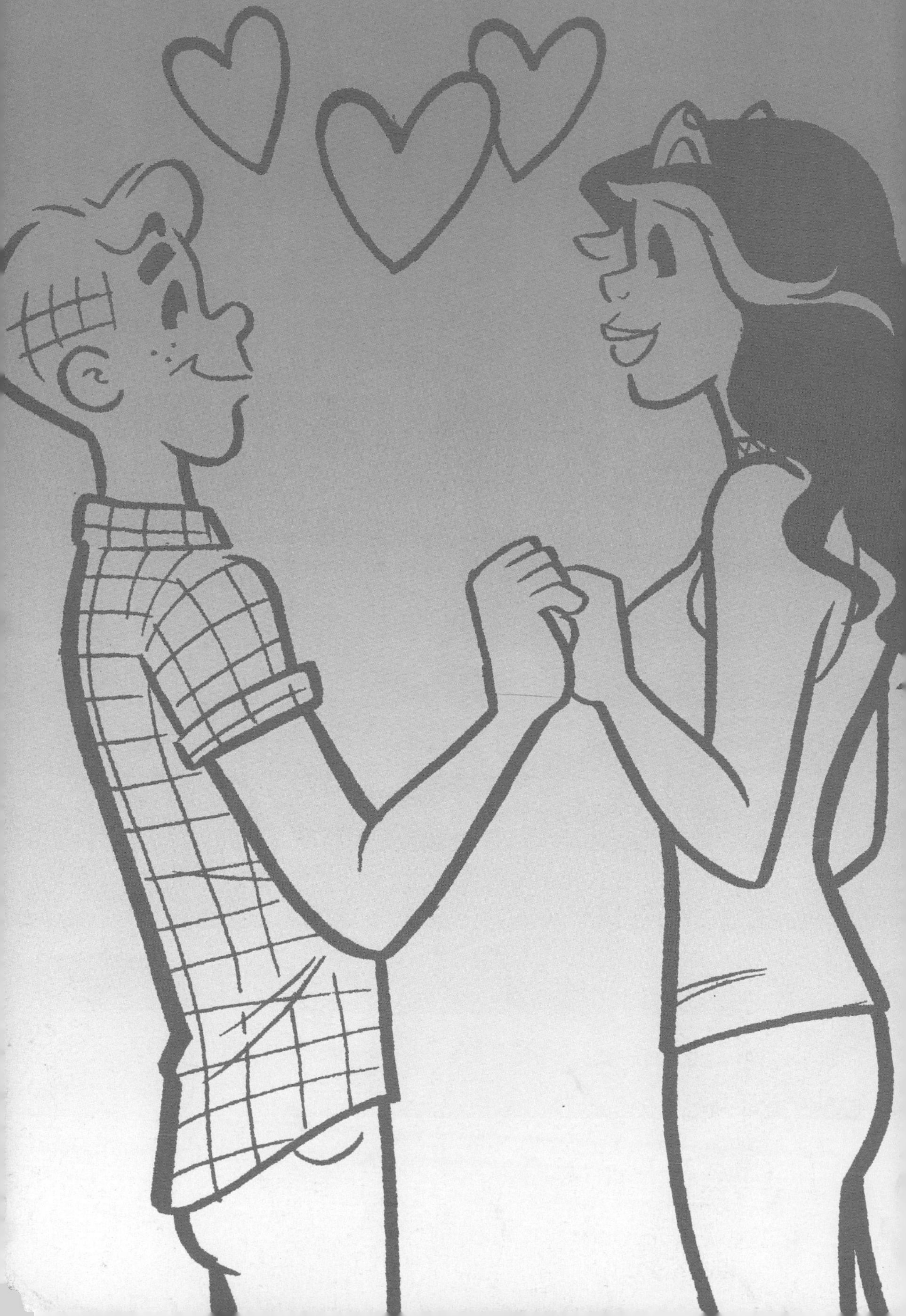

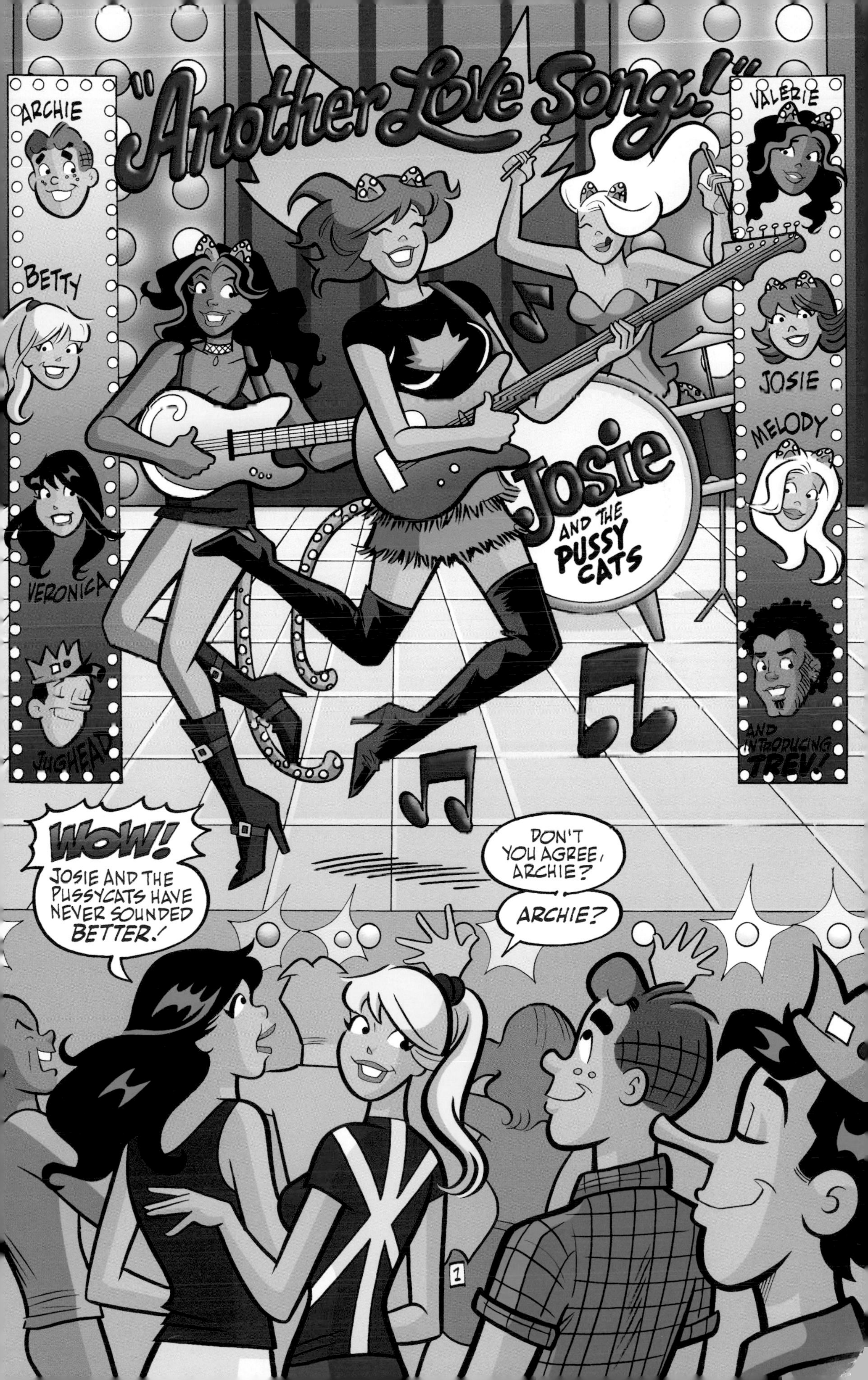
"Another Love Song!"
ARCHIE
BETTY
VERONICA
JUGHEAD
VALERIE
JOSIE
MELODY
AND INTRODUCING TREV!
JOSIE AND THE PUSSY CATS
WOW! JOSIE AND THE PUSSYCATS HAVE NEVER SOUNDED BETTER!
DON'T YOU AGREE, ARCHIE?
ARCHIE?
1

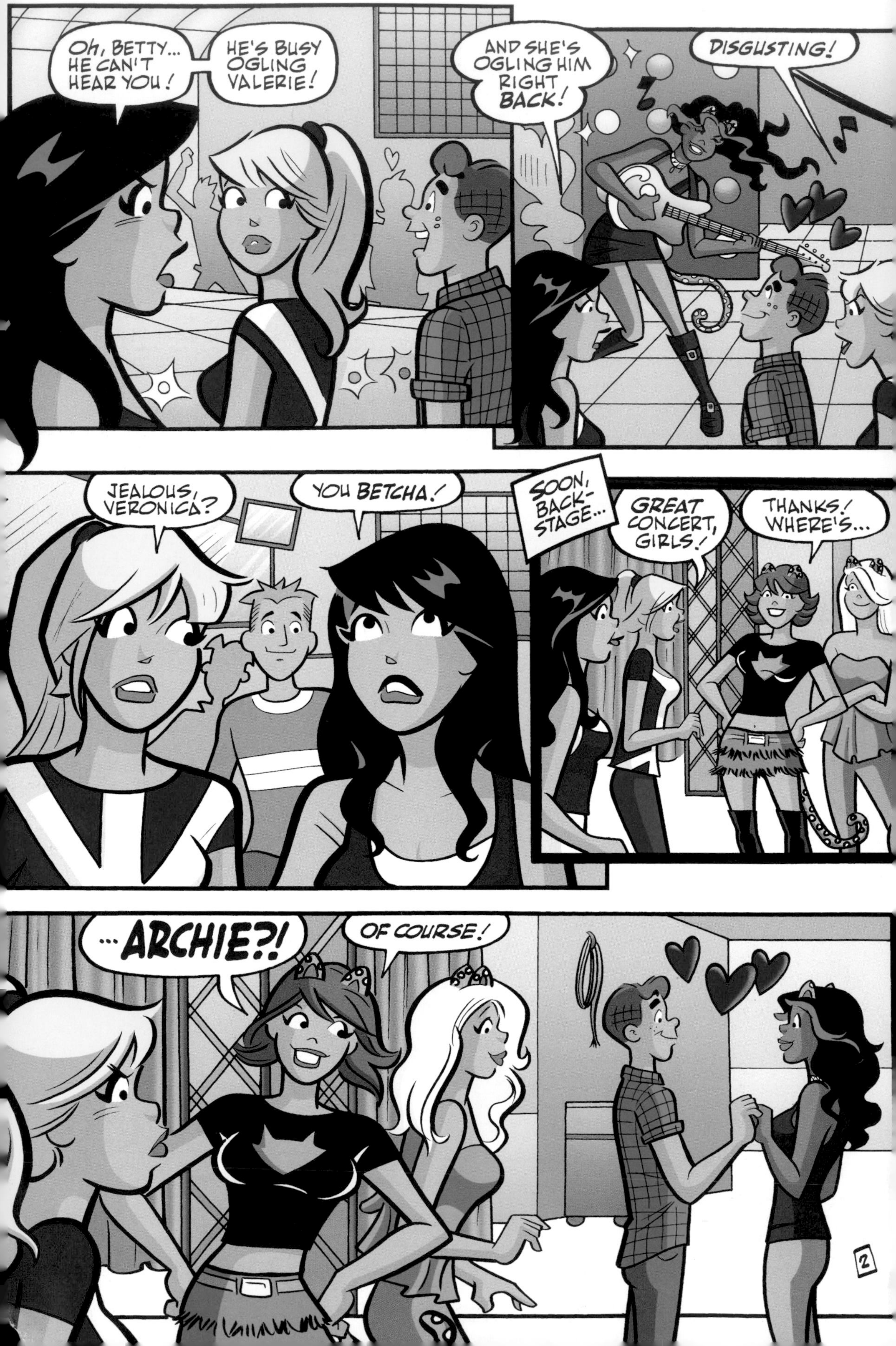

Oh, BETTY... HE CAN'T HEAR YOU!
HE'S BUSY OGLING VALERIE!
AND SHE'S OGLING HIM RIGHT BACK!
DISGUSTING!
JEALOUS, VERONICA?
YOU BETCHA!
SOON, BACK-STAGE...
GREAT CONCERT, GIRLS!
THANKS! WHERE'S...
...ARCHIE?!
OF COURSE!
2

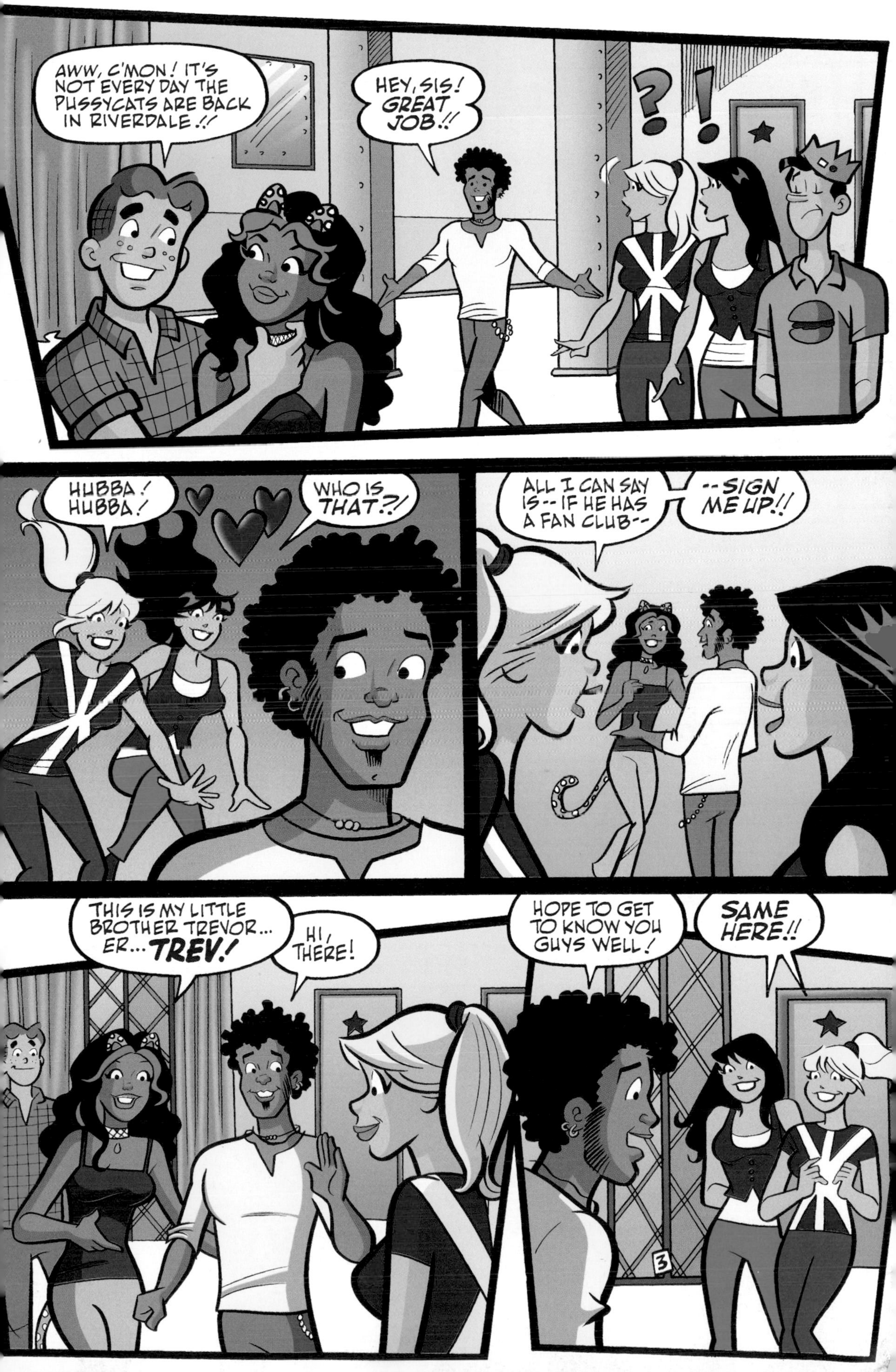
AWW, C'MON! IT'S NOT EVERY DAY THE PUSSYCATS ARE BACK IN RIVERDALE!!
HEY, SIS! GREAT JOB!!
?
!
HUBBA! HUBBA!
WHO IS THAT?!
ALL I CAN SAY IS-- IF HE HAS A FAN CLUB--
--SIGN ME UP!!
THIS IS MY LITTLE BROTHER TREVOR... ER... TREV!
HI, THERE!
HOPE TO GET TO KNOW YOU GUYS WELL!
SAME HERE!!
3

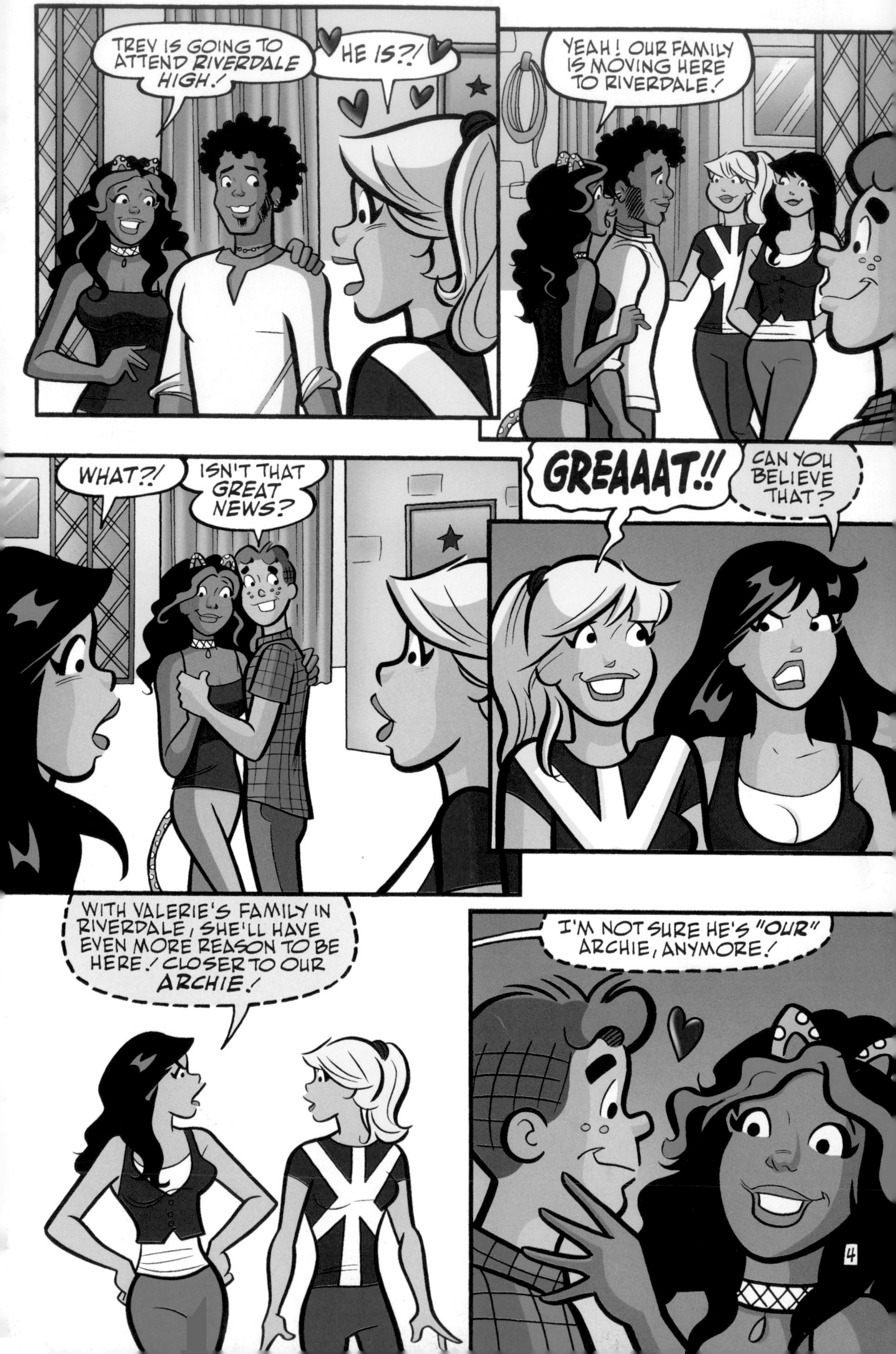

TREV IS GOING TO ATTEND RIVERDALE HIGH!
HE IS?!
YEAH! OUR FAMILY IS MOVING HERE TO RIVERDALE!
WHAT?!
ISN'T THAT GREAT NEWS?
GREAAAT!!
CAN YOU BELIEVE THAT?
WITH VALERIE'S FAMILY IN RIVERDALE, SHE'LL HAVE EVEN MORE REASON TO BE HERE! CLOSER TO OUR ARCHIE!
I'M NOT SURE HE'S "OUR" ARCHIE, ANYMORE!
4

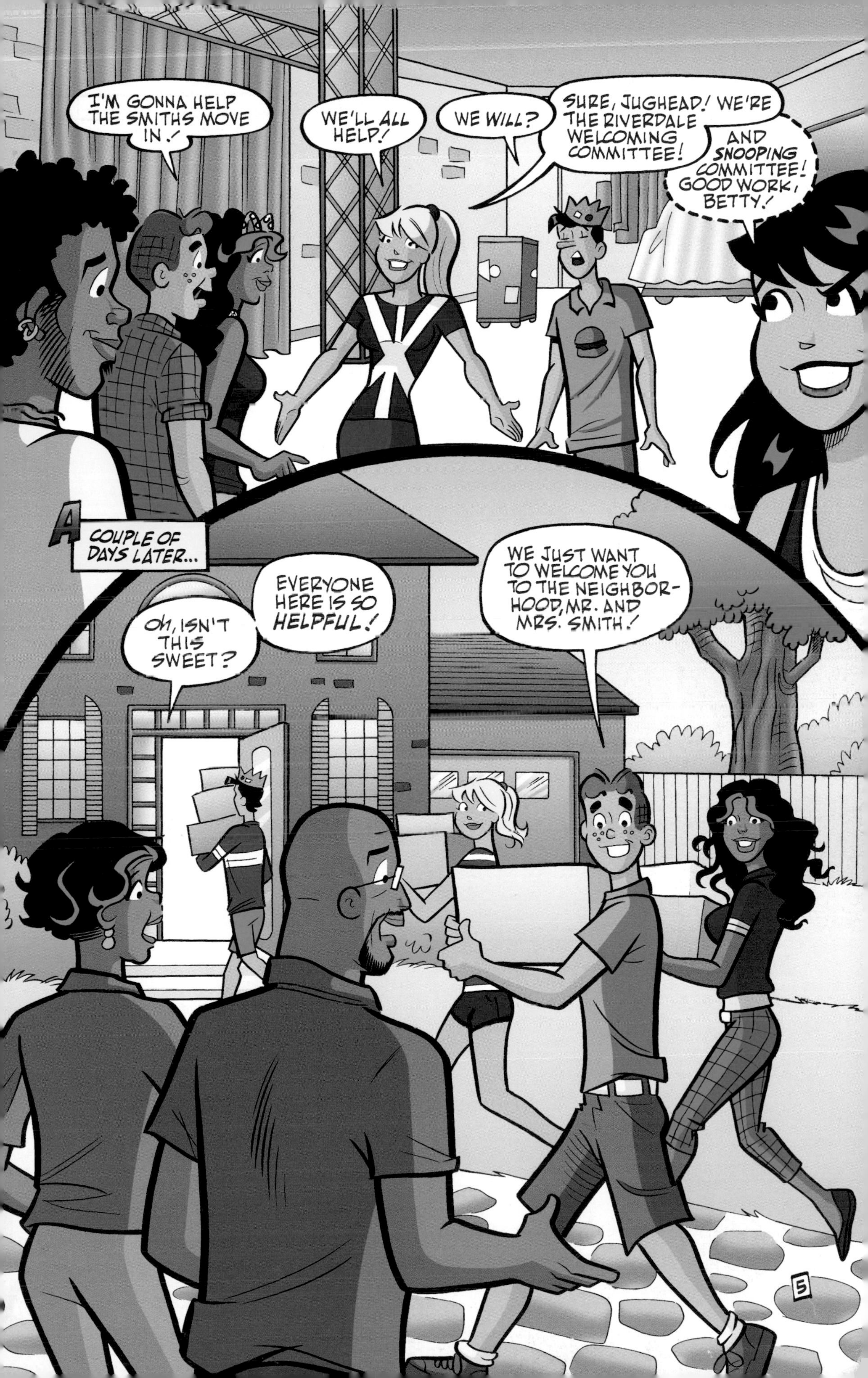

I'M GONNA HELP THE SMITHS MOVE IN!
WE'LL ALL HELP!
WE WILL?
SURE, JUGHEAD! WE'RE THE RIVERDALE WELCOMING COMMITTEE!
AND SNOOPING COMMITTEE! GOOD WORK, BETTY!
A COUPLE OF DAYS LATER...
OH, ISN'T THIS SWEET?
EVERYONE HERE IS SO HELPFUL!
WE JUST WANT TO WELCOME YOU TO THE NEIGHBORHOOD, MR. AND MRS. SMITH!

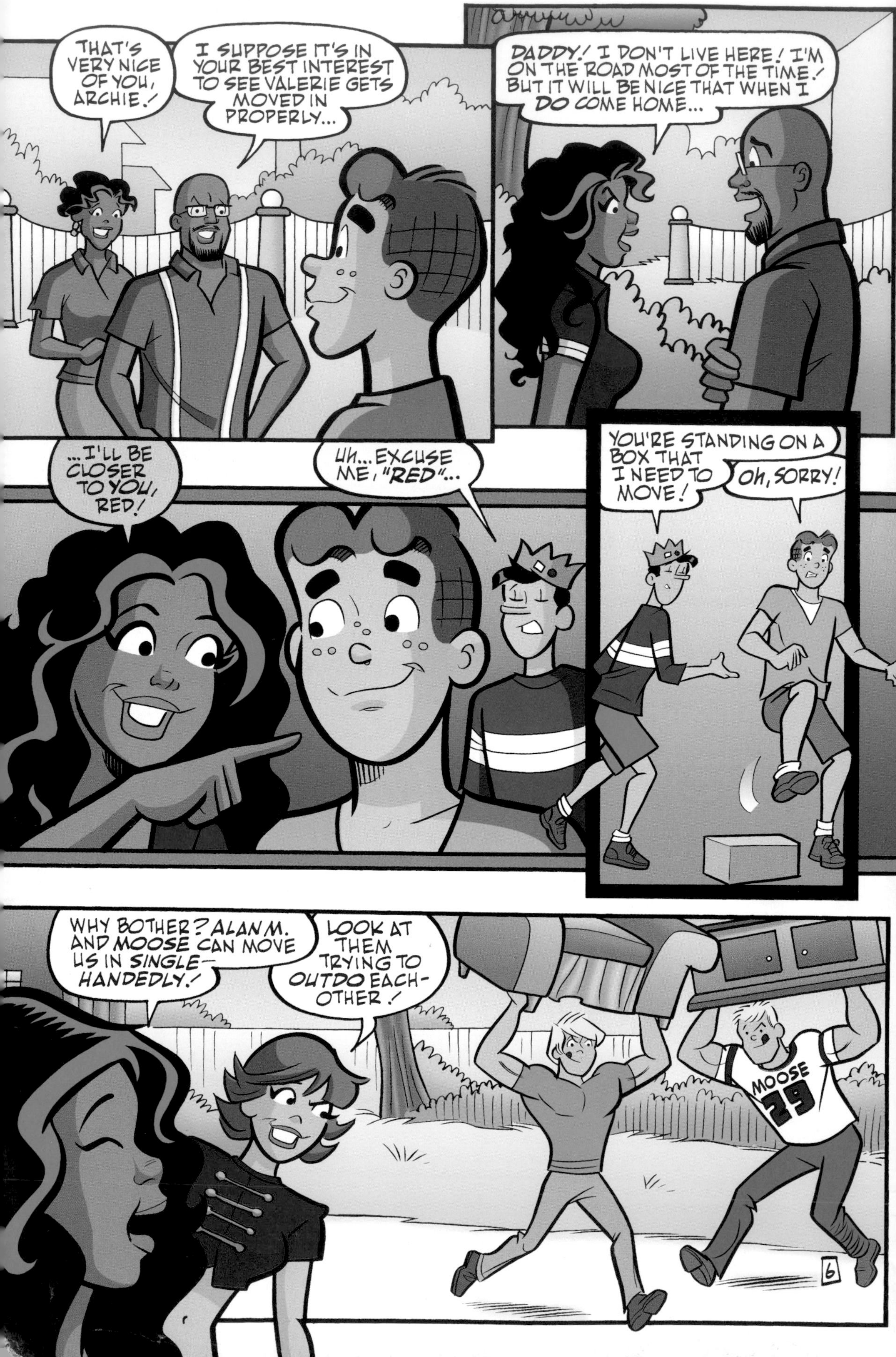
THAT'S VERY NICE OF YOU, ARCHIE!
I SUPPOSE IT'S IN YOUR BEST INTEREST TO SEE VALERIE GETS MOVED IN PROPERLY...
DADDY! I DON'T LIVE HERE! I'M ON THE ROAD MOST OF THE TIME! BUT IT WILL BE NICE THAT WHEN I DO COME HOME...
...I'LL BE CLOSER TO YOU, RED!
Uh... EXCUSE ME, "RED"...
YOU'RE STANDING ON A BOX THAT I NEED TO MOVE!
Oh, SORRY!
WHY BOTHER? ALAN M. AND MOOSE CAN MOVE US IN SINGLE-HANDEDLY!
LOOK AT THEM TRYING TO OUTDO EACH-OTHER!
MOOSE
29
6

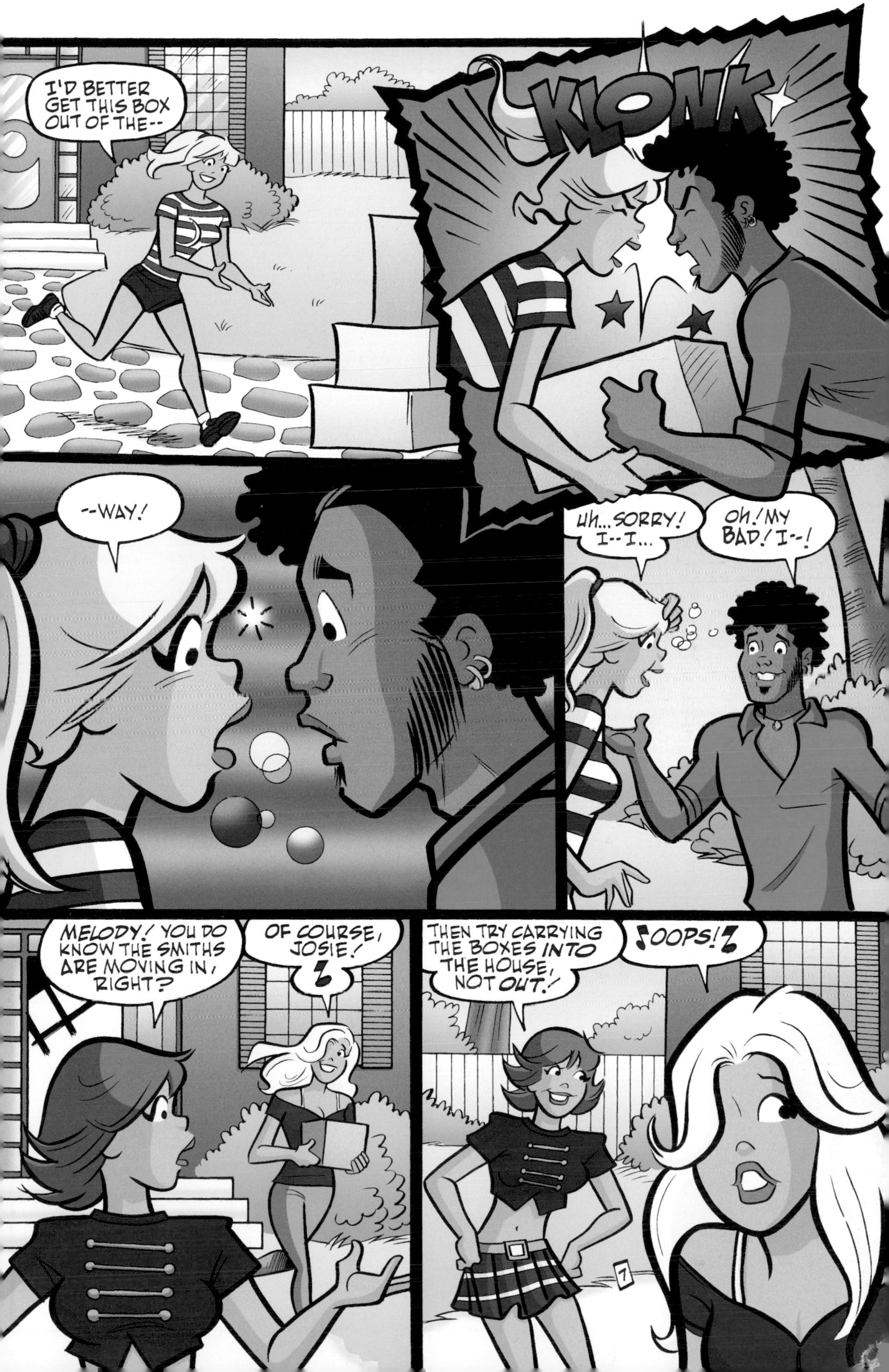

I'D BETTER GET THIS BOX OUT OF THE--
KLONK
--WAY!
uh... SORRY! I--I...
Oh! MY BAD! I--!
MELODY! YOU DO KNOW THE SMITHS ARE MOVING IN, RIGHT?
OF COURSE, JOSIE!
THEN TRY CARRYING THE BOXES INTO THE HOUSE, NOT OUT!
OOPS!
7

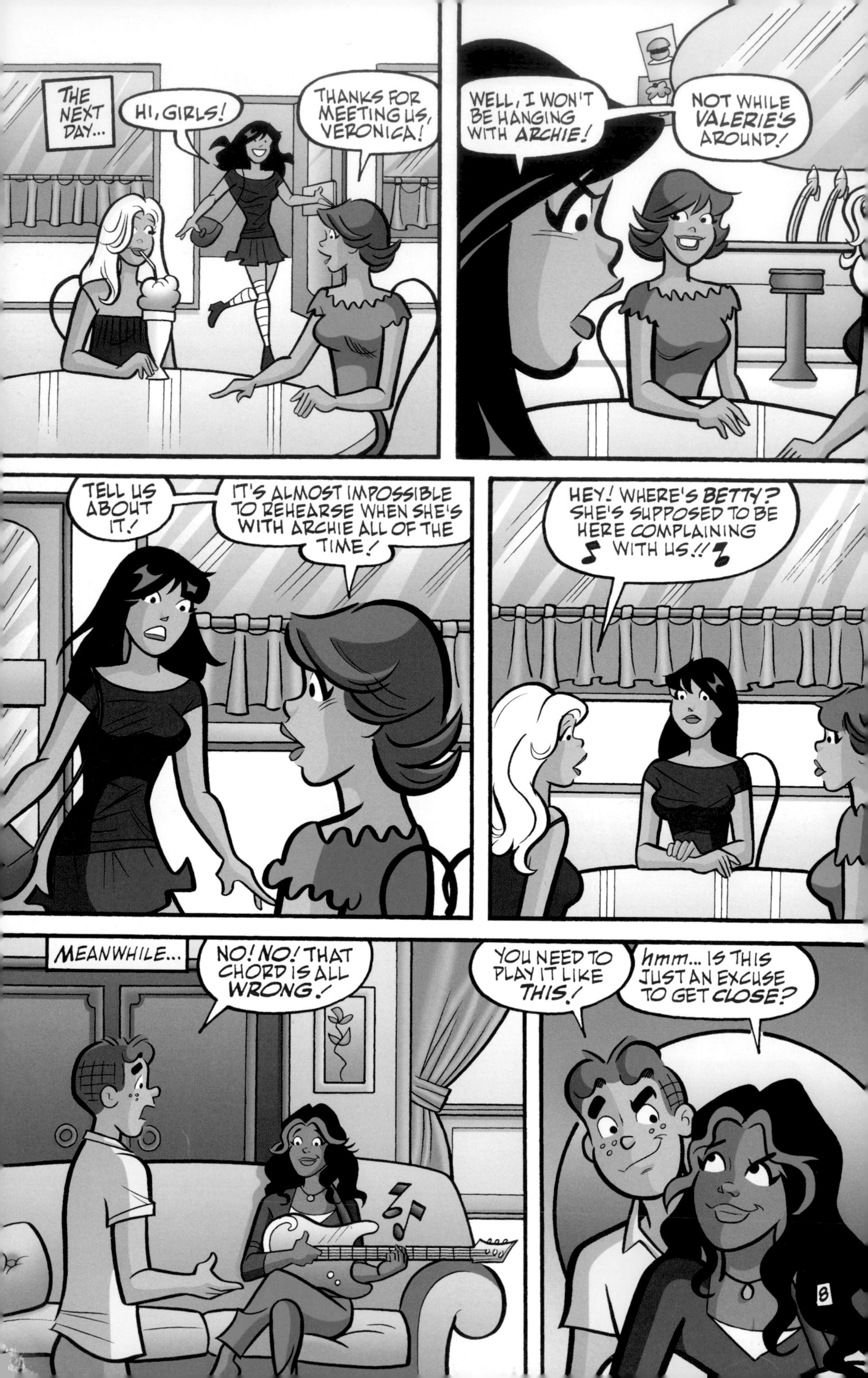
THE NEXT DAY...
HI, GIRLS!
THANKS FOR MEETING US, VERONICA!
WELL, I WON'T BE HANGING WITH ARCHIE!
NOT WHILE VALERIE'S AROUND!
TELL US ABOUT IT!
IT'S ALMOST IMPOSSIBLE TO REHEARSE WHEN SHE'S WITH ARCHIE ALL OF THE TIME!
HEY! WHERE'S BETTY? SHE'S SUPPOSED TO BE HERE COMPLAINING WITH US!!
MEANWHILE...
NO! NO! THAT CHORD IS ALL WRONG!
YOU NEED TO PLAY IT LIKE THIS!
hmm... IS THIS JUST AN EXCUSE TO GET CLOSE?
8

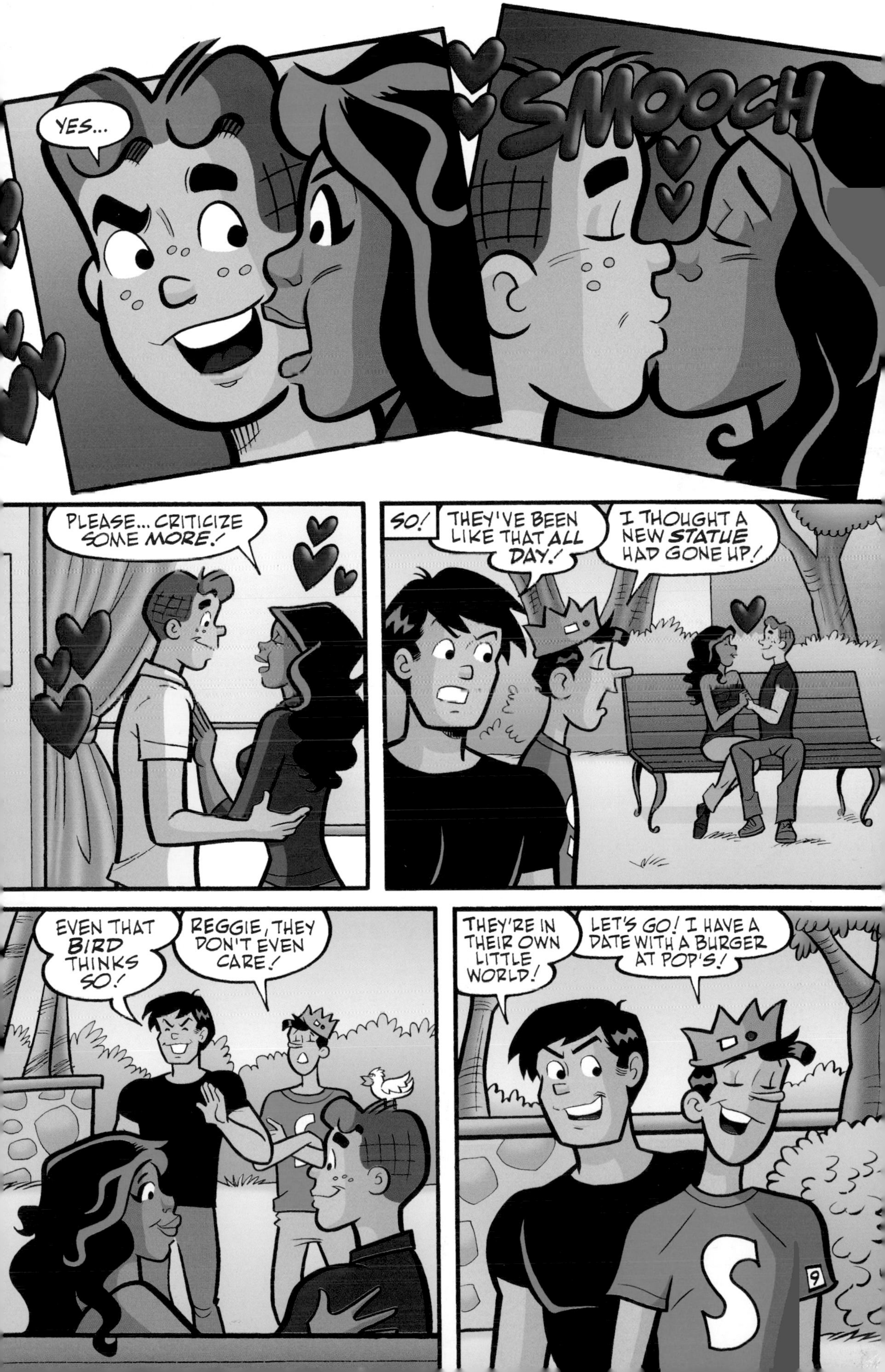
YES...
SMOOCH
PLEASE... CRITICIZE SOME MORE!
SO!
THEY'VE BEEN LIKE THAT ALL DAY!
I THOUGHT A NEW STATUE HAD GONE UP!
EVEN THAT BIRD THINKS SO!
REGGIE, THEY DON'T EVEN CARE!
THEY'RE IN THEIR OWN LITTLE WORLD!
LET'S GO! I HAVE A DATE WITH A BURGER AT POP'S!
S
9

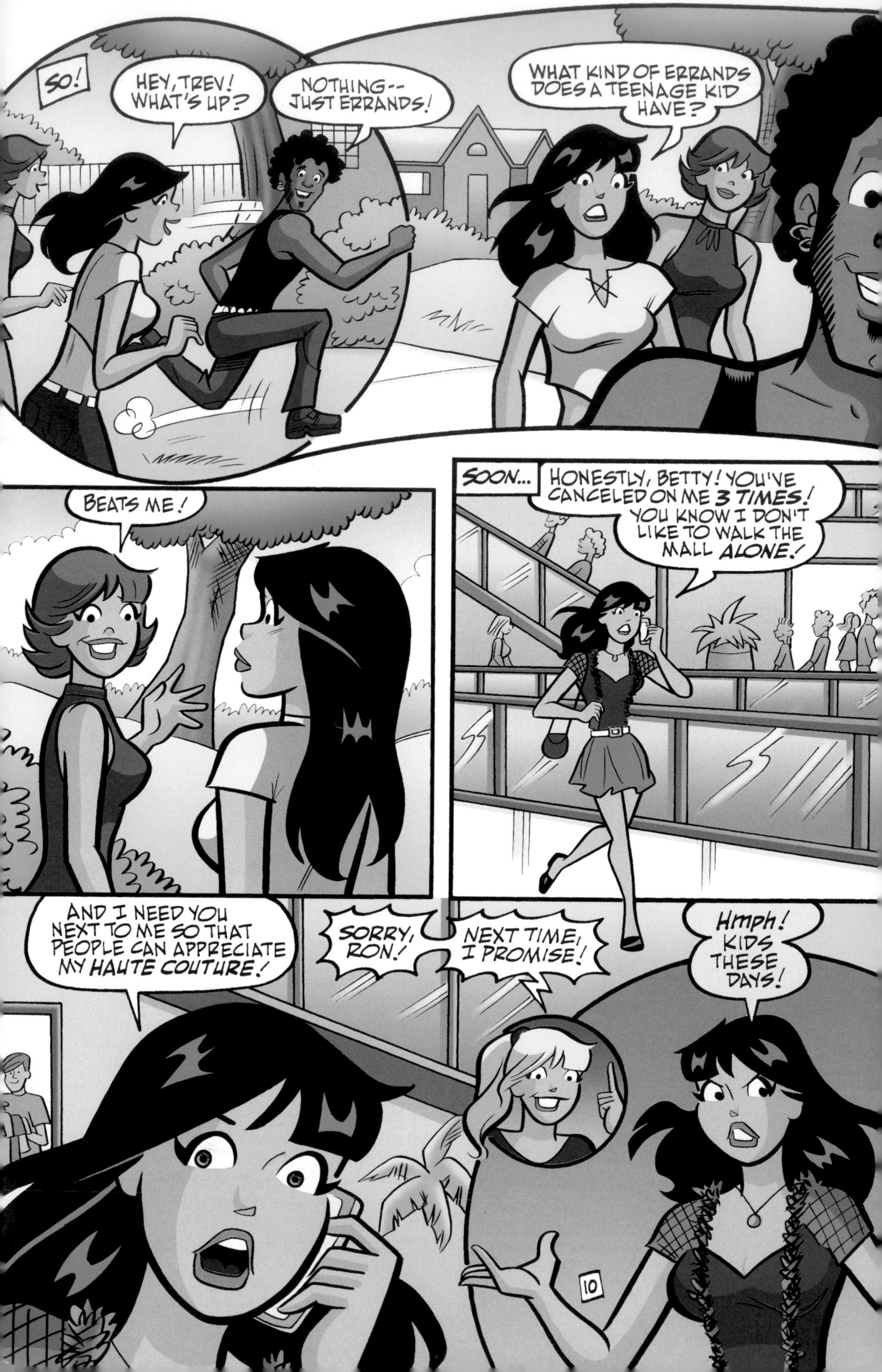
SO!
HEY, TREV! WHAT'S UP?
NOTHING-- JUST ERRANDS!
WHAT KIND OF ERRANDS DOES A TEENAGE KID HAVE?
BEATS ME!
SOON...
HONESTLY, BETTY! YOU'VE CANCELED ON ME 3 TIMES! YOU KNOW I DON'T LIKE TO WALK THE MALL ALONE!
AND I NEED YOU NEXT TO ME SO THAT PEOPLE CAN APPRECIATE MY HAUTE COUTURE!
SORRY, RON!
NEXT TIME, I PROMISE!
Hmph! KIDS THESE DAYS!
10

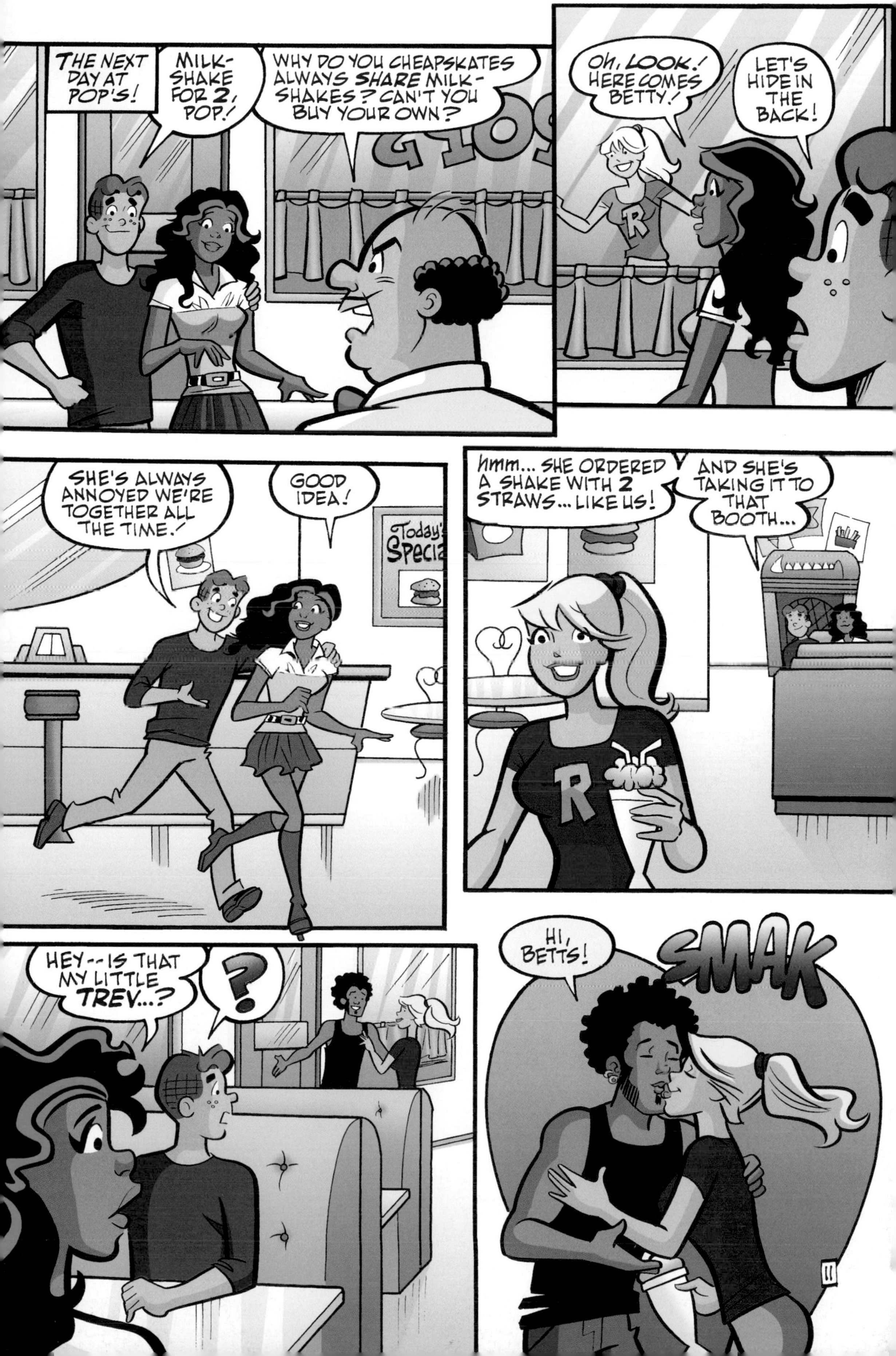
THE NEXT DAY AT POP'S!
MILK-SHAKE FOR 2, POP!
WHY DO YOU CHEAPSKATES ALWAYS SHARE MILK-SHAKES? CAN'T YOU BUY YOUR OWN?
POP'S
Oh, LOOK! HERE COMES BETTY!
LET'S HIDE IN THE BACK!
SHE'S ALWAYS ANNOYED WE'RE TOGETHER ALL THE TIME!
GOOD IDEA!
Today's Specia
hmm... SHE ORDERED A SHAKE WITH 2 STRAWS... LIKE US!
AND SHE'S TAKING IT TO THAT BOOTH...
R
HEY--IS THAT MY LITTLE TREV...?
?
HI, BETTS!
SMAK
11

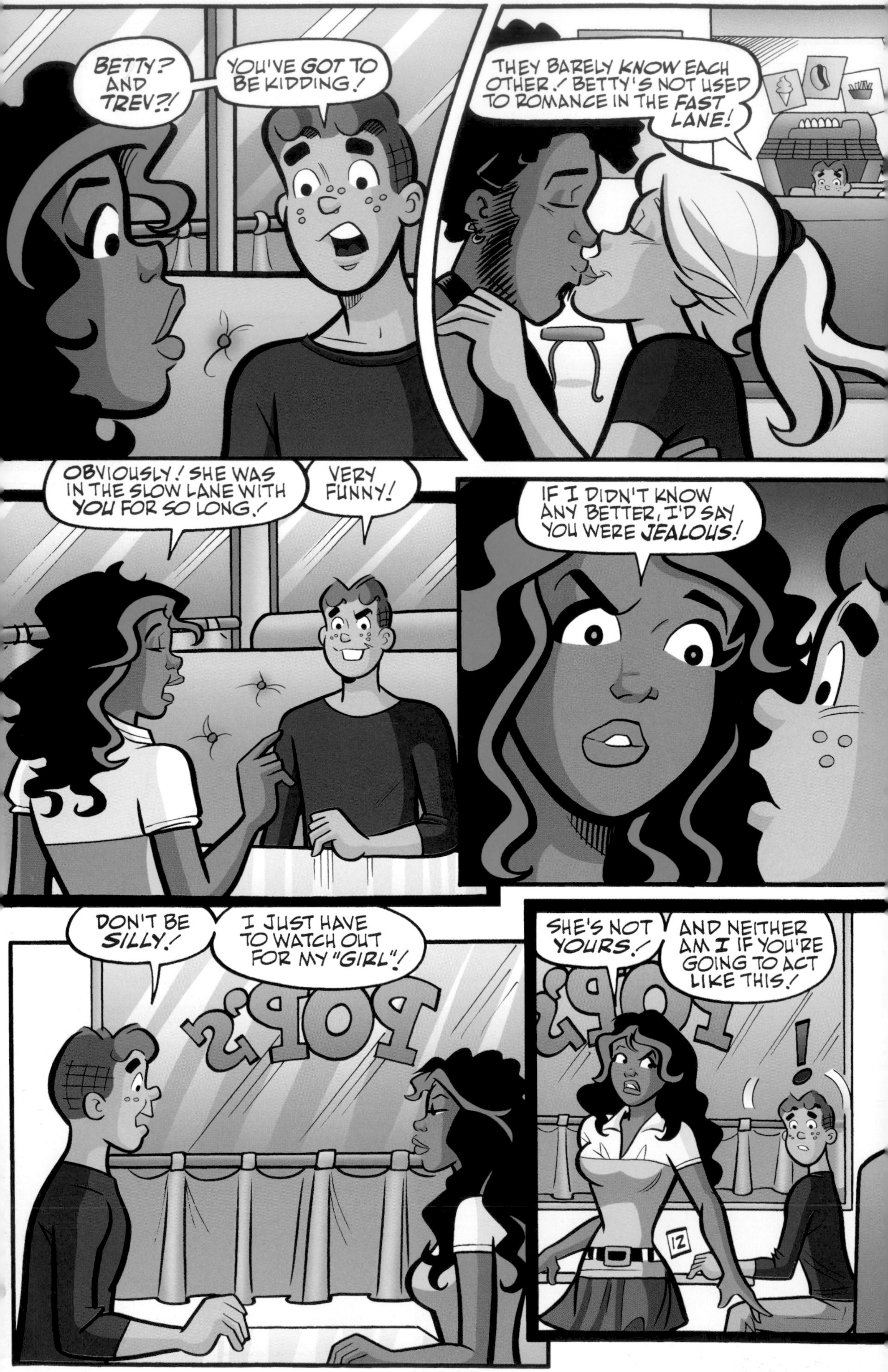
BETTY? AND TREV?!
YOU'VE GOT TO BE KIDDING!
THEY BARELY KNOW EACH OTHER! BETTY'S NOT USED TO ROMANCE IN THE FAST LANE!
OBVIOUSLY! SHE WAS IN THE SLOW LANE WITH YOU FOR SO LONG!
VERY FUNNY!
IF I DIDN'T KNOW ANY BETTER, I'D SAY YOU WERE JEALOUS!
DON'T BE SILLY!
I JUST HAVE TO WATCH OUT FOR MY "GIRL"!
POP'S
SHE'S NOT YOURS!
AND NEITHER AM I IF YOU'RE GOING TO ACT LIKE THIS!
!
12

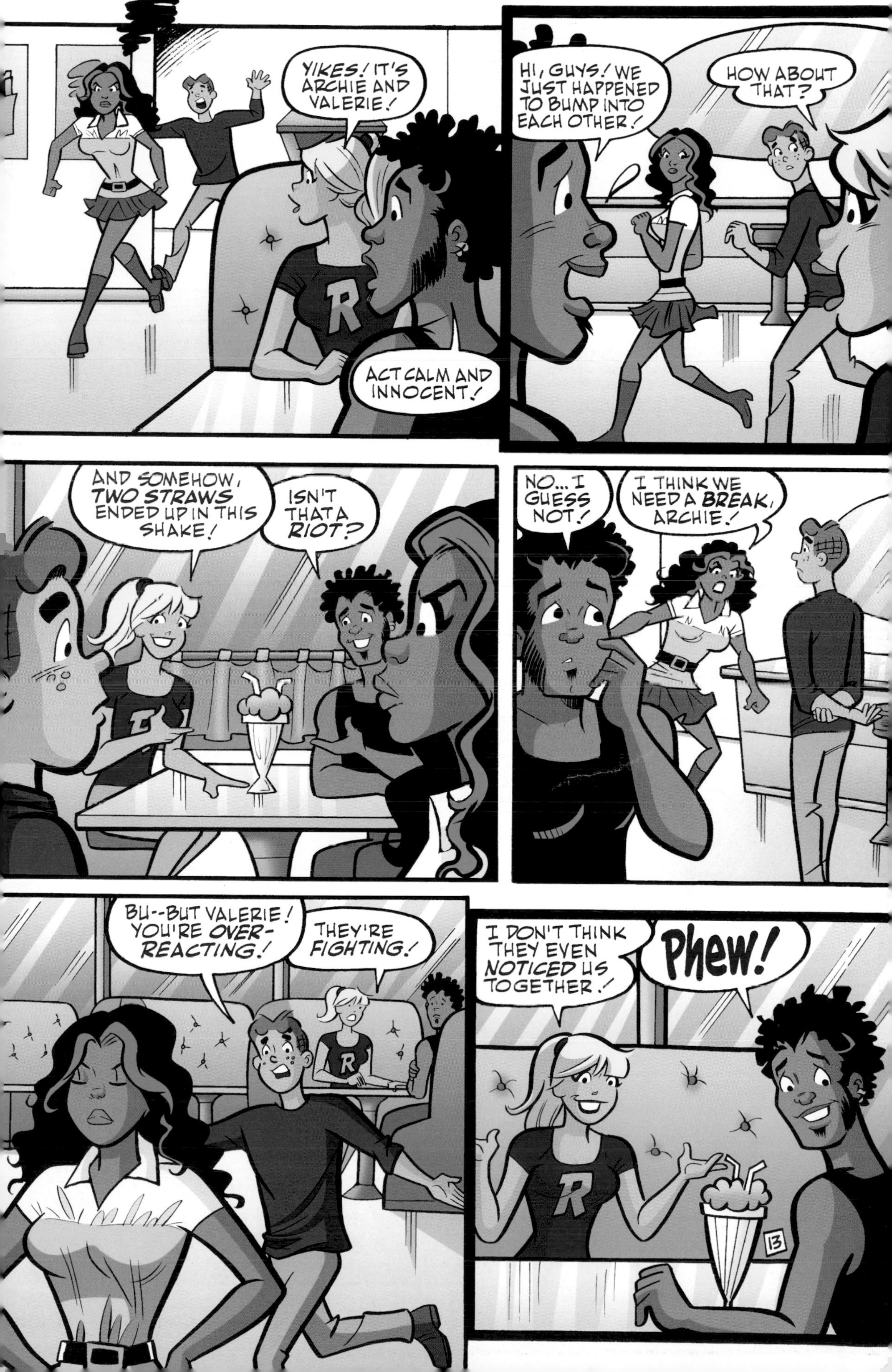
YIKES! IT'S ARCHIE AND VALERIE!
ACT CALM AND INNOCENT!
HI, GUYS! WE JUST HAPPENED TO BUMP INTO EACH OTHER!
HOW ABOUT THAT?
AND SOMEHOW, TWO STRAWS ENDED UP IN THIS SHAKE!
ISN'T THAT A RIOT?
NO... I GUESS NOT!
I THINK WE NEED A BREAK, ARCHIE!
BU--BUT VALERIE! YOU'RE OVER-REACTING!
THEY'RE FIGHTING!
I DON'T THINK THEY EVEN NOTICED US TOGETHER.
Phew!
13

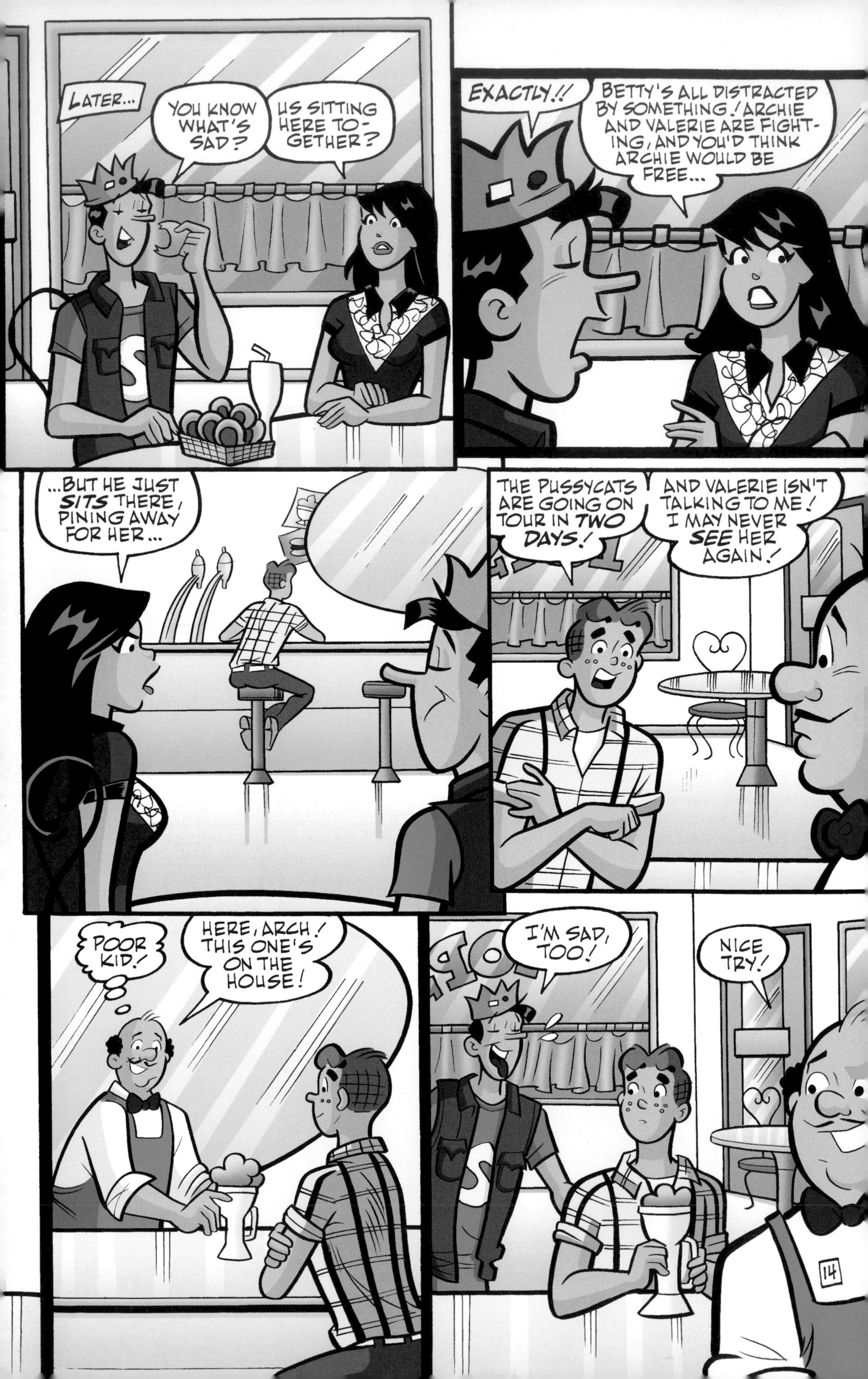
LATER...
YOU KNOW WHAT'S SAD?
US SITTING HERE TOGETHER?
EXACTLY!!
BETTY'S ALL DISTRACTED BY SOMETHING! ARCHIE AND VALERIE ARE FIGHTING, AND YOU'D THINK ARCHIE WOULD BE FREE...
...BUT HE JUST SITS THERE, PINING AWAY FOR HER...
THE PUSSYCATS ARE GOING ON TOUR IN TWO DAYS!
AND VALERIE ISN'T TALKING TO ME! I MAY NEVER SEE HER AGAIN!
POOR KID!
HERE, ARCH! THIS ONE'S ON THE HOUSE!
I'M SAD, TOO!
NICE TRY!
14

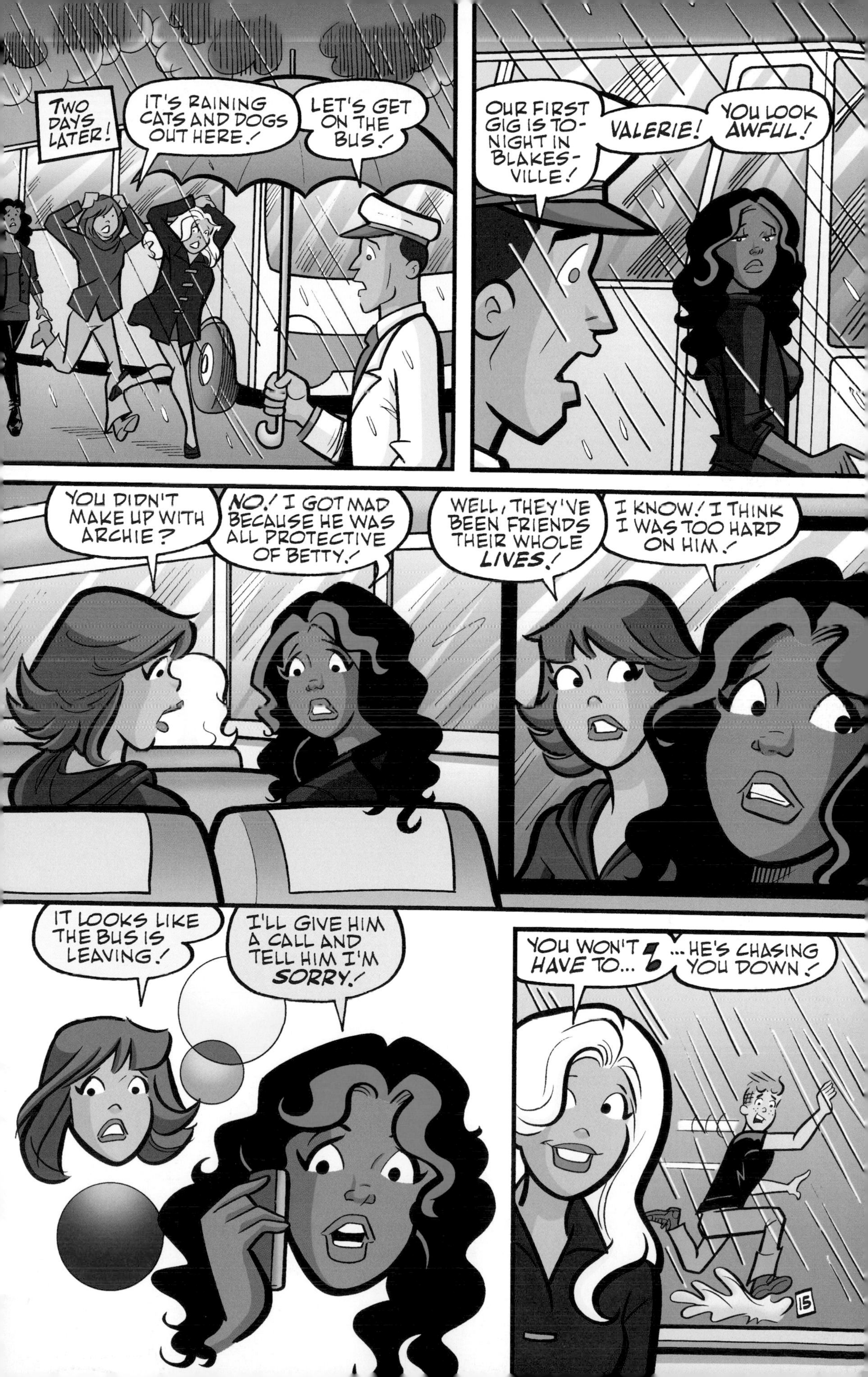

TWO DAYS LATER!
IT'S RAINING CATS AND DOGS OUT HERE!
LET'S GET ON THE BUS!
OUR FIRST GIG IS TO-NIGHT IN BLAKES-VILLE!
VALERIE!
YOU LOOK AWFUL!
YOU DIDN'T MAKE UP WITH ARCHIE?
NO! I GOT MAD BECAUSE HE WAS ALL PROTECTIVE OF BETTY!
WELL, THEY'VE BEEN FRIENDS THEIR WHOLE LIVES!
I KNOW! I THINK I WAS TOO HARD ON HIM!
IT LOOKS LIKE THE BUS IS LEAVING!
I'LL GIVE HIM A CALL AND TELL HIM I'M SORRY!
YOU WON'T HAVE TO...
...HE'S CHASING YOU DOWN!
15

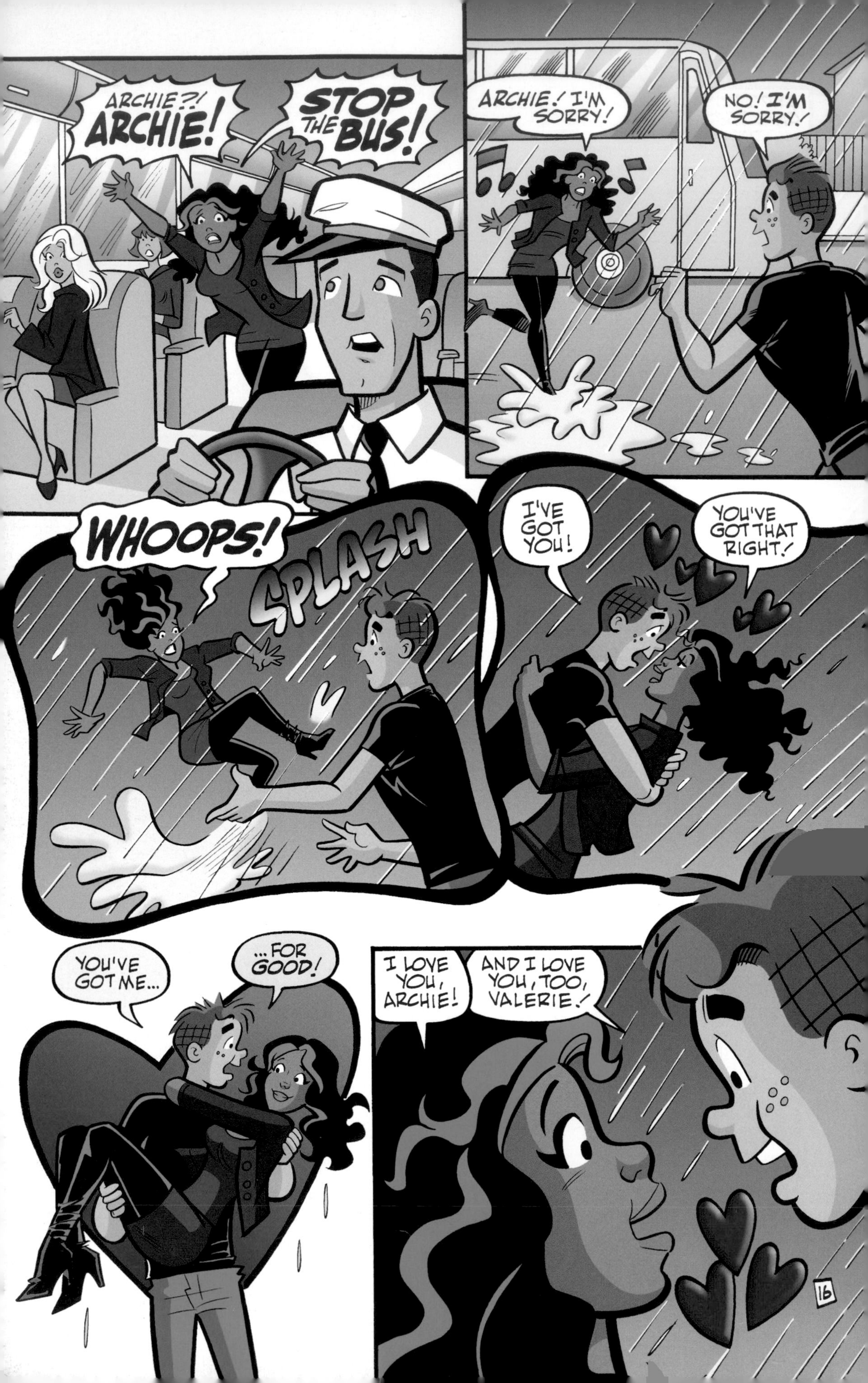
ARCHIE?! ARCHIE!
STOP THE BUS!
ARCHIE! I'M SORRY!
NO! I'M SORRY!
WHOOPS!
SPLASH
I'VE GOT YOU!
YOU'VE GOT THAT RIGHT!
YOU'VE GOT ME...
...FOR GOOD!
I LOVE YOU, ARCHIE!
AND I LOVE YOU, TOO, VALERIE!

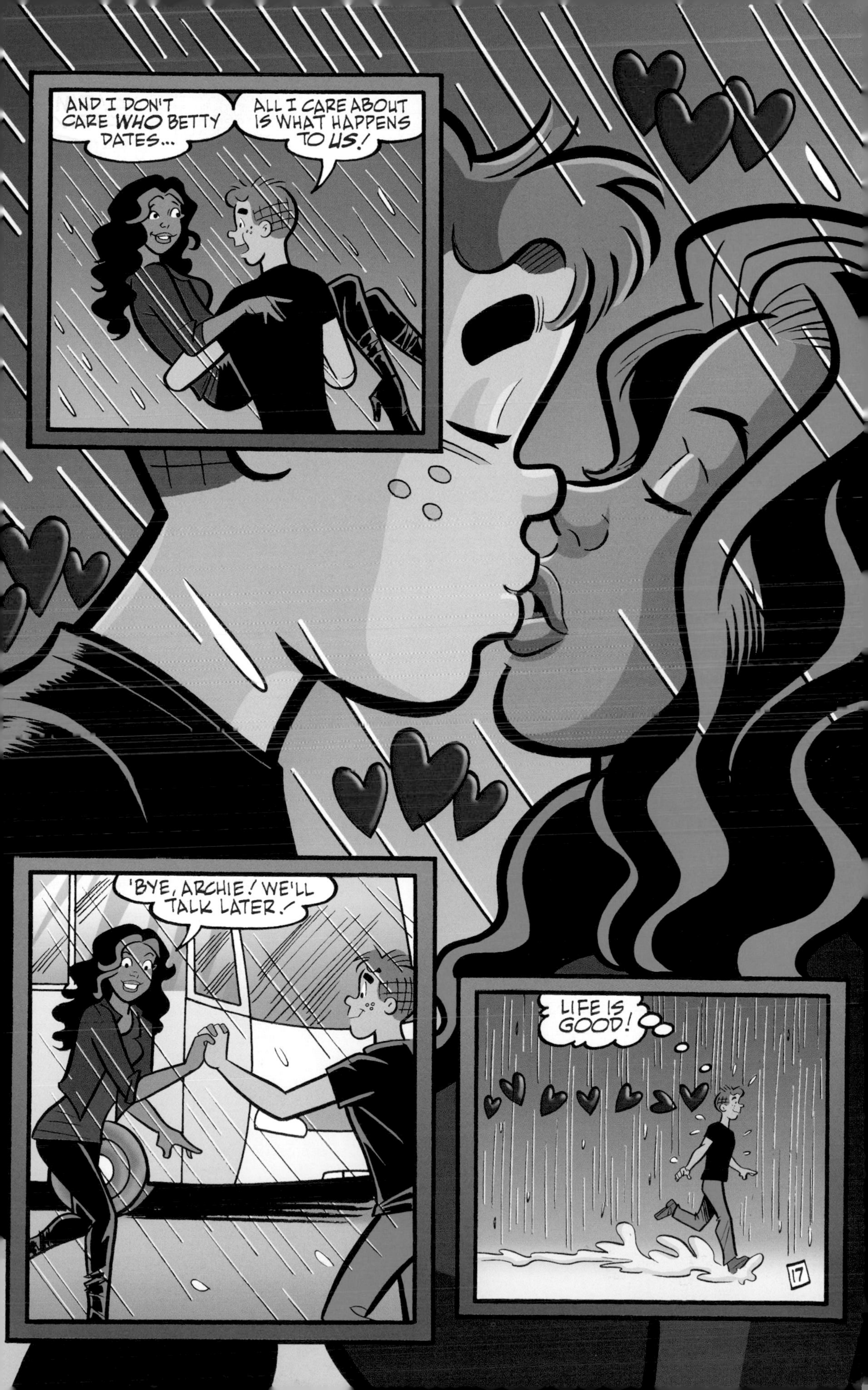
AND I DON'T CARE WHO BETTY DATES...
ALL I CARE ABOUT IS WHAT HAPPENS TO US!
'BYE, ARCHIE! WE'LL TALK LATER!
LIFE IS GOOD!
17

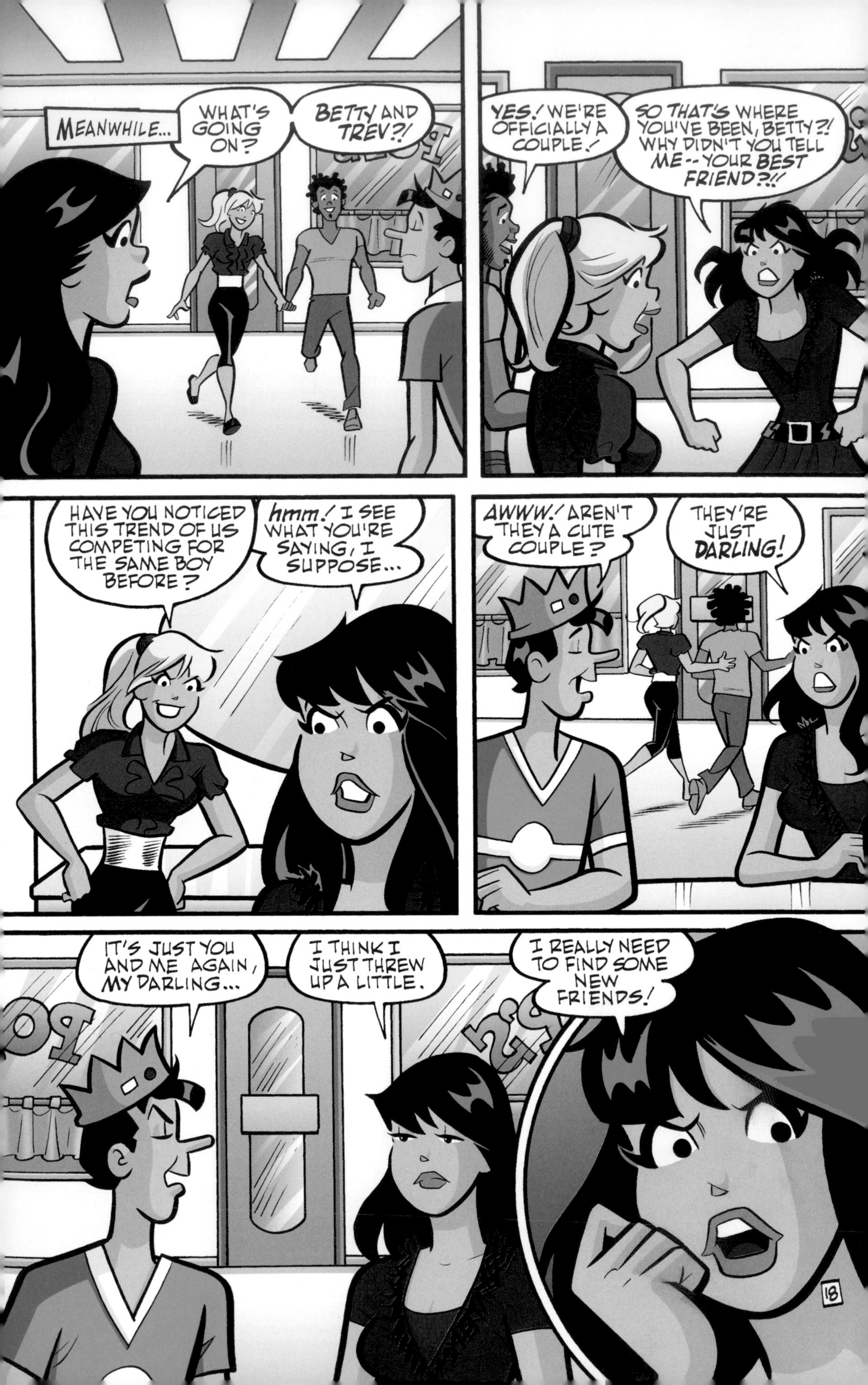
MEANWHILE...
WHAT'S GOING ON?
BETTY AND TREV?!
YES! WE'RE OFFICIALLY A COUPLE!
SO THAT'S WHERE YOU'VE BEEN, BETTY?! WHY DIDN'T YOU TELL ME -- YOUR BEST FRIEND?!!
HAVE YOU NOTICED THIS TREND OF US COMPETING FOR THE SAME BOY BEFORE?
hmm! I SEE WHAT YOU'RE SAYING, I SUPPOSE...
AWWW! AREN'T THEY A CUTE COUPLE?
THEY'RE JUST DARLING!
IT'S JUST YOU AND ME AGAIN, MY DARLING...
I THINK I JUST THREW UP A LITTLE.
I REALLY NEED TO FIND SOME NEW FRIENDS!
18

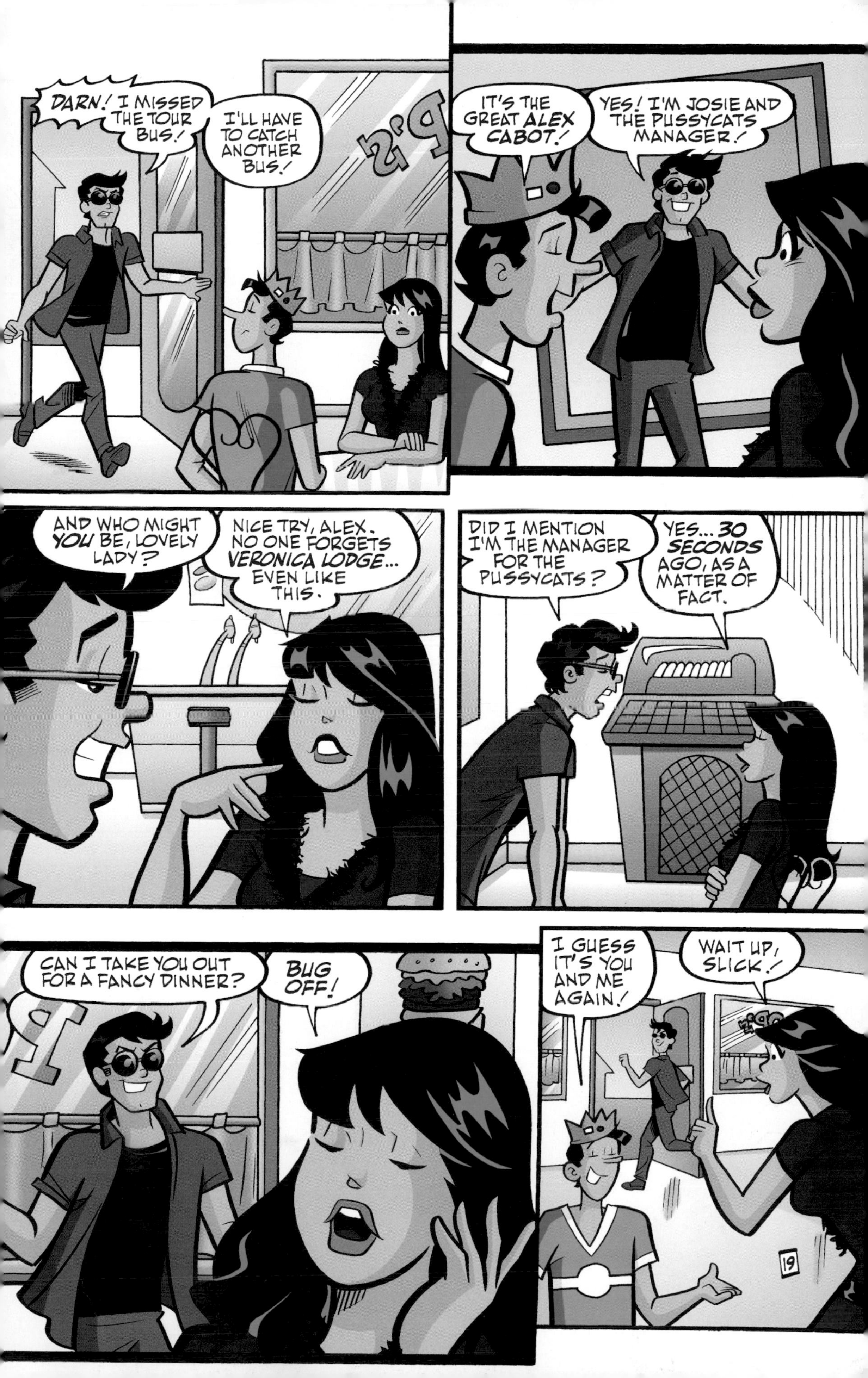
DARN! I MISSED THE TOUR BUS!
I'LL HAVE TO CATCH ANOTHER BUS!
IT'S THE GREAT ALEX CABOT!
YES! I'M JOSIE AND THE PUSSYCATS MANAGER!
AND WHO MIGHT YOU BE, LOVELY LADY?
NICE TRY, ALEX. NO ONE FORGETS VERONICA LODGE... EVEN LIKE THIS.
DID I MENTION I'M THE MANAGER FOR THE PUSSYCATS?
YES... 30 SECONDS AGO, AS A MATTER OF FACT.
CAN I TAKE YOU OUT FOR A FANCY DINNER?
BUG OFF!
I GUESS IT'S YOU AND ME AGAIN!
WAIT UP, SLICK!
19

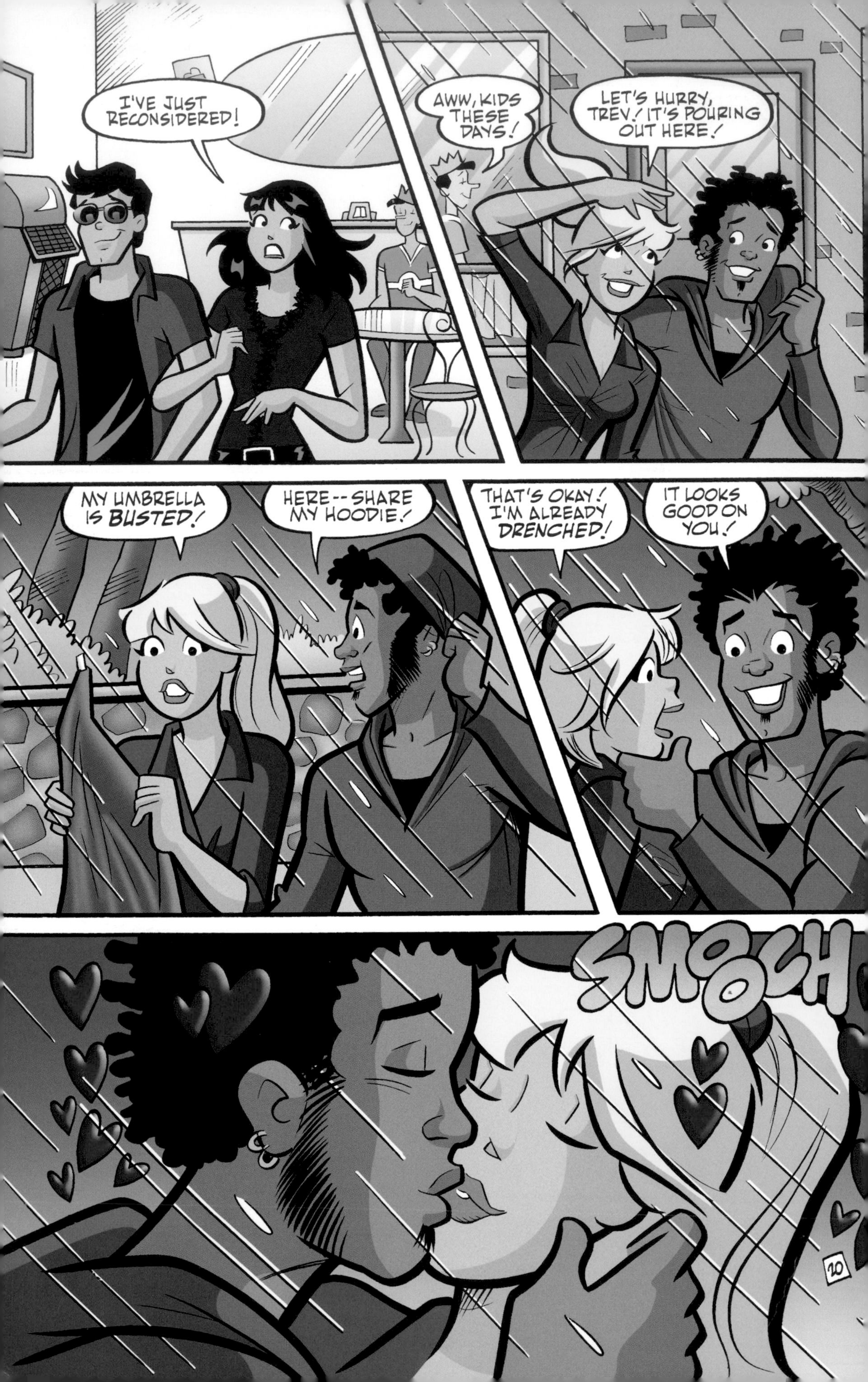
I'VE JUST RECONSIDERED!
AWW, KIDS THESE DAYS!
LET'S HURRY, TREV! IT'S POURING OUT HERE!
MY UMBRELLA IS BUSTED!
HERE-- SHARE MY HOODIE!
THAT'S OKAY! I'M ALREADY DRENCHED!
IT LOOKS GOOD ON YOU!
SMOOCH
20

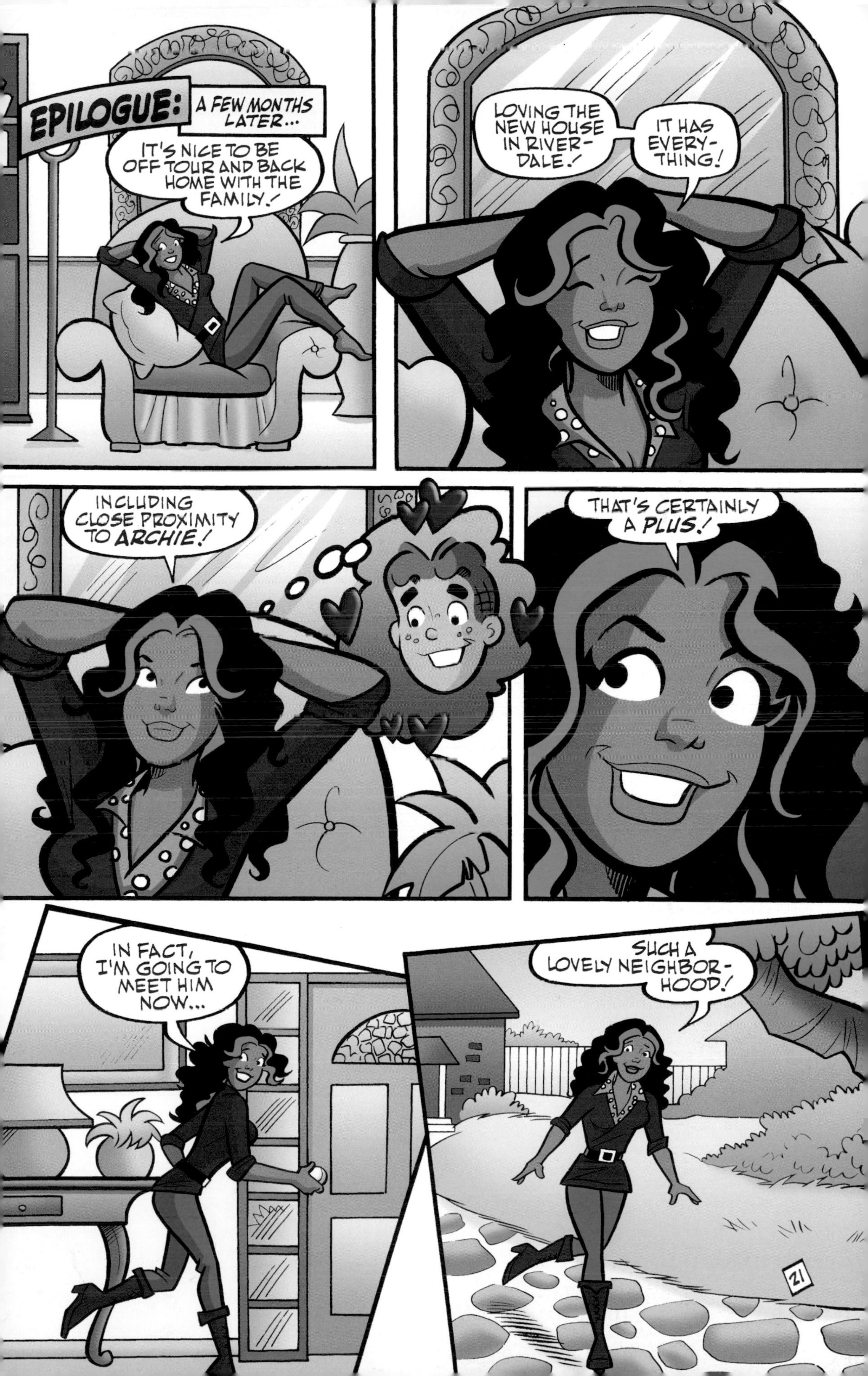
EPILOGUE:
A FEW MONTHS LATER...
IT'S NICE TO BE OFF TOUR AND BACK HOME WITH THE FAMILY!
LOVING THE NEW HOUSE IN RIVER-DALE!
IT HAS EVERY-THING!
INCLUDING CLOSE PROXIMITY TO ARCHIE!
THAT'S CERTAINLY A PLUS!
IN FACT, I'M GOING TO MEET HIM NOW...
SUCH A LOVELY NEIGHBOR-HOOD!
21

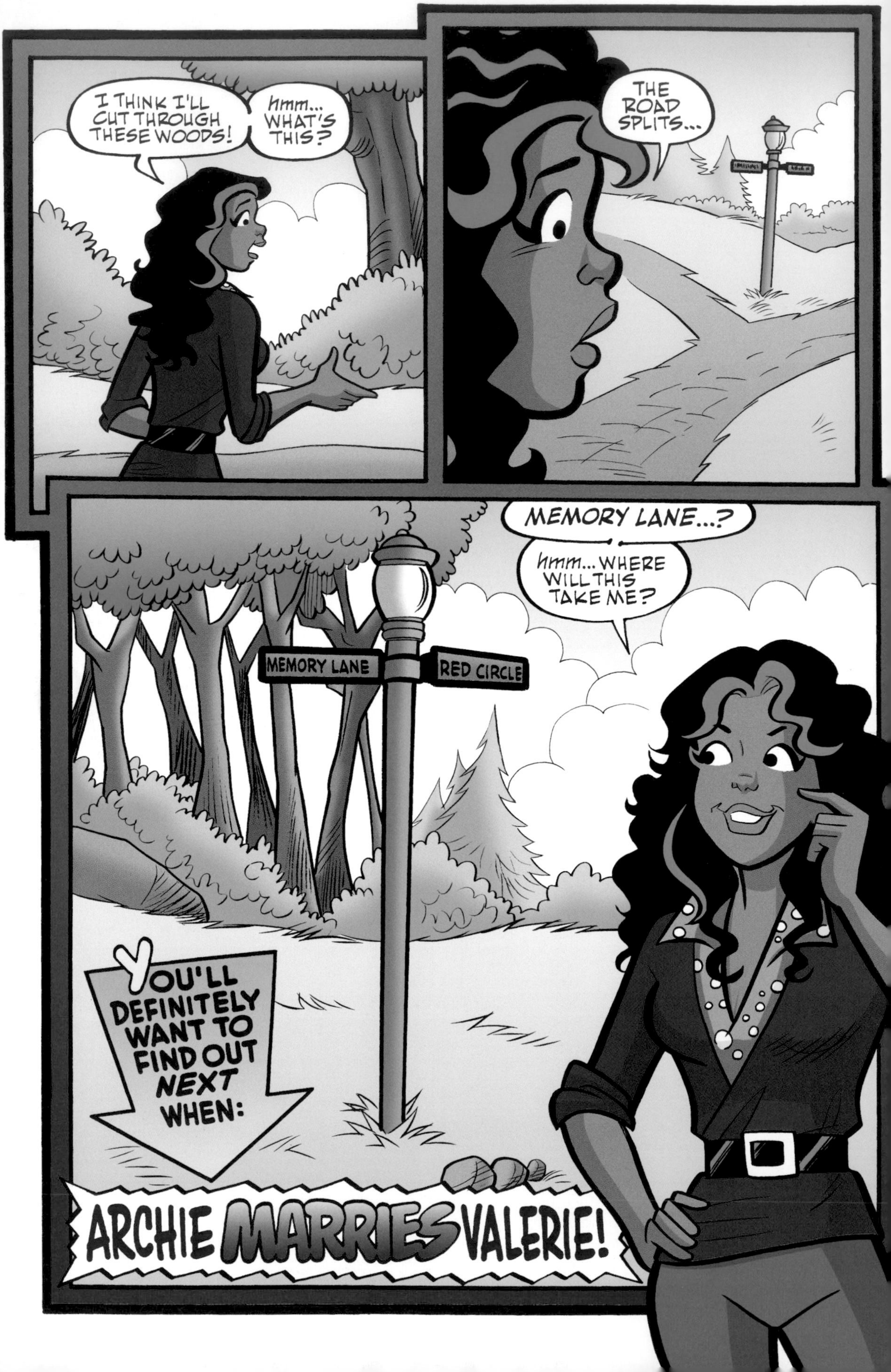

I THINK I'LL CUT THROUGH THESE WOODS!
hmm... WHAT'S THIS?
THE ROAD SPLITS...
MEMORY LANE...?
hmm... WHERE WILL THIS TAKE ME?
MEMORY LANE
RED CIRCLE
YOU'LL DEFINITELY WANT TO FIND OUT NEXT WHEN:
ARCHIE MARRIES VALERIE!

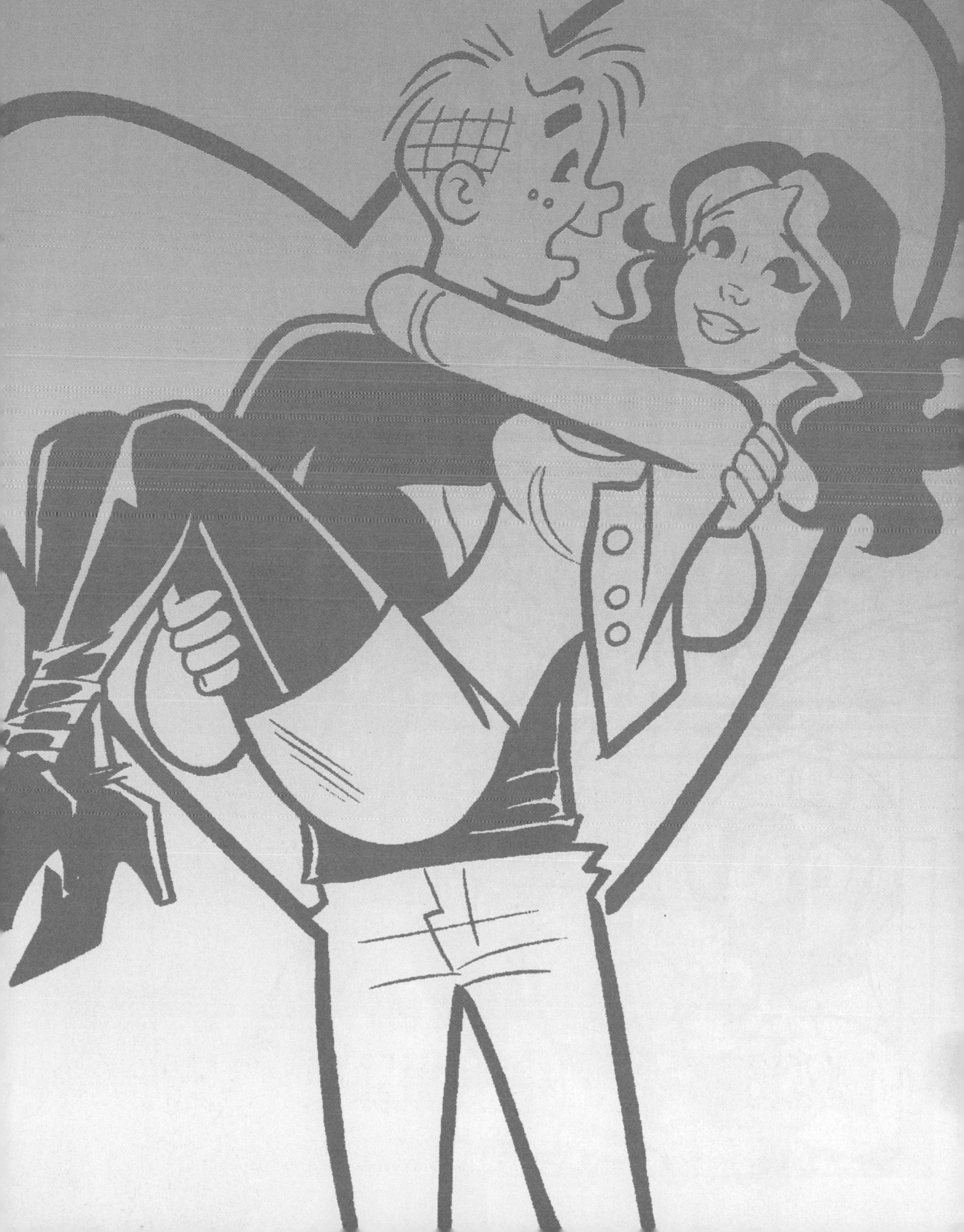

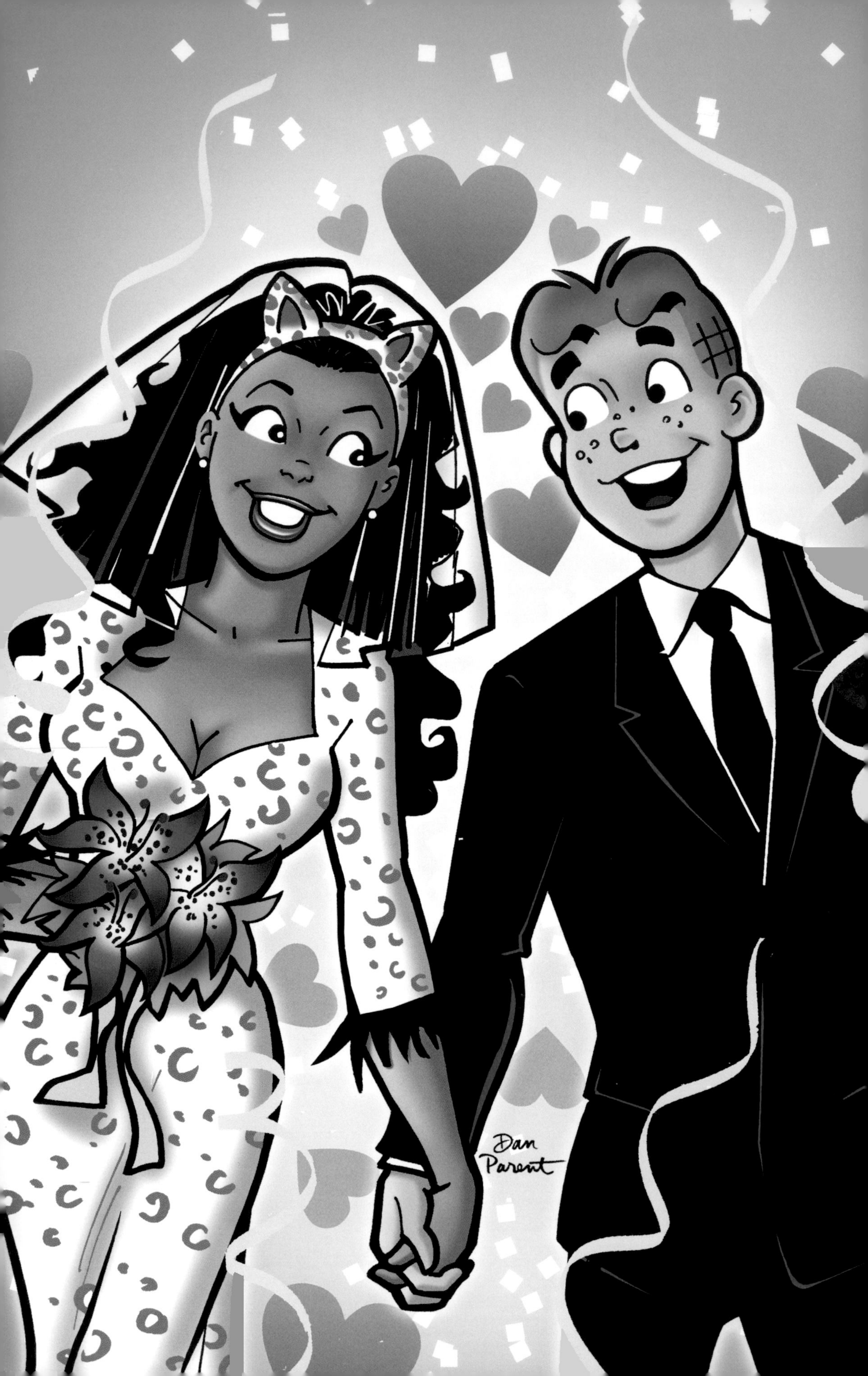
Dan
Parent

Chapter Two: With this Ring

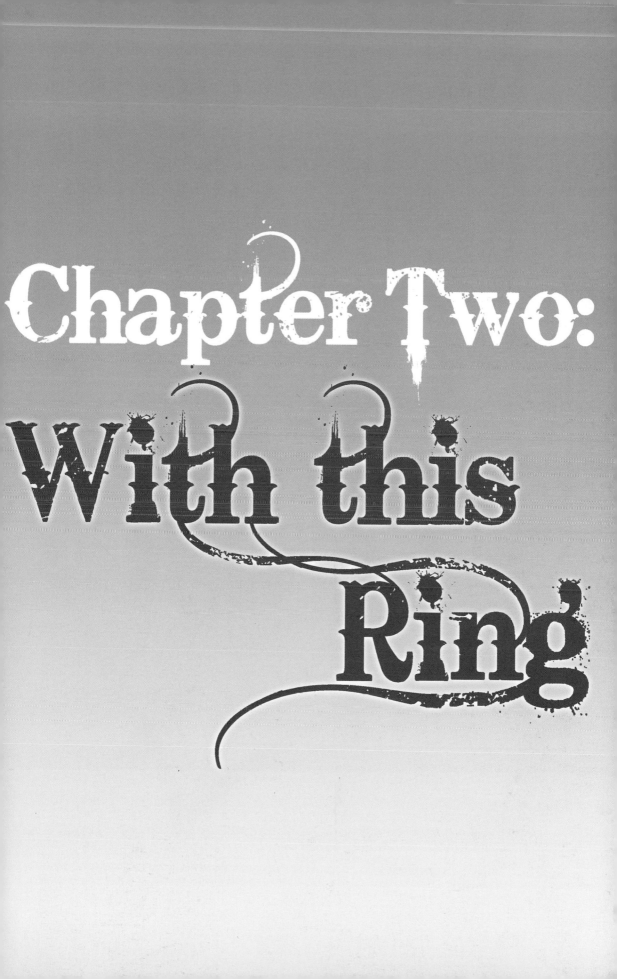

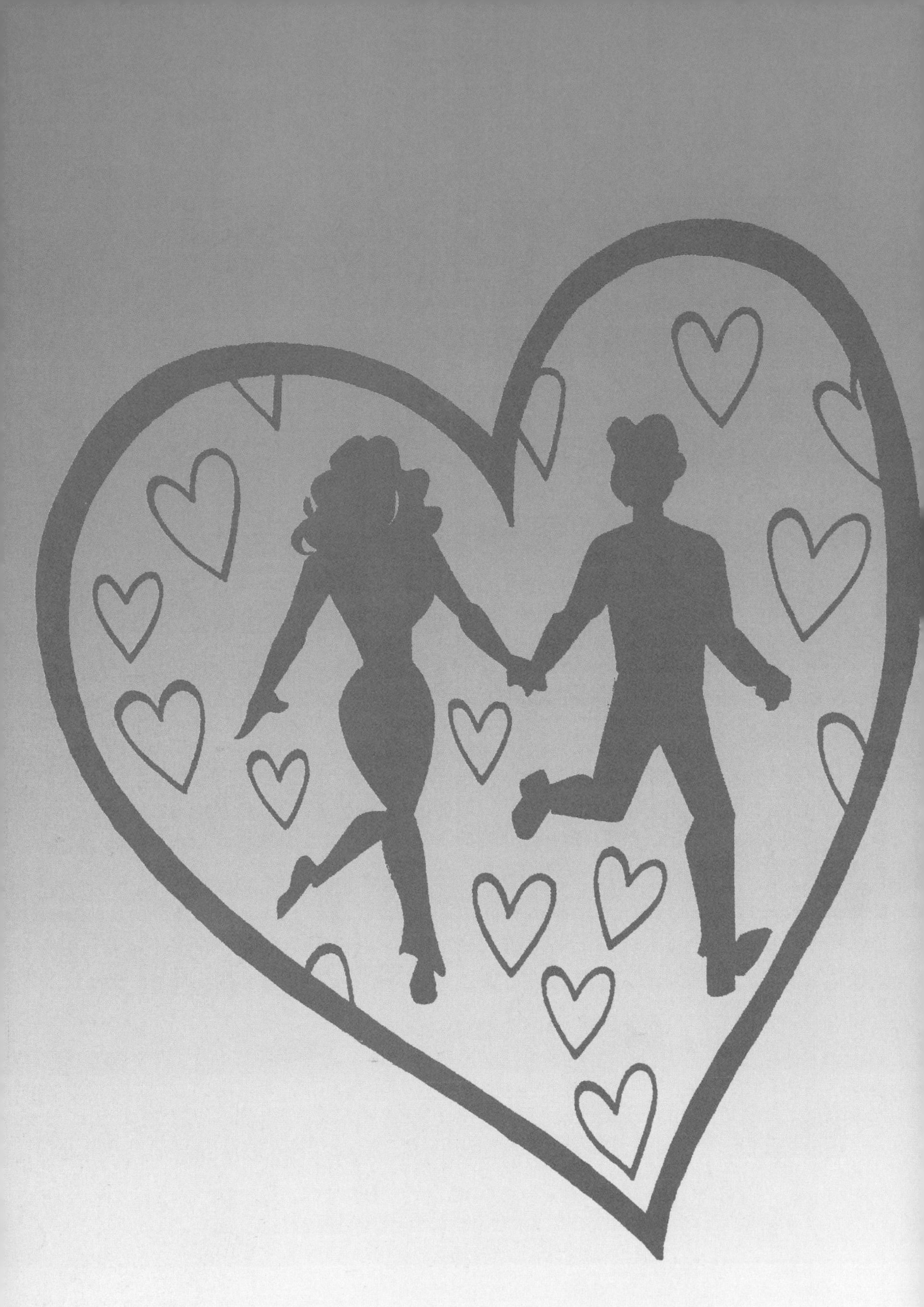

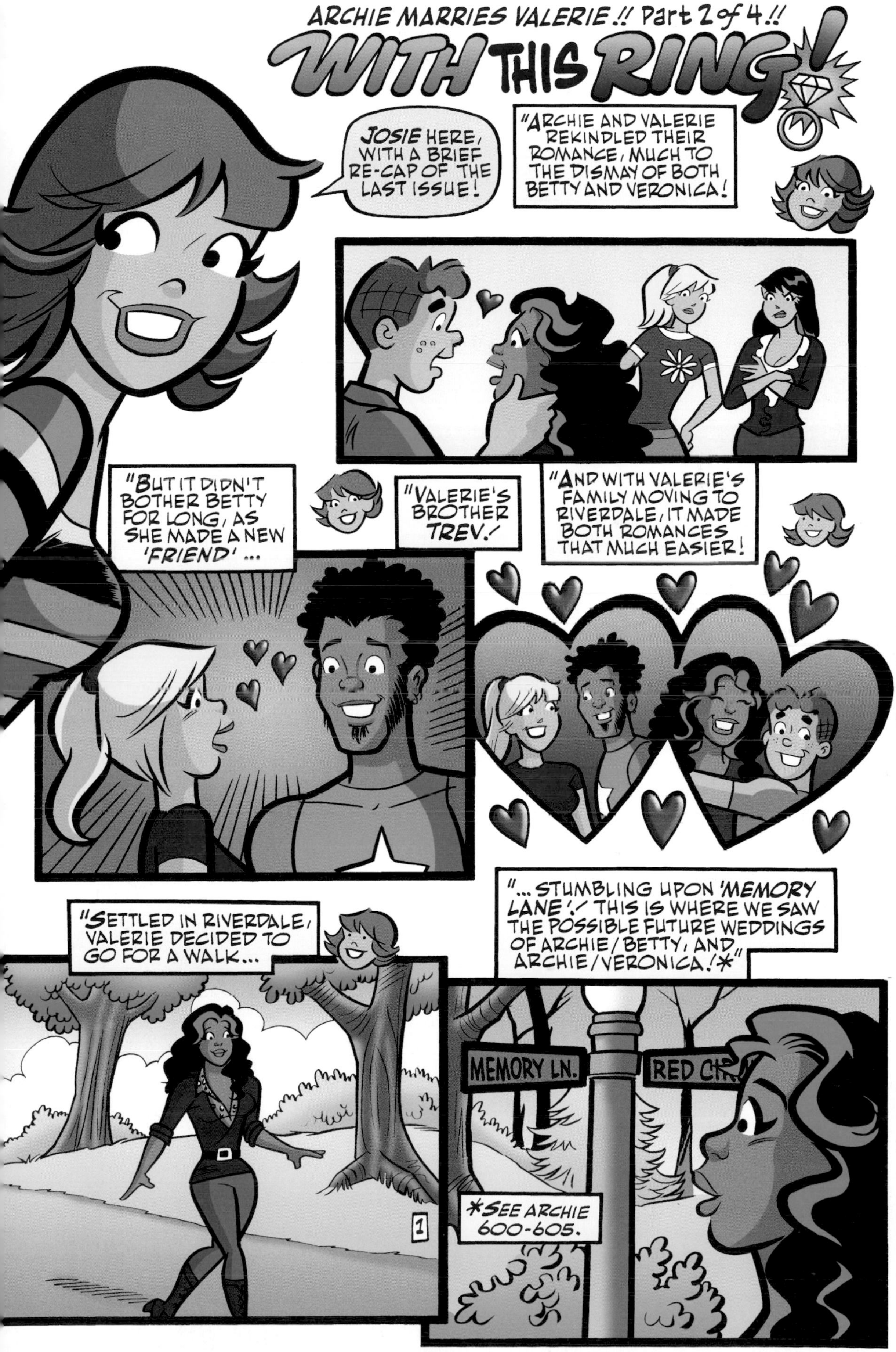

ARCHIE MARRIES VALERIE !! Part 2 of 4 !!
WITH THIS RING!
JOSIE HERE, WITH A BRIEF RE-CAP OF THE LAST ISSUE!
"ARCHIE AND VALERIE REKINDLED THEIR ROMANCE, MUCH TO THE DISMAY OF BOTH BETTY AND VERONICA!
"BUT IT DIDN'T BOTHER BETTY FOR LONG, AS SHE MADE A NEW 'FRIEND' ...
"VALERIE'S BROTHER TREV!
"AND WITH VALERIE'S FAMILY MOVING TO RIVERDALE, IT MADE BOTH ROMANCES THAT MUCH EASIER!
"SETTLED IN RIVERDALE, VALERIE DECIDED TO GO FOR A WALK...
1
"... STUMBLING UPON 'MEMORY LANE'! THIS IS WHERE WE SAW THE POSSIBLE FUTURE WEDDINGS OF ARCHIE / BETTY, AND ARCHIE / VERONICA!*"
MEMORY LN.
*SEE ARCHIE 600-605.

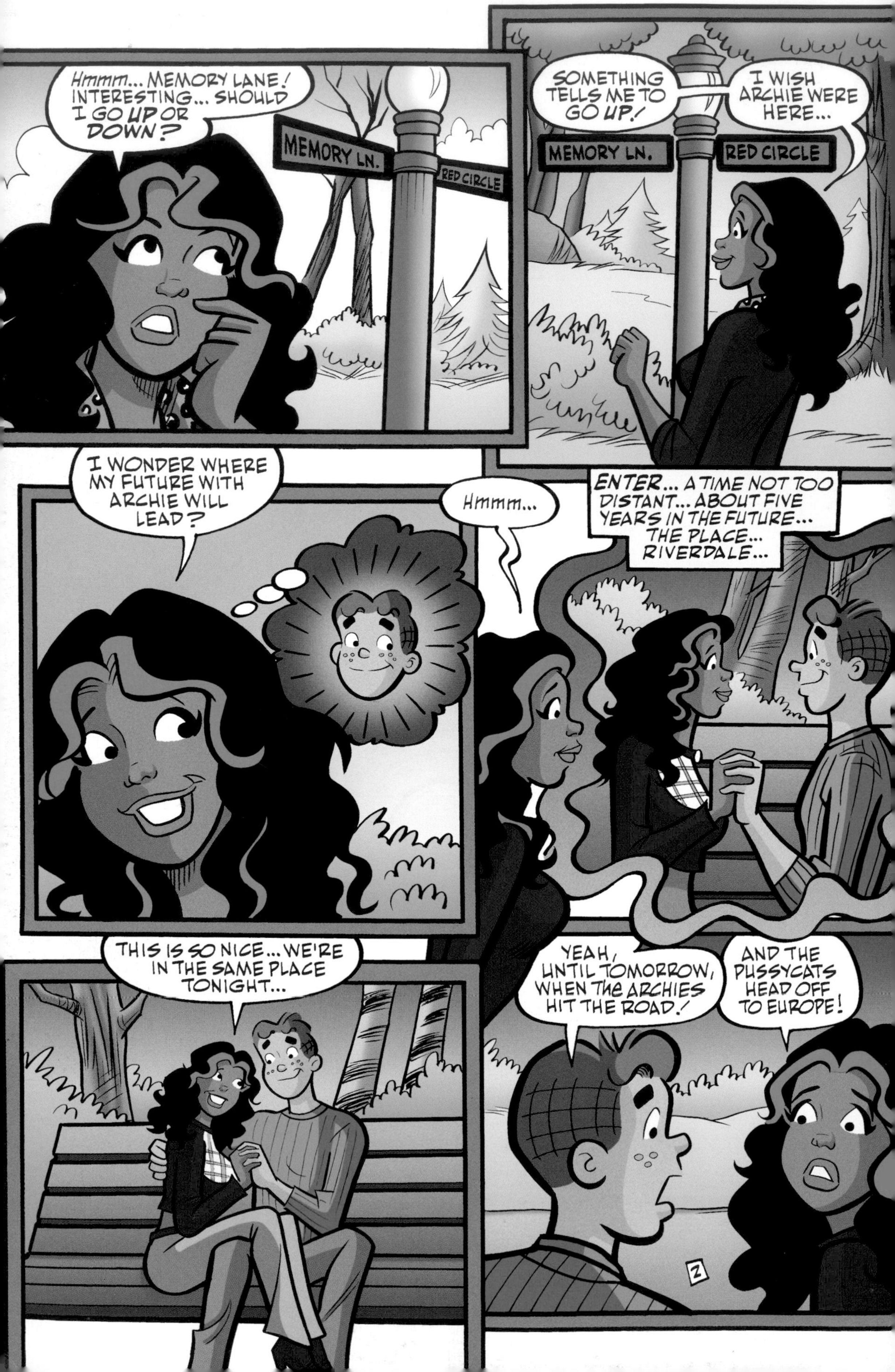
Hmmm... MEMORY LANE! INTERESTING... SHOULD I GO UP OR DOWN?
MEMORY LN.
RED CIRCLE
SOMETHING TELLS ME TO GO UP!
I WISH ARCHIE WERE HERE...
MEMORY LN.
RED CIRCLE
I WONDER WHERE MY FUTURE WITH ARCHIE WILL LEAD?
Hmmm...
ENTER... A TIME NOT TOO DISTANT... ABOUT FIVE YEARS IN THE FUTURE... THE PLACE... RIVERDALE...
THIS IS SO NICE... WE'RE IN THE SAME PLACE TONIGHT...
YEAH, UNTIL TOMORROW, WHEN THE ARCHIES HIT THE ROAD!
AND THE PUSSYCATS HEAD OFF TO EUROPE!
2

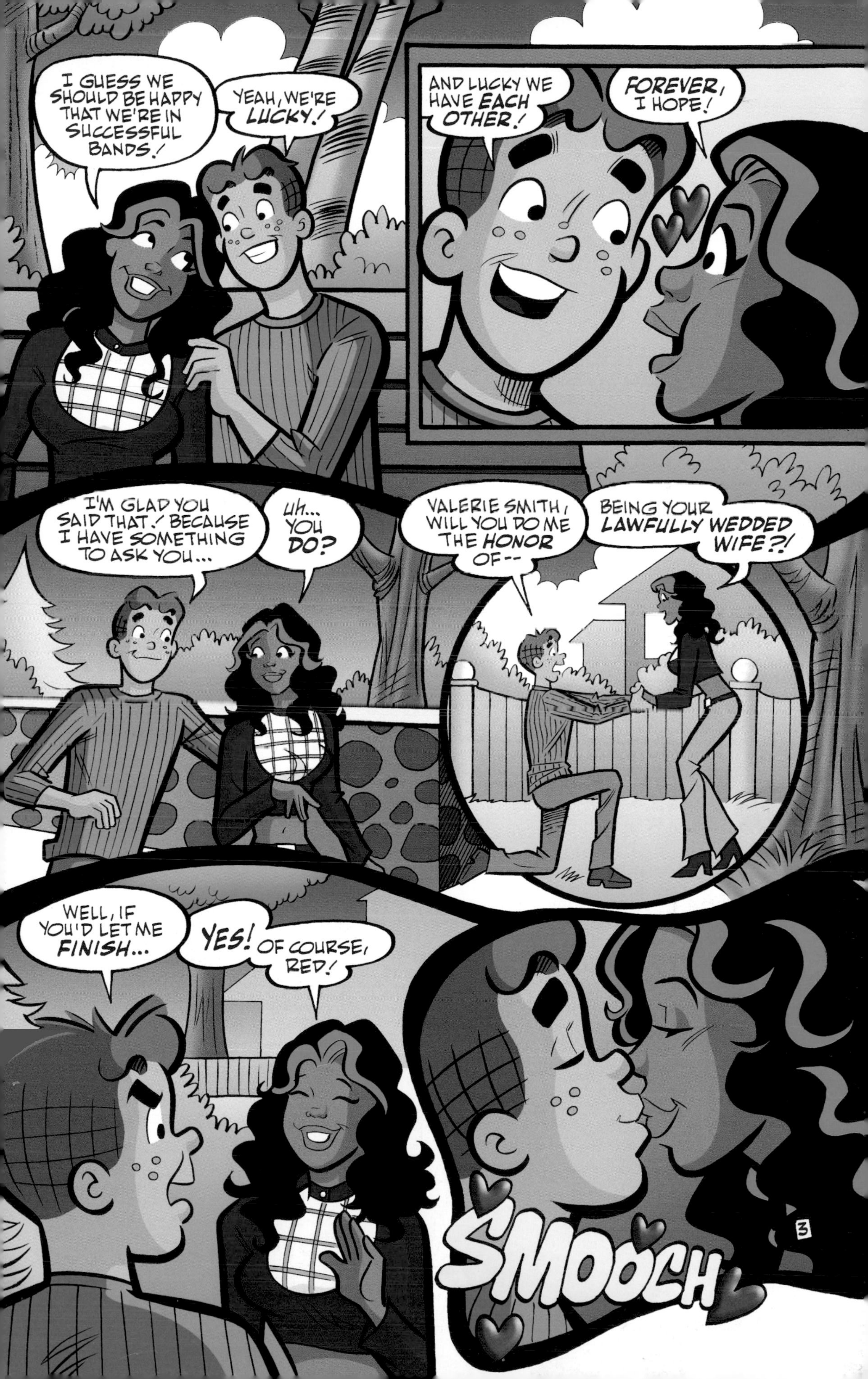
I GUESS WE SHOULD BE HAPPY THAT WE'RE IN SUCCESSFUL BANDS!
YEAH, WE'RE LUCKY!
AND LUCKY WE HAVE EACH OTHER!
FOREVER, I HOPE!
I'M GLAD YOU SAID THAT! BECAUSE I HAVE SOMETHING TO ASK YOU...
UH... YOU DO?
VALERIE SMITH, WILL YOU DO ME THE HONOR OF--
BEING YOUR LAWFULLY WEDDED WIFE?!
WELL, IF YOU'D LET ME FINISH...
YES! OF COURSE, RED!
SMOOCH
3

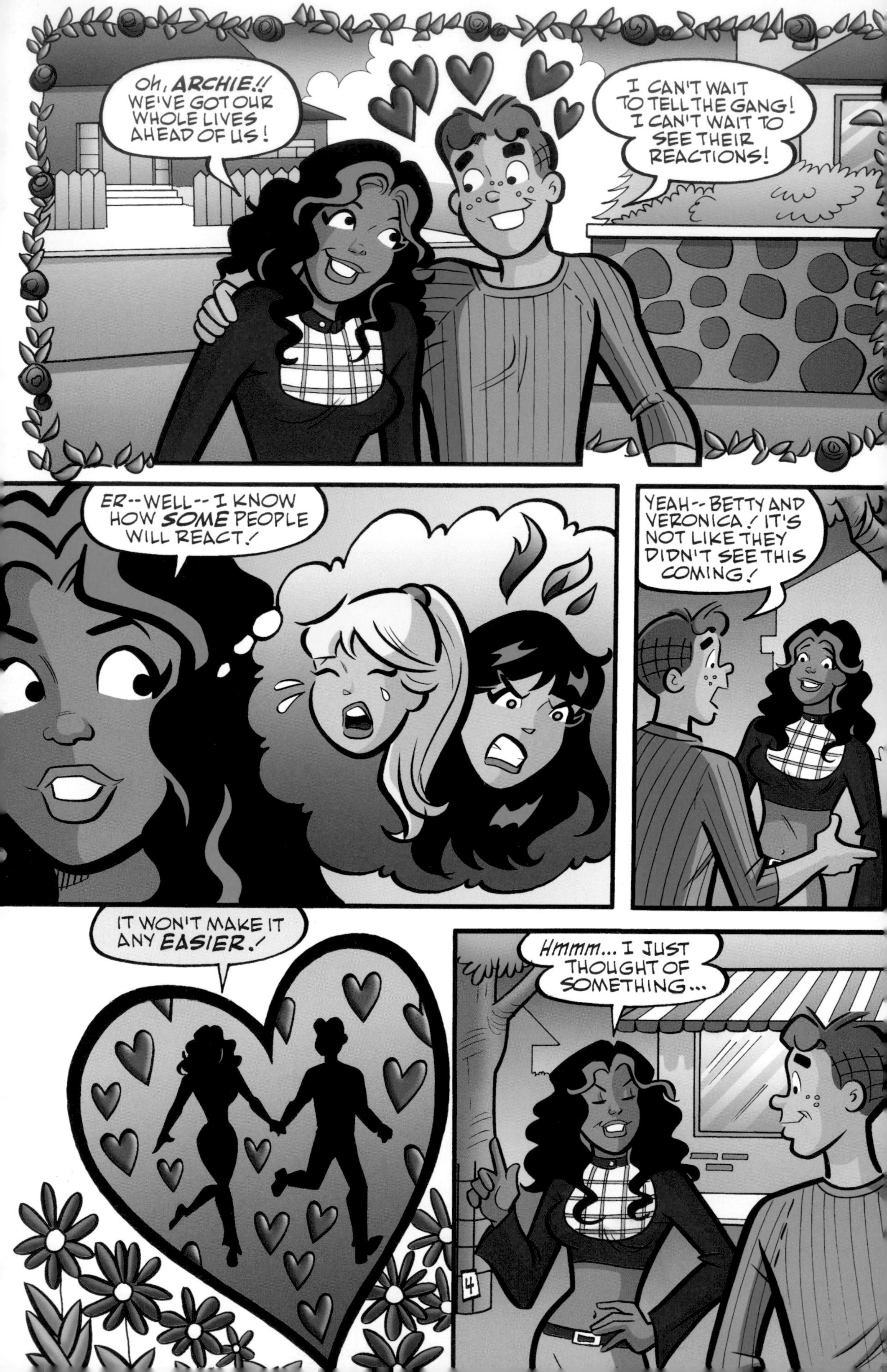

Oh, ARCHIE!! WE'VE GOT OUR WHOLE LIVES AHEAD OF US!
I CAN'T WAIT TO TELL THE GANG! I CAN'T WAIT TO SEE THEIR REACTIONS!
ER--WELL--I KNOW HOW SOME PEOPLE WILL REACT!
YEAH--BETTY AND VERONICA! IT'S NOT LIKE THEY DIDN'T SEE THIS COMING!
IT WON'T MAKE IT ANY EASIER!
Hmmm... I JUST THOUGHT OF SOMETHING...

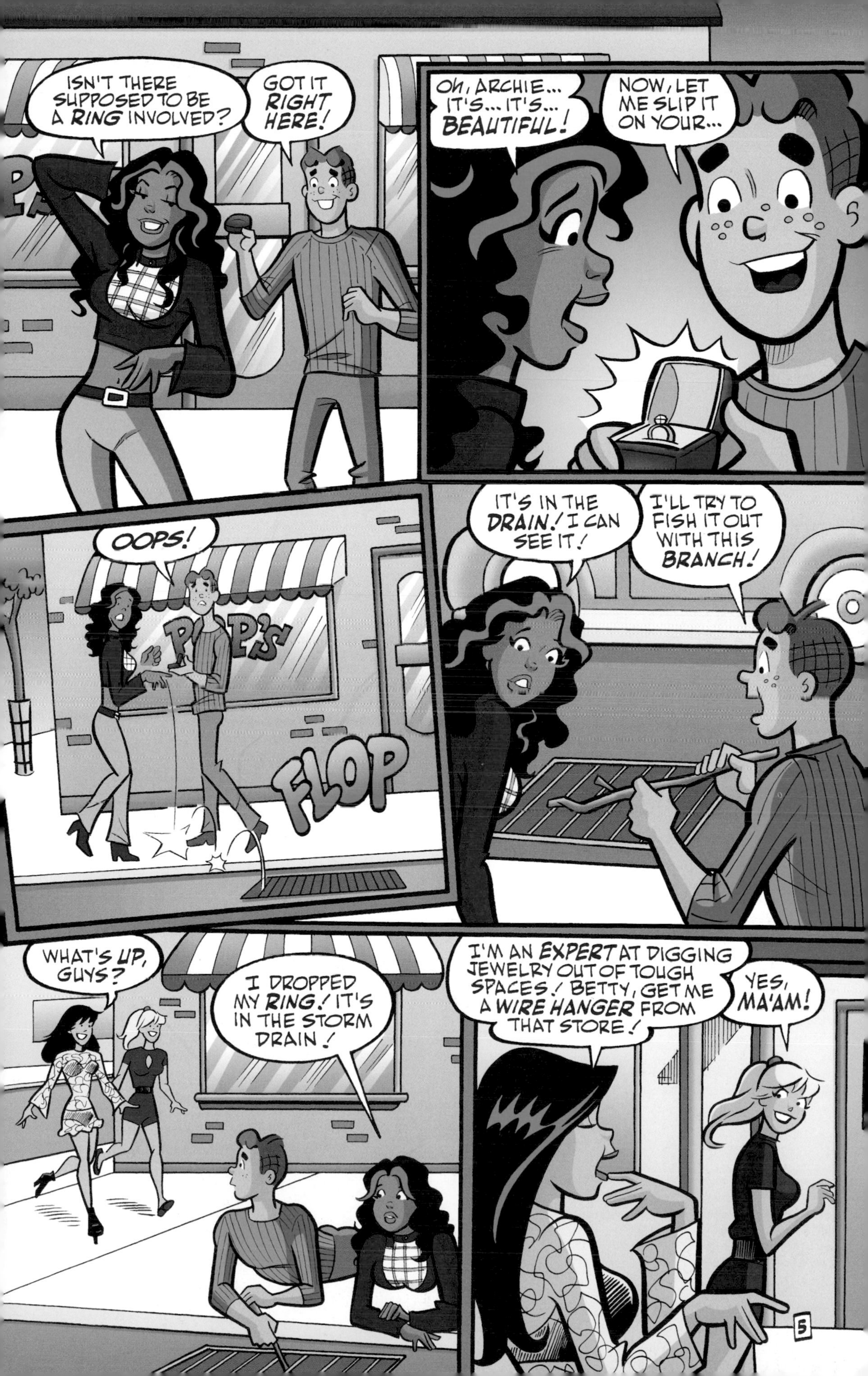

ISN'T THERE SUPPOSED TO BE A RING INVOLVED?
GOT IT RIGHT HERE!
Oh, ARCHIE... IT'S... IT'S... BEAUTIFUL!
NOW, LET ME SLIP IT ON YOUR...
OOPS!
POP'S
FLOP
IT'S IN THE DRAIN! I CAN SEE IT!
I'LL TRY TO FISH IT OUT WITH THIS BRANCH!
WHAT'S UP, GUYS?
I DROPPED MY RING! IT'S IN THE STORM DRAIN!
I'M AN EXPERT AT DIGGING JEWELRY OUT OF TOUGH SPACES! BETTY, GET ME A WIRE HANGER FROM THAT STORE!
YES, MA'AM!

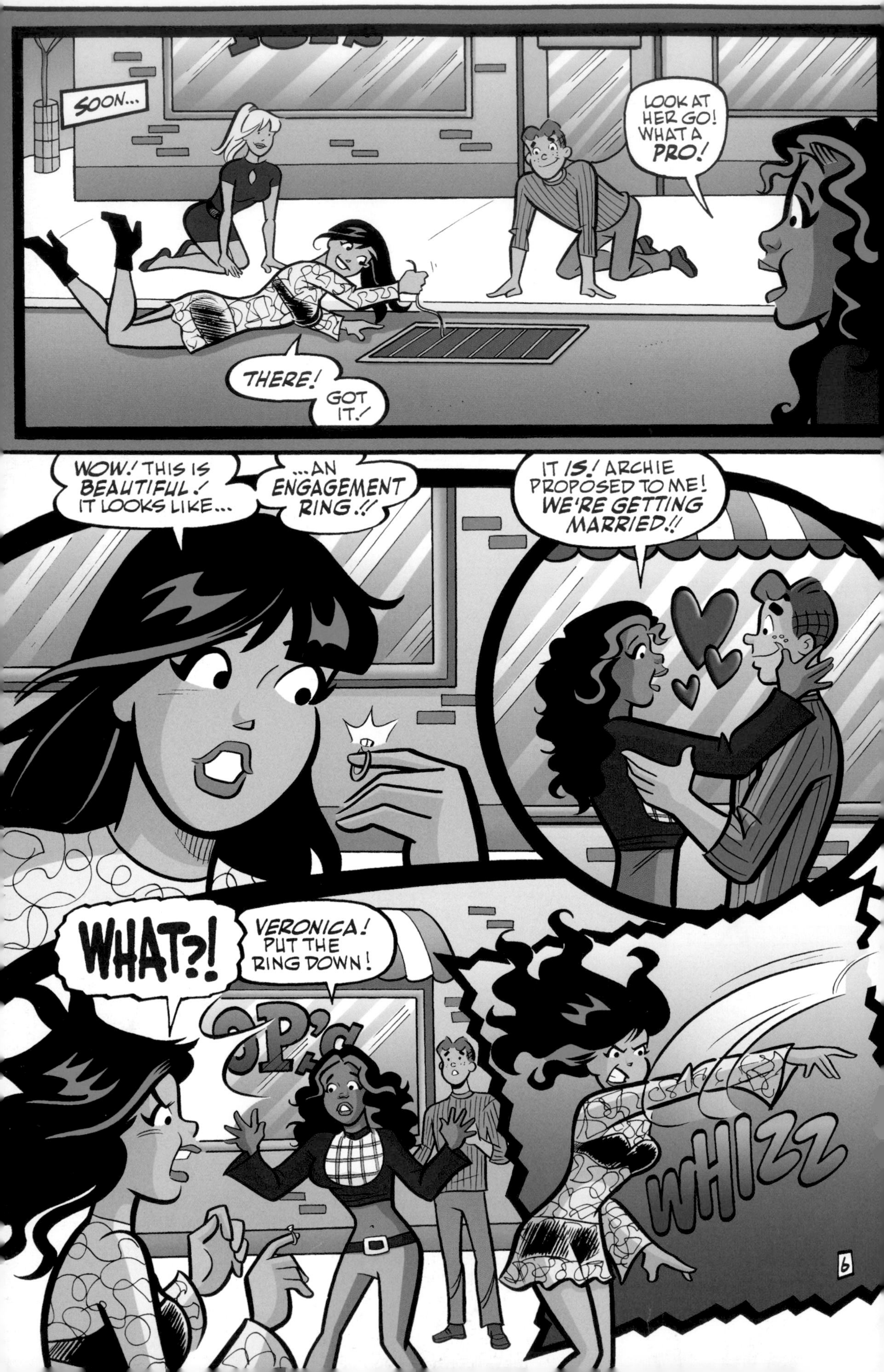
SOON...
LOOK AT HER GO! WHAT A PRO!
THERE!
GOT IT.!
WOW! THIS IS BEAUTIFUL! IT LOOKS LIKE...
...AN ENGAGEMENT RING.!!
IT IS! ARCHIE PROPOSED TO ME! WE'RE GETTING MARRIED!!
WHAT?!
VERONICA! PUT THE RING DOWN!
WHIZZ
6

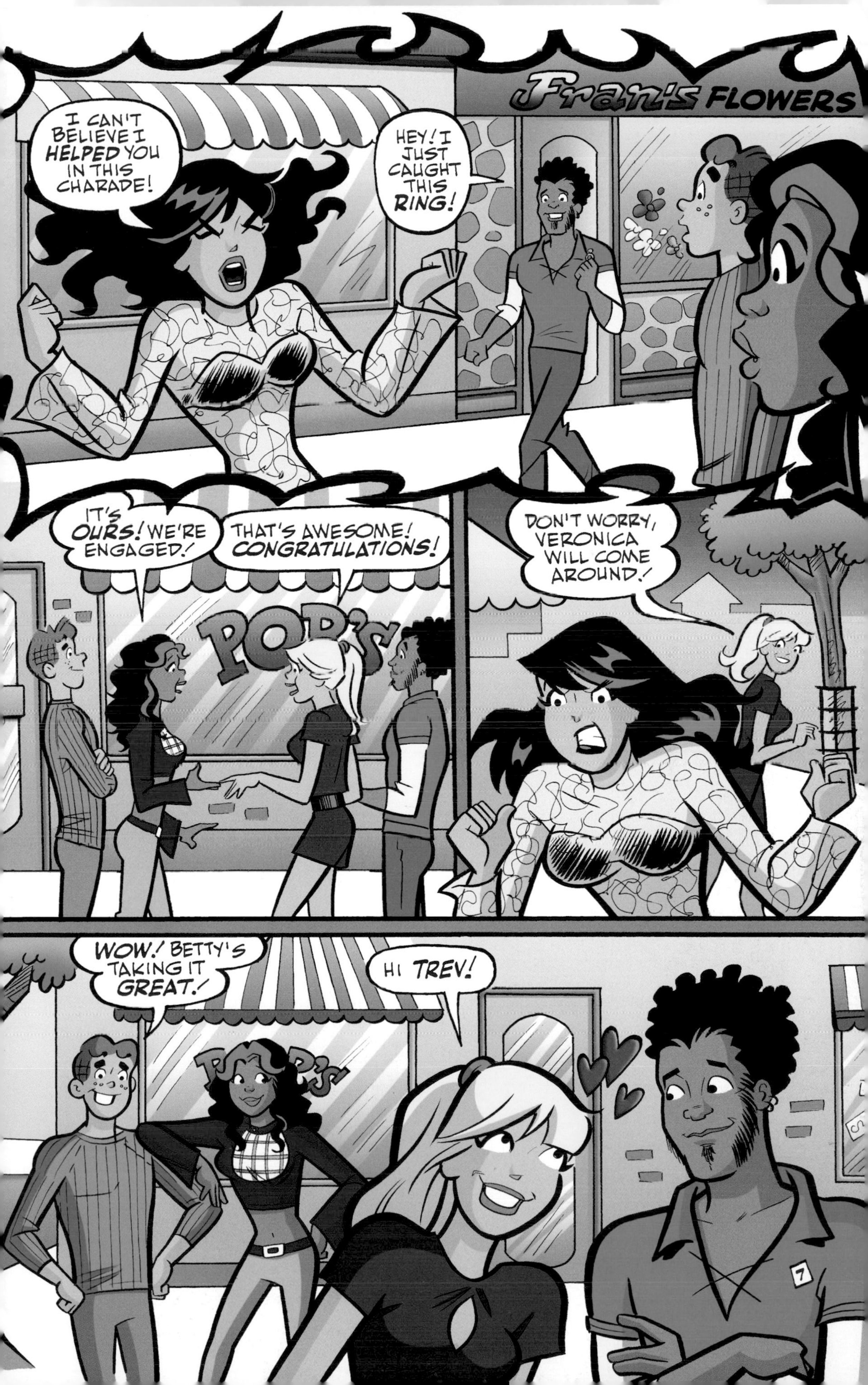
Fran's FLOWERS
I CAN'T BELIEVE I HELPED YOU IN THIS CHARADE!
HEY! I JUST CAUGHT THIS RING!
IT'S OURS! WE'RE ENGAGED!
THAT'S AWESOME! CONGRATULATIONS!
POP'S
DON'T WORRY, VERONICA WILL COME AROUND!
WOW! BETTY'S TAKING IT GREAT!
HI TREV!
7

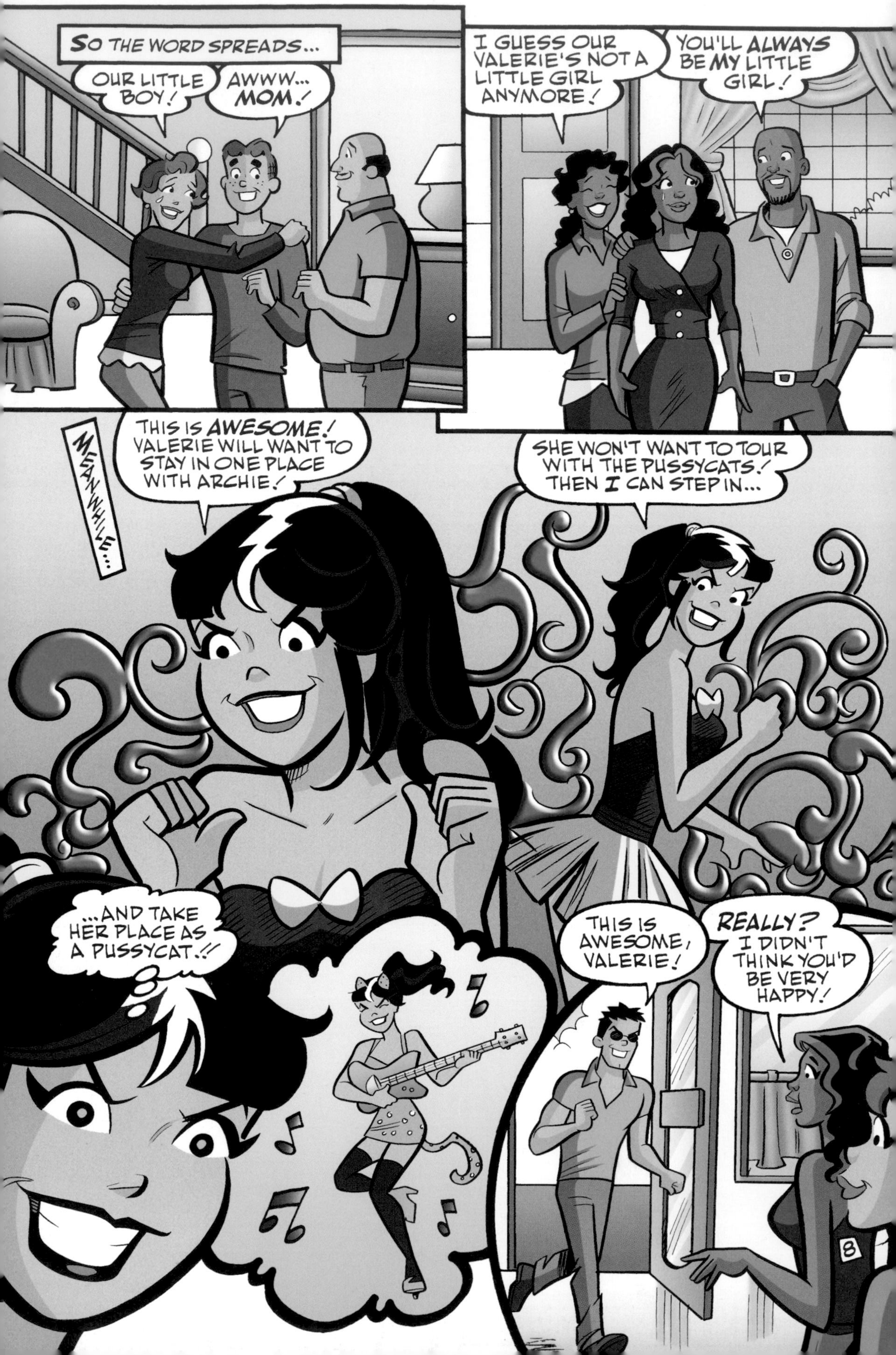
SO THE WORD SPREADS...
OUR LITTLE BOY!
AWWW... MOM!
I GUESS OUR VALERIE'S NOT A LITTLE GIRL ANYMORE!
YOU'LL ALWAYS BE MY LITTLE GIRL!
MEANWHILE...
THIS IS AWESOME! VALERIE WILL WANT TO STAY IN ONE PLACE WITH ARCHIE!
SHE WON'T WANT TO TOUR WITH THE PUSSYCATS! THEN I CAN STEP IN...
...AND TAKE HER PLACE AS A PUSSYCAT!!
THIS IS AWESOME, VALERIE!
REALLY? I DIDN'T THINK YOU'D BE VERY HAPPY!
8

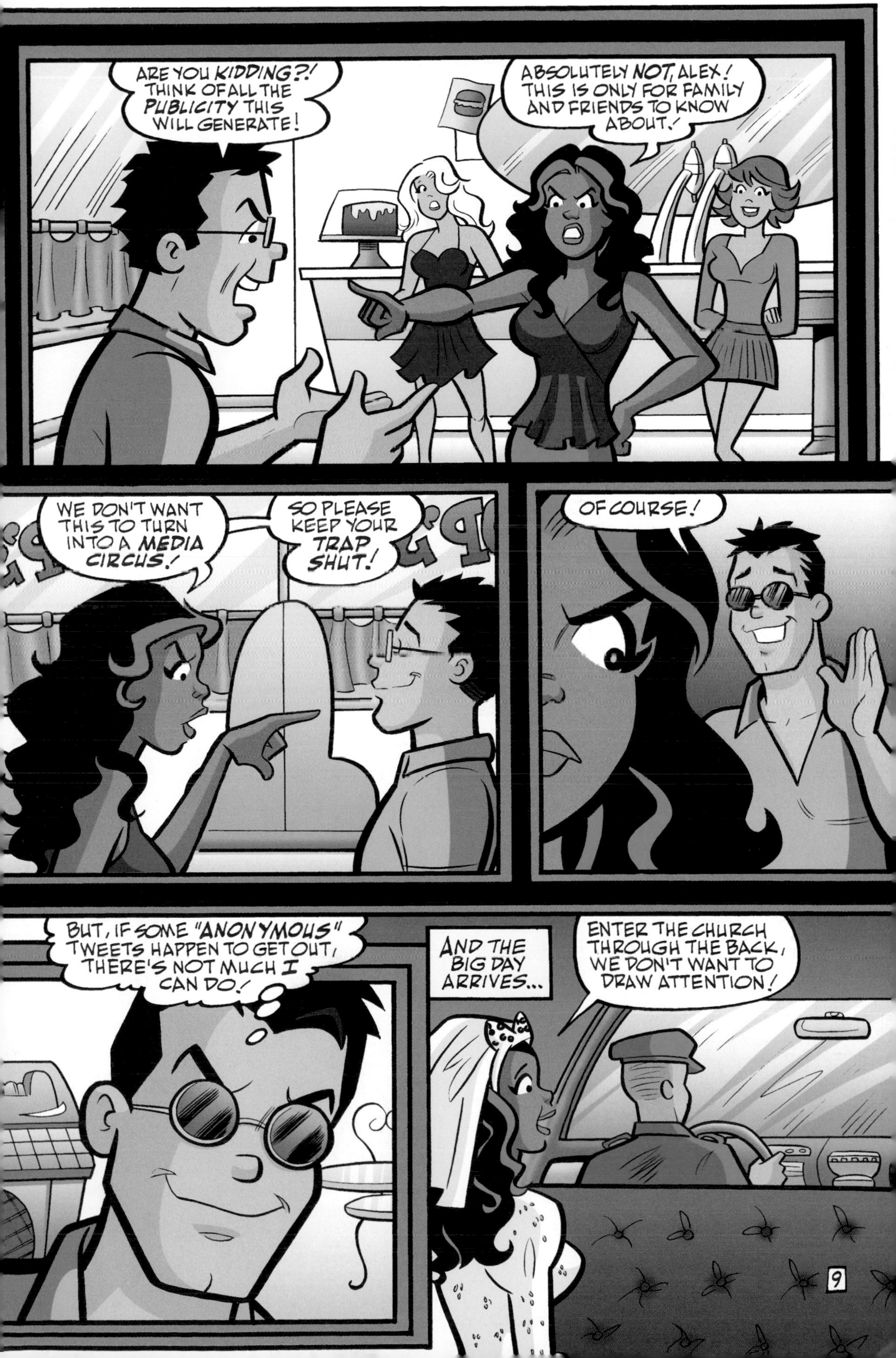
ARE YOU KIDDING?! THINK OF ALL THE PUBLICITY THIS WILL GENERATE!
ABSOLUTELY NOT, ALEX! THIS IS ONLY FOR FAMILY AND FRIENDS TO KNOW ABOUT!
WE DON'T WANT THIS TO TURN INTO A MEDIA CIRCUS!
SO PLEASE KEEP YOUR TRAP SHUT!
OF COURSE!
BUT, IF SOME "ANONYMOUS" TWEETS HAPPEN TO GET OUT, THERE'S NOT MUCH I CAN DO!
AND THE BIG DAY ARRIVES...
ENTER THE CHURCH THROUGH THE BACK, WE DON'T WANT TO DRAW ATTENTION!

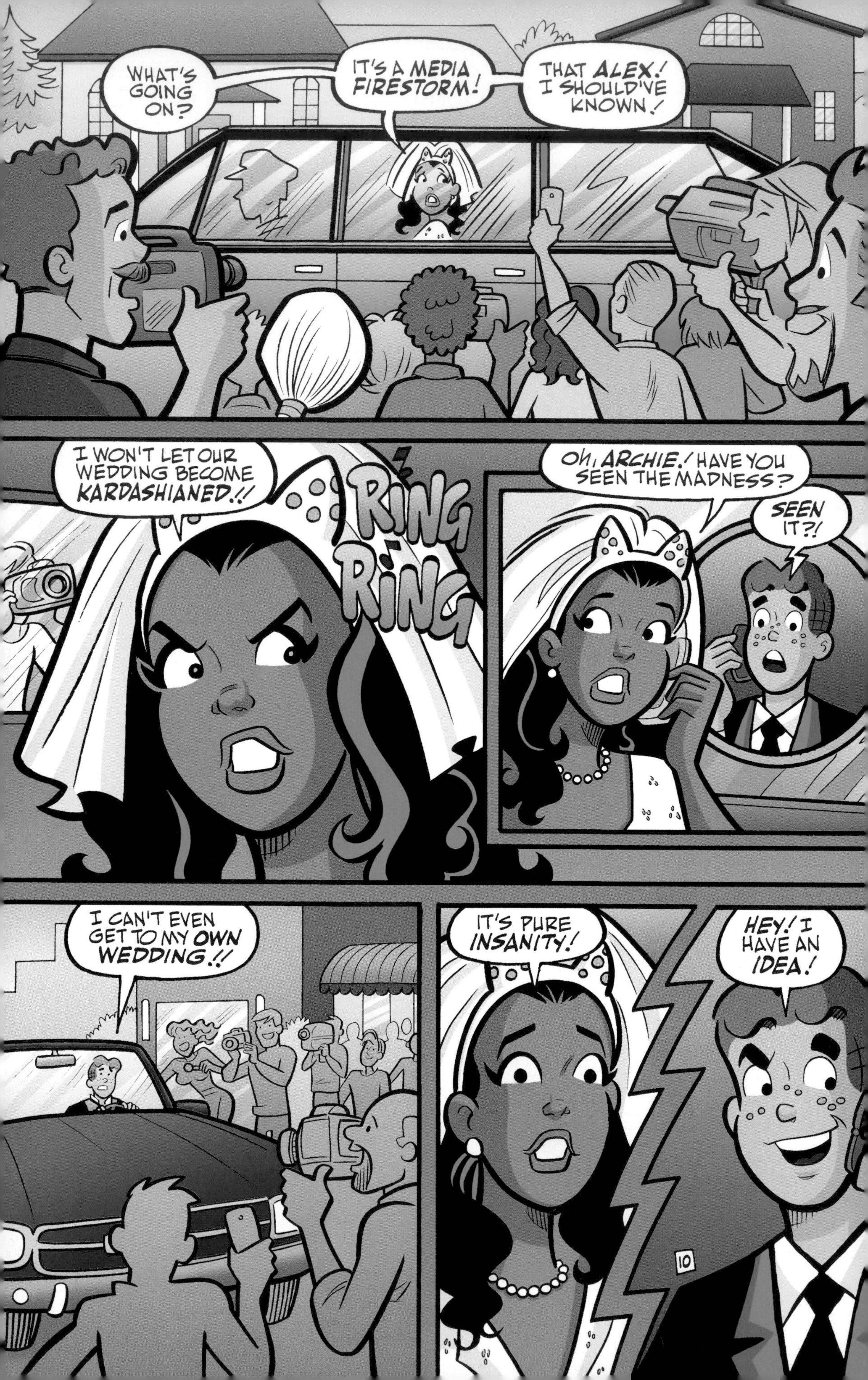
WHAT'S GOING ON?
IT'S A MEDIA FIRESTORM!
THAT ALEX! I SHOULD'VE KNOWN!
I WON'T LET OUR WEDDING BECOME KARDASHIANED!!
RING RING
Oh, ARCHIE! HAVE YOU SEEN THE MADNESS?
SEEN IT?!
I CAN'T EVEN GET TO MY OWN WEDDING!!
IT'S PURE INSANITY!
HEY! I HAVE AN IDEA!
10

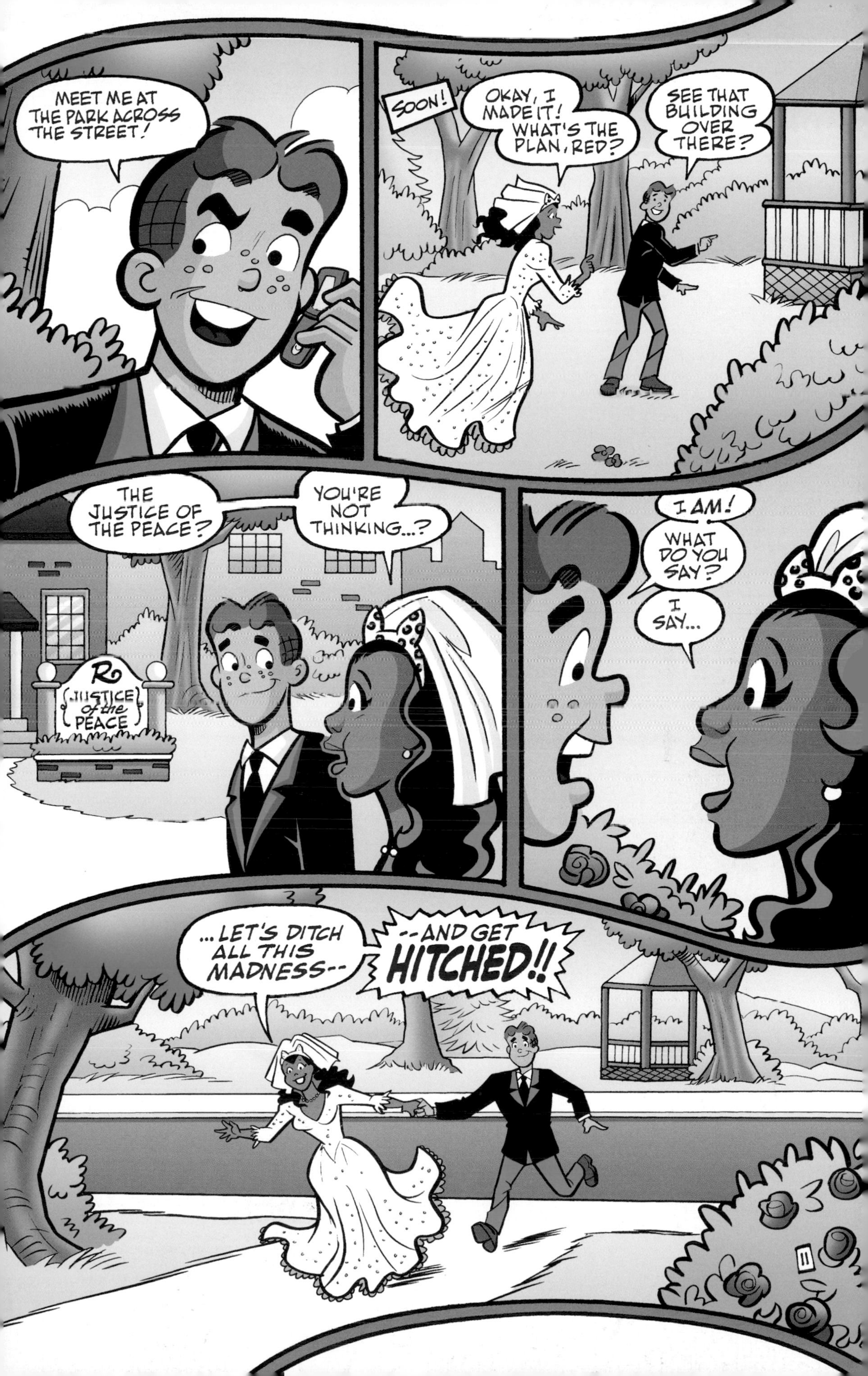
MEET ME AT THE PARK ACROSS THE STREET!
SOON!
OKAY, I MADE IT! WHAT'S THE PLAN, RED?
SEE THAT BUILDING OVER THERE?
THE JUSTICE OF THE PEACE?
YOU'RE NOT THINKING...?
JUSTICE of the PEACE
I AM!
WHAT DO YOU SAY?
I SAY...
...LET'S DITCH ALL THIS MADNESS--
--AND GET HITCHED!!
11

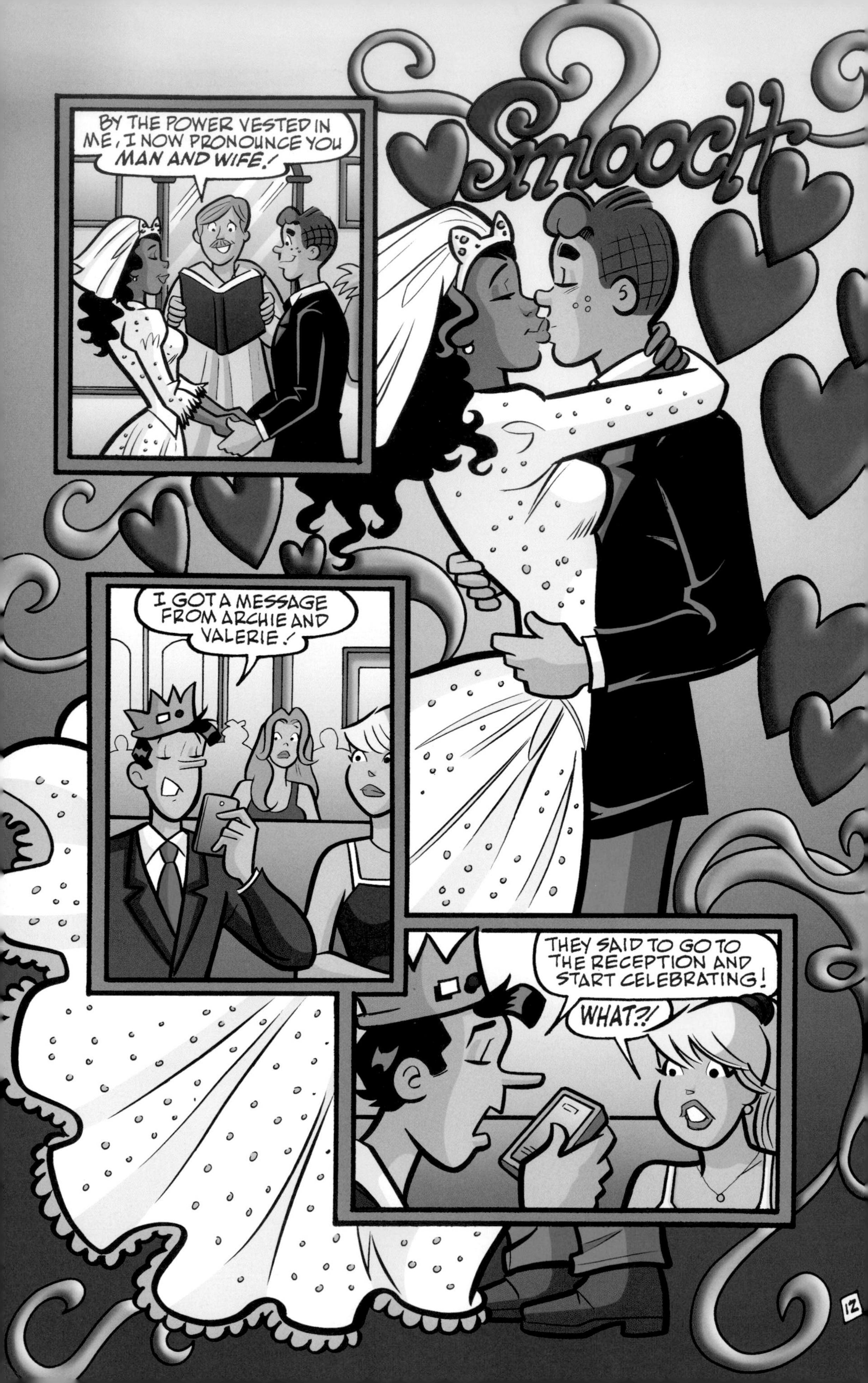
BY THE POWER VESTED IN ME, I NOW PRONOUNCE YOU MAN AND WIFE!
SMOOCH
I GOT A MESSAGE FROM ARCHIE AND VALERIE!
THEY SAID TO GO TO THE RECEPTION AND START CELEBRATING!
WHAT?!
12

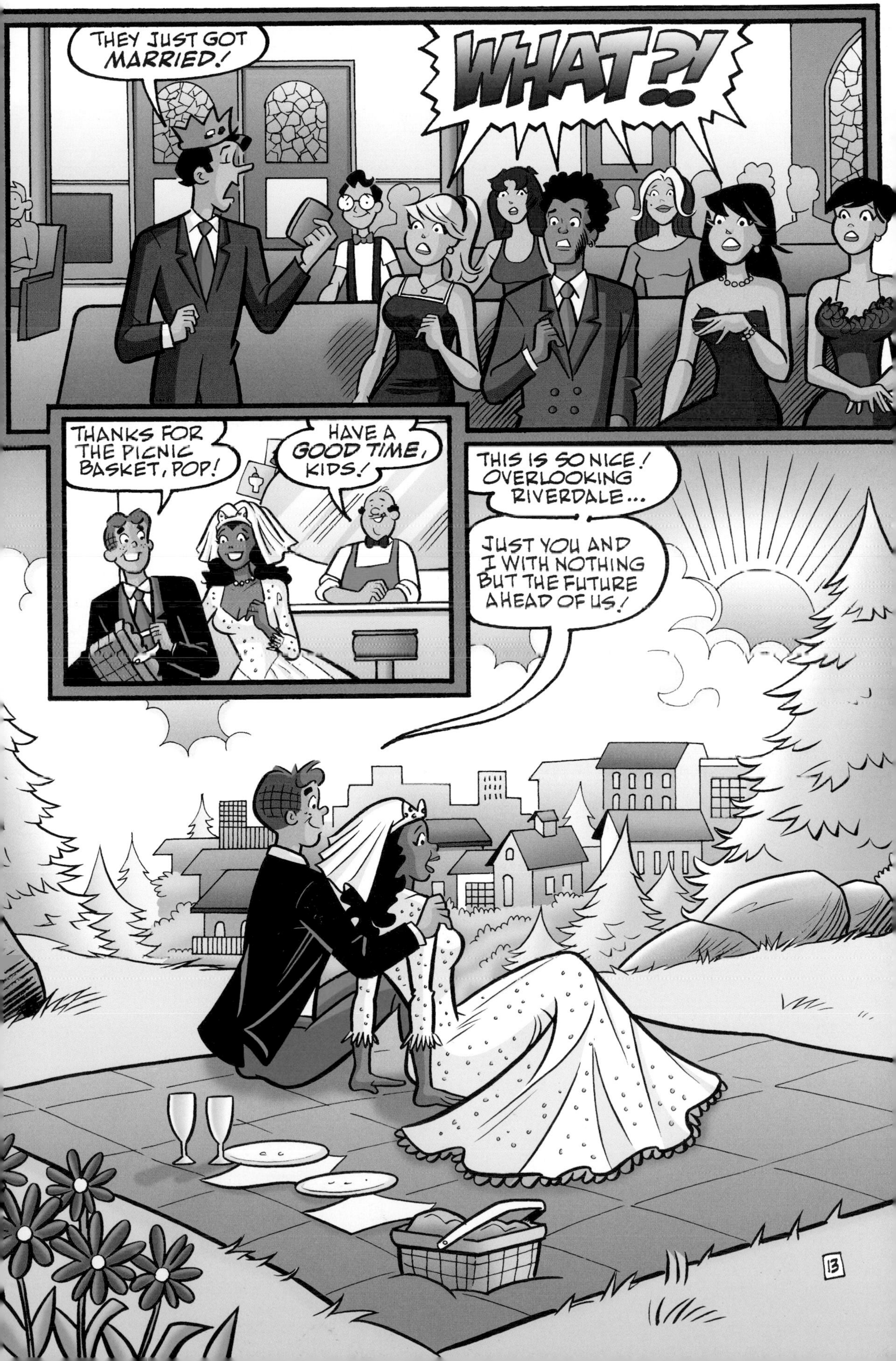
THEY JUST GOT MARRIED!
WHAT?!
THANKS FOR THE PICNIC BASKET, POP!
HAVE A GOOD TIME, KIDS!
THIS IS SO NICE! OVERLOOKING RIVERDALE...
JUST YOU AND I WITH NOTHING BUT THE FUTURE AHEAD OF US!
13

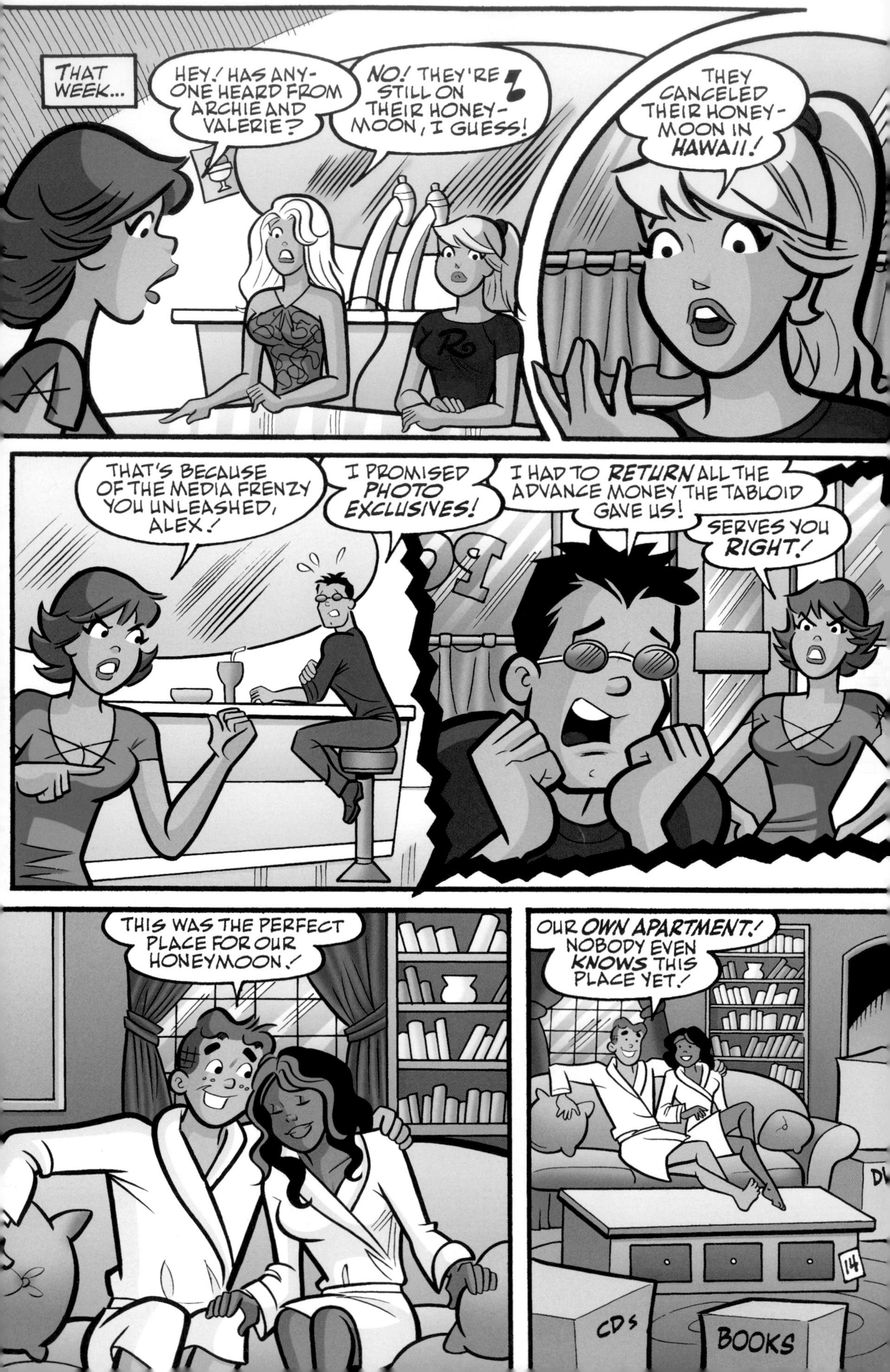
THAT WEEK...
HEY! HAS ANYONE HEARD FROM ARCHIE AND VALERIE?
NO! THEY'RE STILL ON THEIR HONEYMOON, I GUESS!
THEY CANCELED THEIR HONEYMOON IN HAWAII!
THAT'S BECAUSE OF THE MEDIA FRENZY YOU UNLEASHED, ALEX!
I PROMISED PHOTO EXCLUSIVES!
I HAD TO RETURN ALL THE ADVANCE MONEY THE TABLOID GAVE US!
SERVES YOU RIGHT!
THIS WAS THE PERFECT PLACE FOR OUR HONEYMOON!
OUR OWN APARTMENT! NOBODY EVEN KNOWS THIS PLACE YET!
CDs
BOOKS

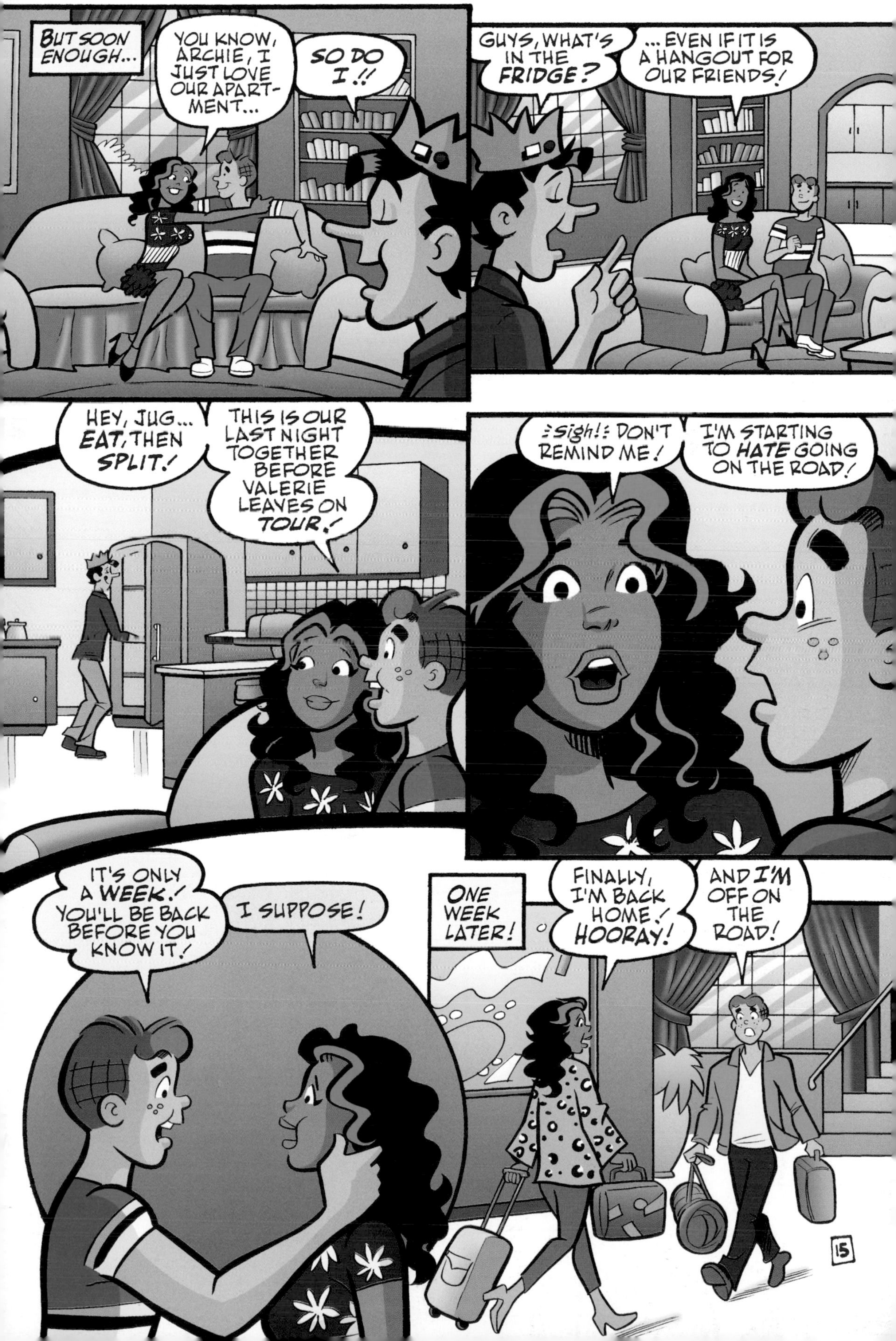
BUT SOON ENOUGH...
YOU KNOW, ARCHIE, I JUST LOVE OUR APARTMENT...
SO DO I!!
GUYS, WHAT'S IN THE FRIDGE?
...EVEN IF IT IS A HANGOUT FOR OUR FRIENDS!
HEY, JUG... EAT, THEN SPLIT!
THIS IS OUR LAST NIGHT TOGETHER BEFORE VALERIE LEAVES ON TOUR!
:sigh!: DON'T REMIND ME!
I'M STARTING TO HATE GOING ON THE ROAD!
IT'S ONLY A WEEK! YOU'LL BE BACK BEFORE YOU KNOW IT!
I SUPPOSE!
ONE WEEK LATER!
FINALLY, I'M BACK HOME! HOORAY!
AND I'M OFF ON THE ROAD!
15

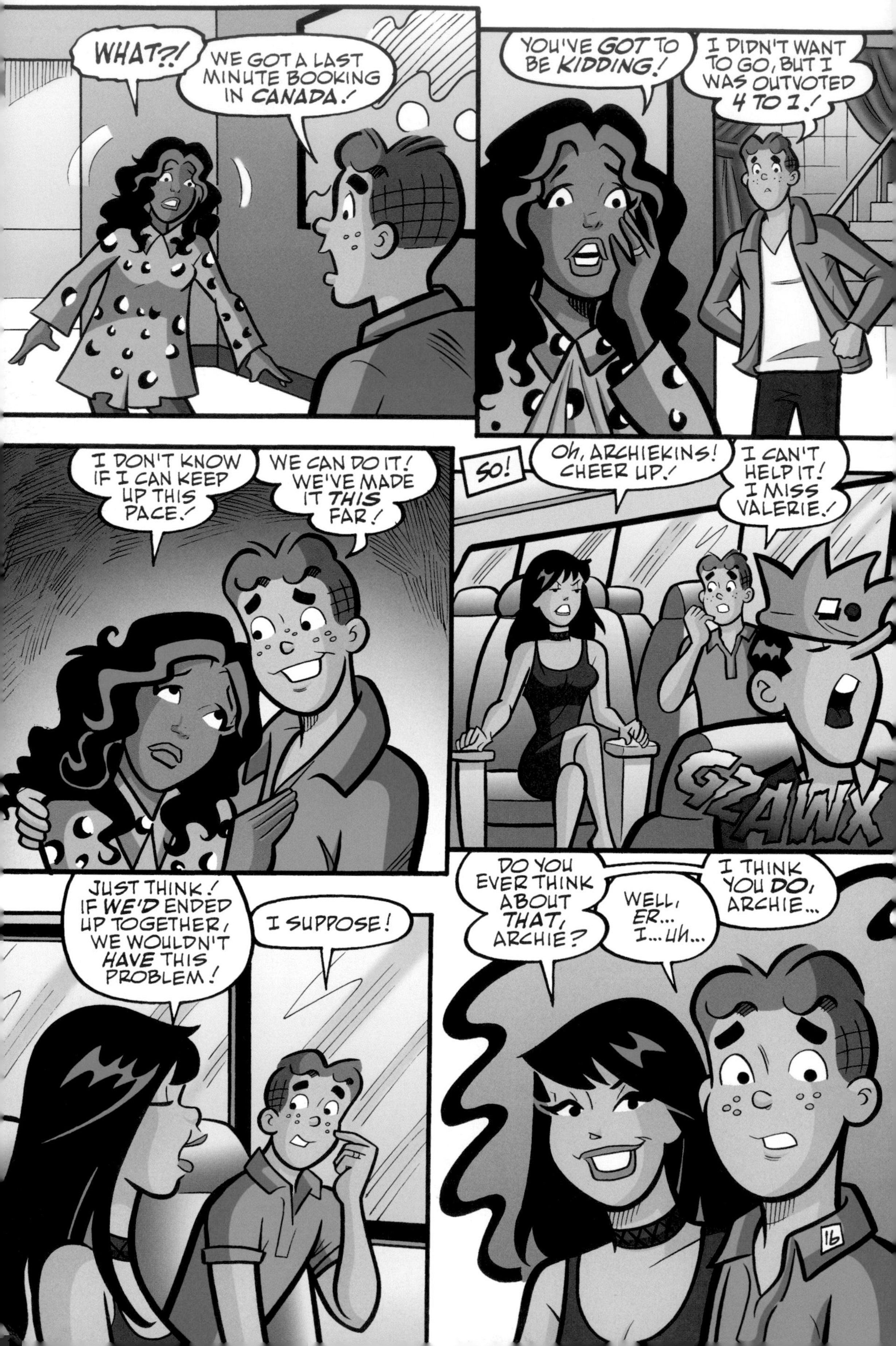

WHAT?!
WE GOT A LAST MINUTE BOOKING IN CANADA!
YOU'VE GOT TO BE KIDDING!
I DIDN'T WANT TO GO, BUT I WAS OUTVOTED 4 TO 1!
I DON'T KNOW IF I CAN KEEP UP THIS PACE!
WE CAN DO IT! WE'VE MADE IT THIS FAR!
SO!
Oh, ARCHIEKINS! CHEER UP!
I CAN'T HELP IT! I MISS VALERIE!
GZAWX
JUST THINK! IF WE'D ENDED UP TOGETHER, WE WOULDN'T HAVE THIS PROBLEM!
I SUPPOSE!
DO YOU EVER THINK ABOUT THAT, ARCHIE?
WELL, ER... I...UH...
I THINK YOU DO, ARCHIE...
16

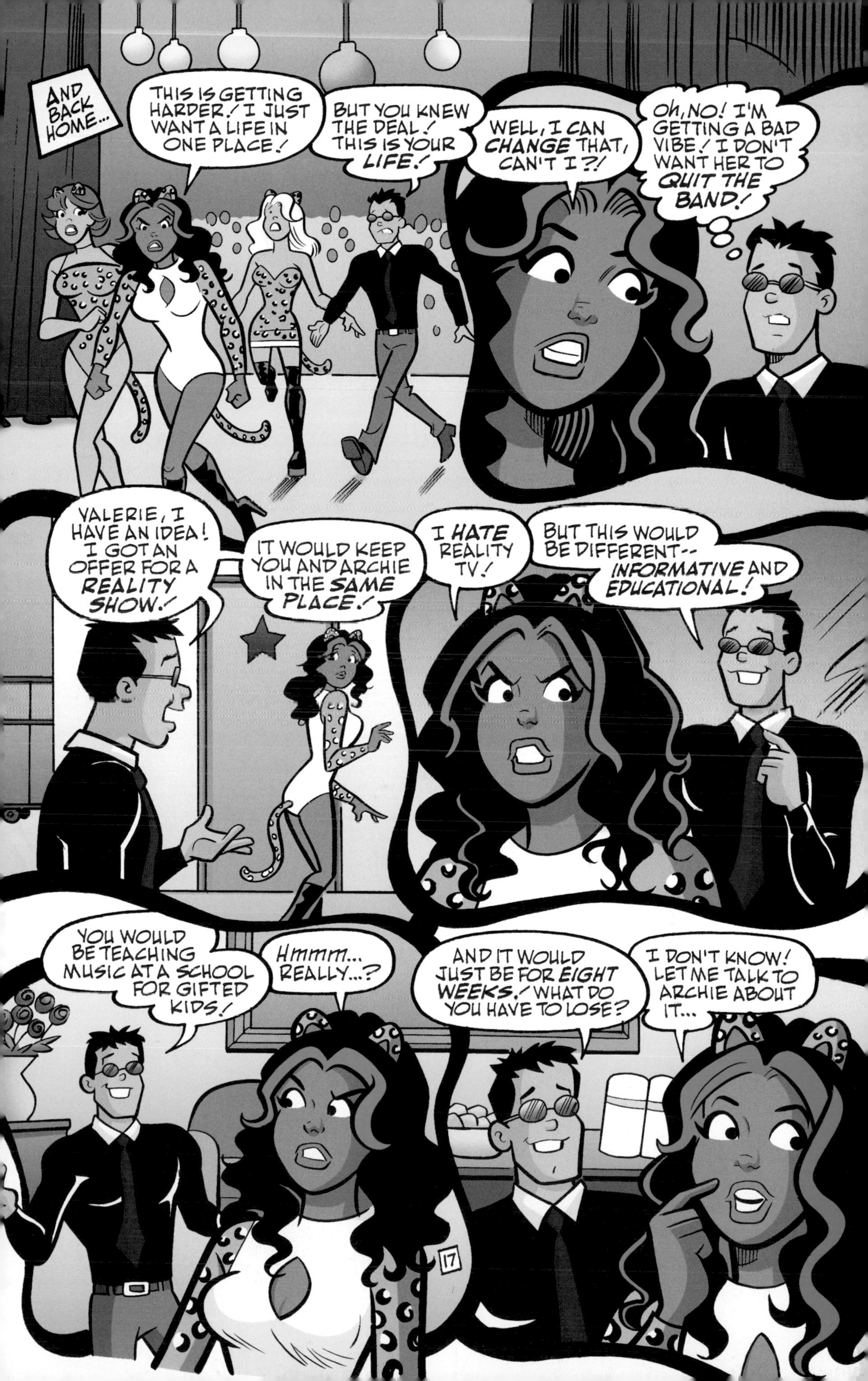
AND BACK HOME...
THIS IS GETTING HARDER! I JUST WANT A LIFE IN ONE PLACE!
BUT YOU KNEW THE DEAL! THIS IS YOUR LIFE!
WELL, I CAN CHANGE THAT, CAN'T I?!
Oh, NO! I'M GETTING A BAD VIBE! I DON'T WANT HER TO QUIT THE BAND!
VALERIE, I HAVE AN IDEA! I GOT AN OFFER FOR A REALITY SHOW!
IT WOULD KEEP YOU AND ARCHIE IN THE SAME PLACE!
I HATE REALITY TV!
BUT THIS WOULD BE DIFFERENT-- INFORMATIVE AND EDUCATIONAL!
YOU WOULD BE TEACHING MUSIC AT A SCHOOL FOR GIFTED KIDS!
Hmmm... REALLY...?
AND IT WOULD JUST BE FOR EIGHT WEEKS! WHAT DO YOU HAVE TO LOSE?
I DON'T KNOW! LET ME TALK TO ARCHIE ABOUT IT...
17

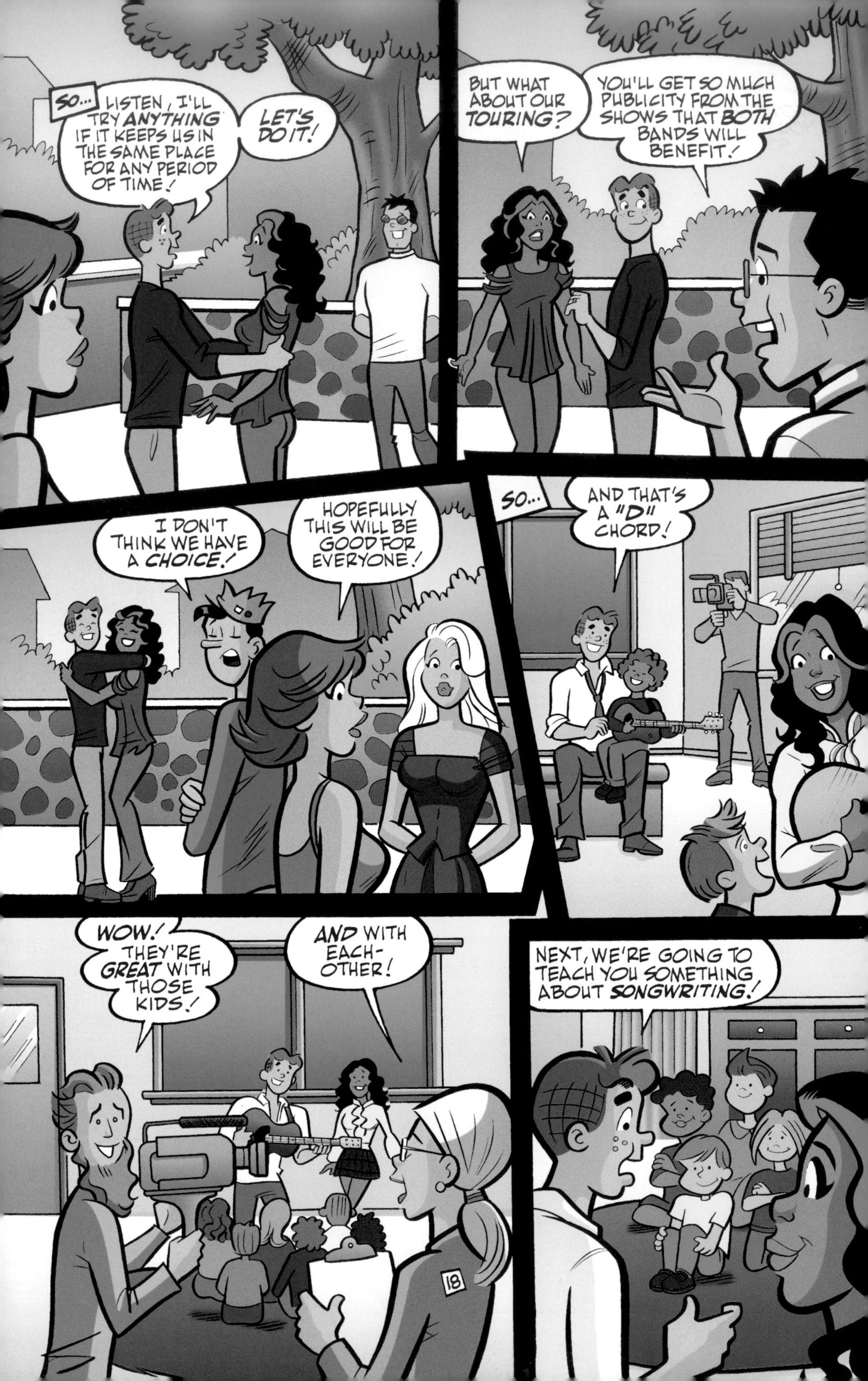
SO...
LISTEN, I'LL TRY ANYTHING IF IT KEEPS US IN THE SAME PLACE FOR ANY PERIOD OF TIME!
LET'S DO IT!
BUT WHAT ABOUT OUR TOURING?
YOU'LL GET SO MUCH PUBLICITY FROM THE SHOWS THAT BOTH BANDS WILL BENEFIT!
I DON'T THINK WE HAVE A CHOICE!
HOPEFULLY THIS WILL BE GOOD FOR EVERYONE!
SO...
AND THAT'S A "D" CHORD!
WOW! THEY'RE GREAT WITH THOSE KIDS!
AND WITH EACH-OTHER!
NEXT, WE'RE GOING TO TEACH YOU SOMETHING ABOUT SONGWRITING!
18

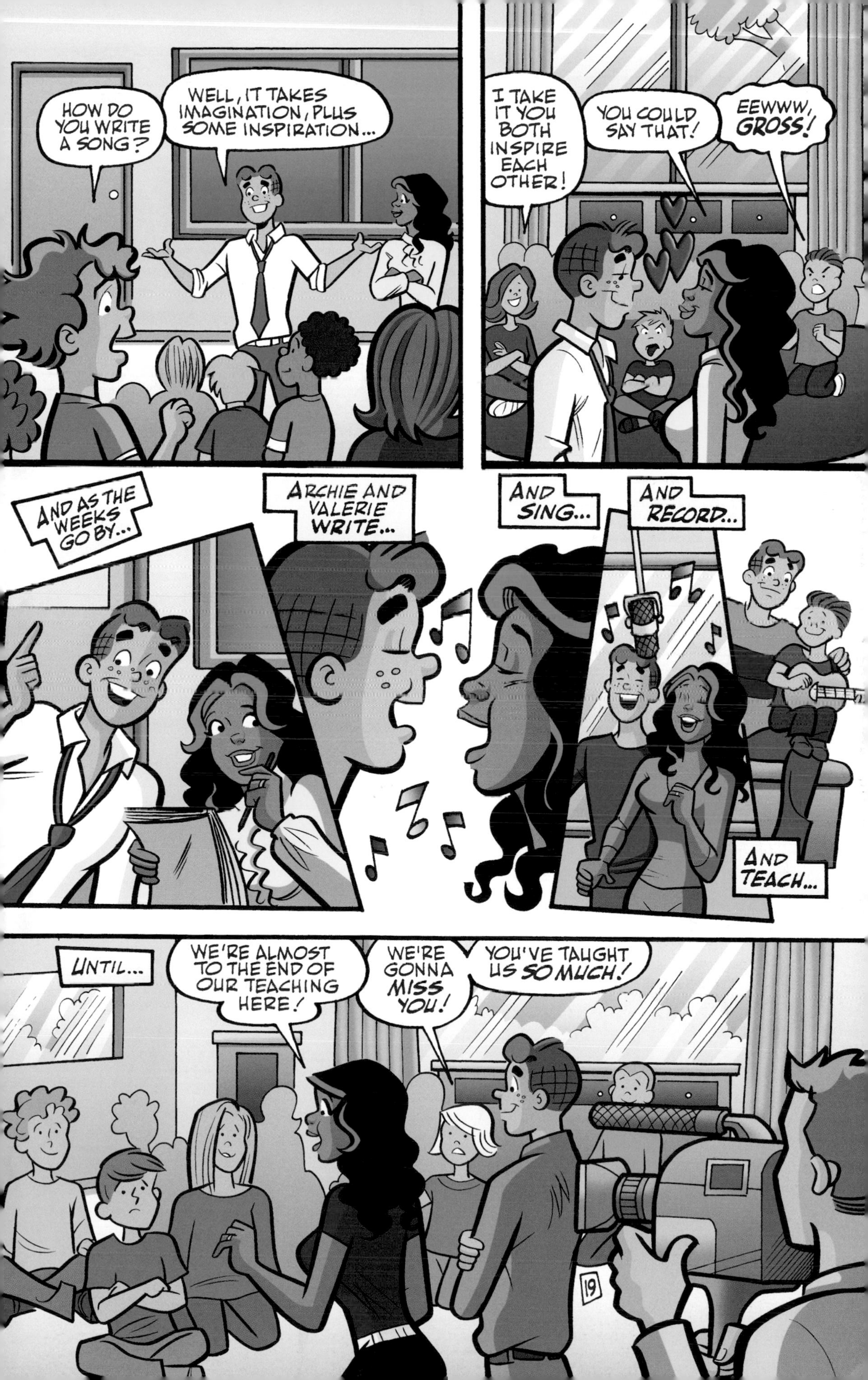
HOW DO YOU WRITE A SONG?
WELL, IT TAKES IMAGINATION, PLUS SOME INSPIRATION...
I TAKE IT YOU BOTH INSPIRE EACH OTHER!
YOU COULD SAY THAT!
EEWWW, GROSS!
AND AS THE WEEKS GO BY...
ARCHIE AND VALERIE WRITE...
AND SING...
AND RECORD...
AND TEACH...
UNTIL...
WE'RE ALMOST TO THE END OF OUR TEACHING HERE!
WE'RE GONNA MISS YOU!
YOU'VE TAUGHT US SO MUCH!
19

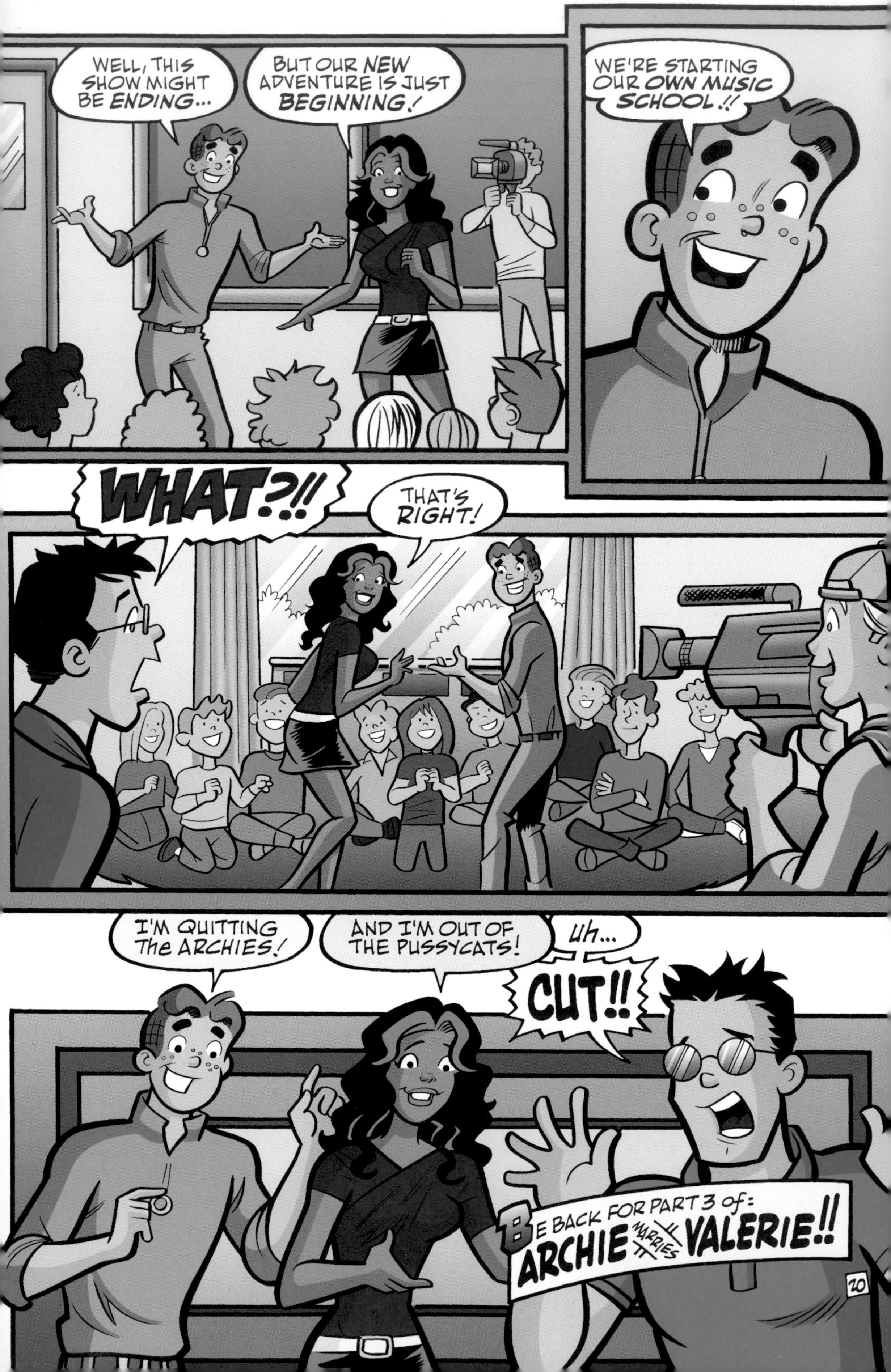

WELL, THIS SHOW MIGHT BE ENDING...
BUT OUR NEW ADVENTURE IS JUST BEGINNING!
WE'RE STARTING OUR OWN MUSIC SCHOOL!!
WHAT?!!
THAT'S RIGHT!
I'M QUITTING THE ARCHIES!
AND I'M OUT OF THE PUSSYCATS!
uh...
CUT!!
BE BACK FOR PART 3 OF: ARCHIE MARRIES VALERIE!!
20

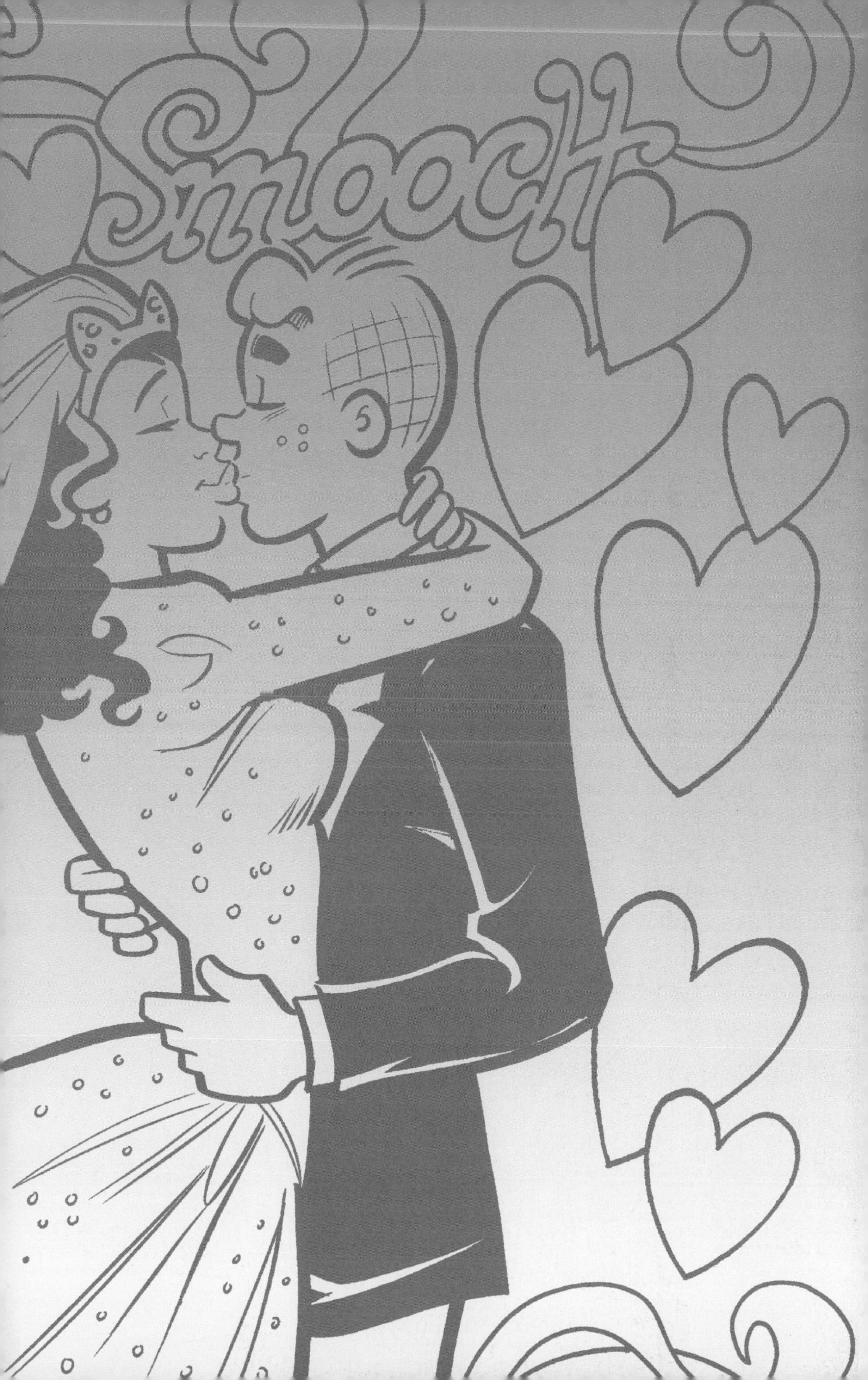
Smooch

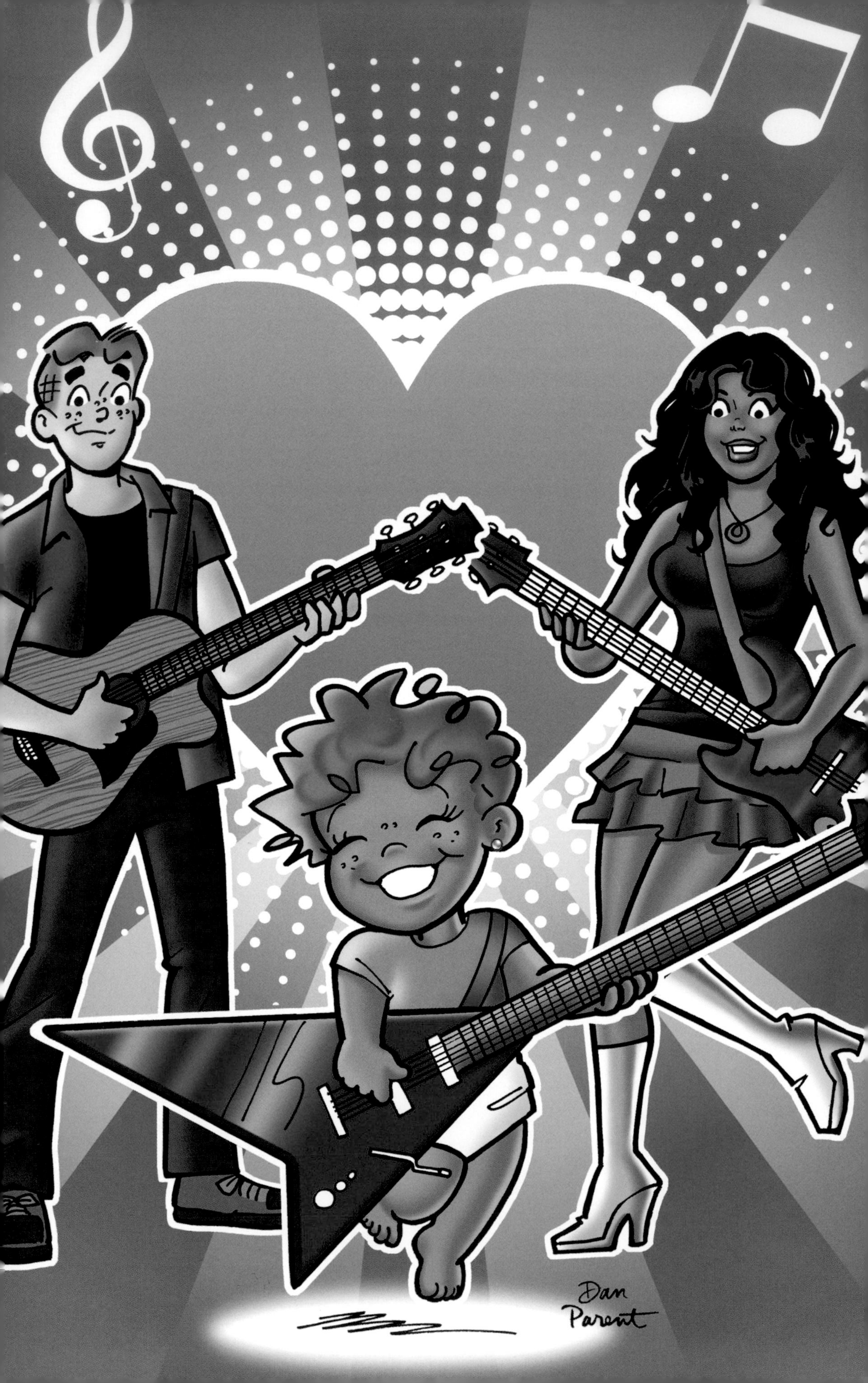
Dan Parent

Chapter Three: A Star is Born

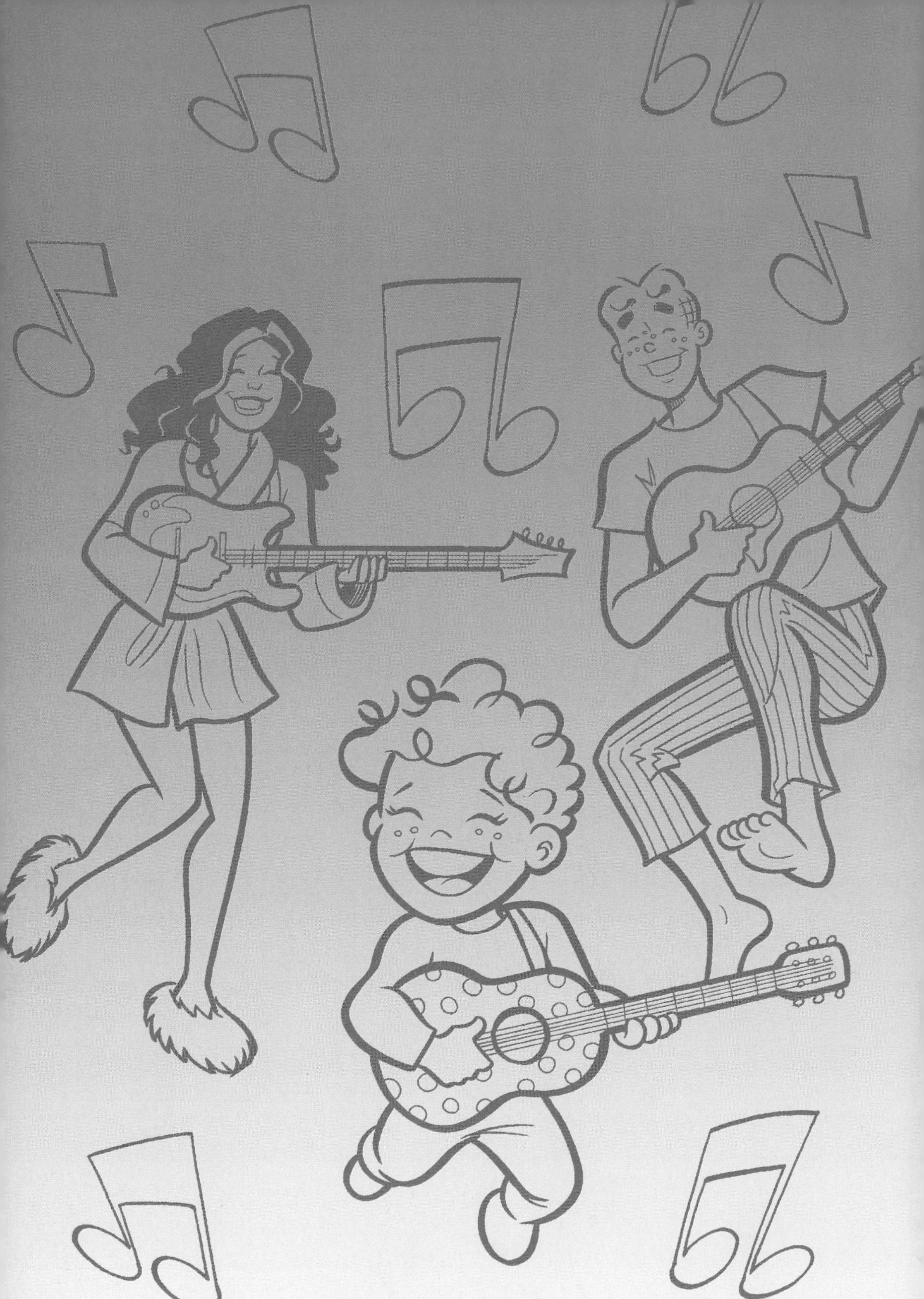

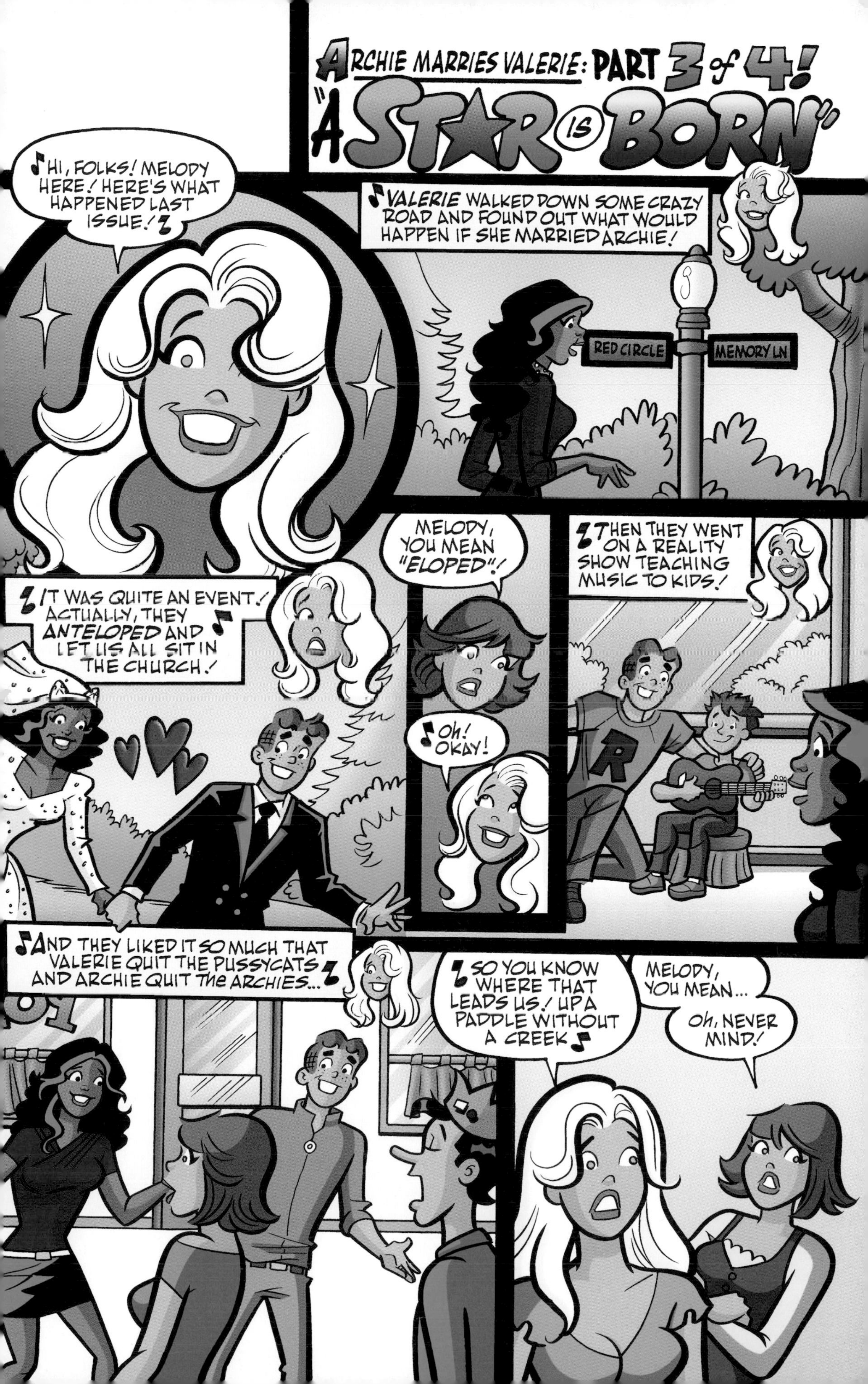
ARCHIE MARRIES VALERIE: PART 3 of 4!
"A STAR IS BORN"
HI, FOLKS! MELODY HERE! HERE'S WHAT HAPPENED LAST ISSUE!
VALERIE WALKED DOWN SOME CRAZY ROAD AND FOUND OUT WHAT WOULD HAPPEN IF SHE MARRIED ARCHIE!
RED CIRCLE
MEMORY LN
IT WAS QUITE AN EVENT! ACTUALLY, THEY ANTELOPED AND LET US ALL SIT IN THE CHURCH!
MELODY, YOU MEAN "ELOPED"!
OH! OKAY!
THEN THEY WENT ON A REALITY SHOW TEACHING MUSIC TO KIDS!
AND THEY LIKED IT SO MUCH THAT VALERIE QUIT THE PUSSYCATS AND ARCHIE QUIT THE ARCHIES...
SO YOU KNOW WHERE THAT LEADS US! UP A PADDLE WITHOUT A CREEK
MELODY, YOU MEAN...
OH, NEVER MIND!

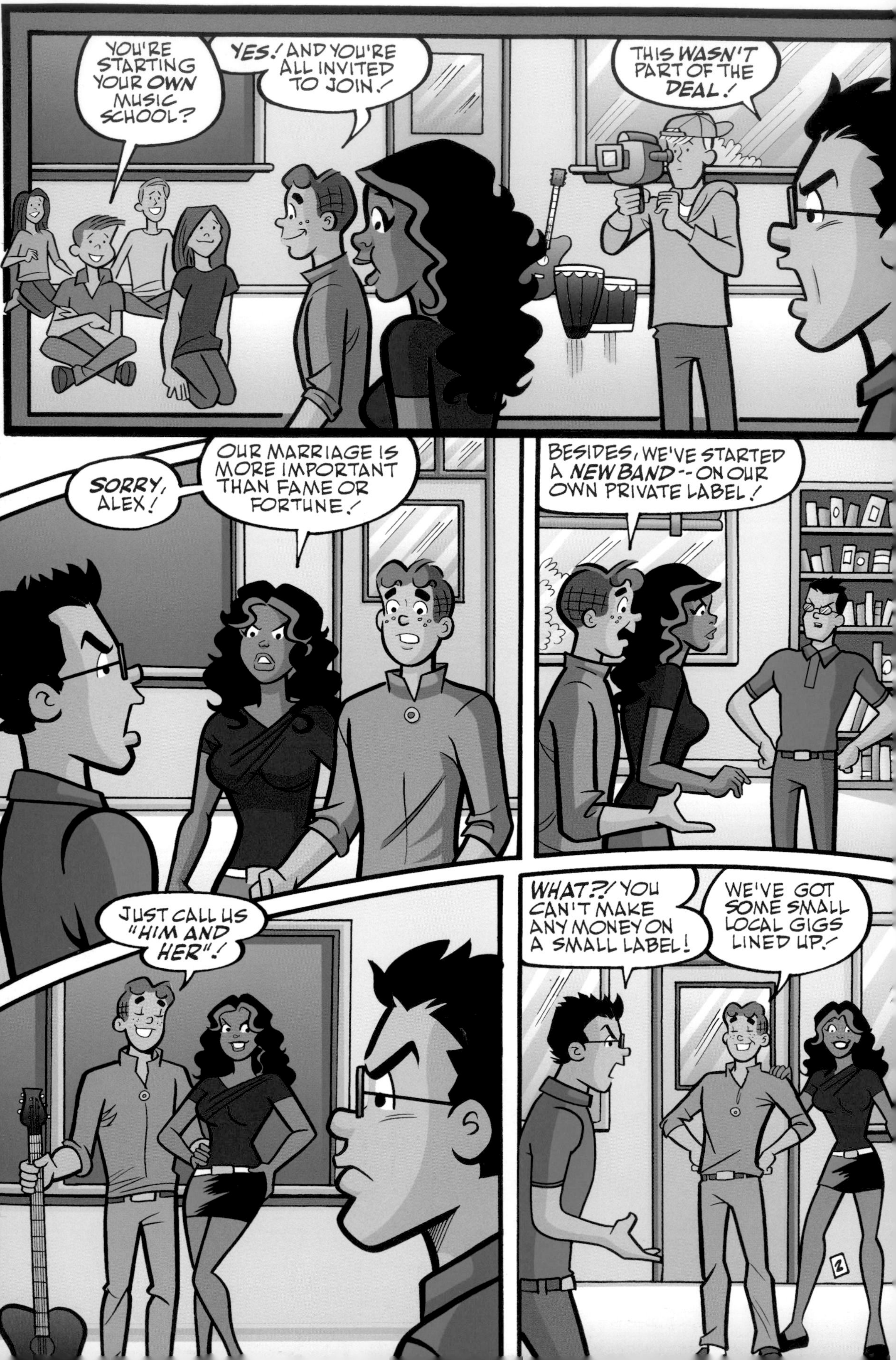
YOU'RE STARTING YOUR OWN MUSIC SCHOOL?
YES! AND YOU'RE ALL INVITED TO JOIN!
THIS WASN'T PART OF THE DEAL!
SORRY, ALEX!
OUR MARRIAGE IS MORE IMPORTANT THAN FAME OR FORTUNE!
BESIDES, WE'VE STARTED A NEW BAND--ON OUR OWN PRIVATE LABEL!
JUST CALL US "HIM AND HER"!
WHAT?! YOU CAN'T MAKE ANY MONEY ON A SMALL LABEL!
WE'VE GOT SOME SMALL LOCAL GIGS LINED UP!
2

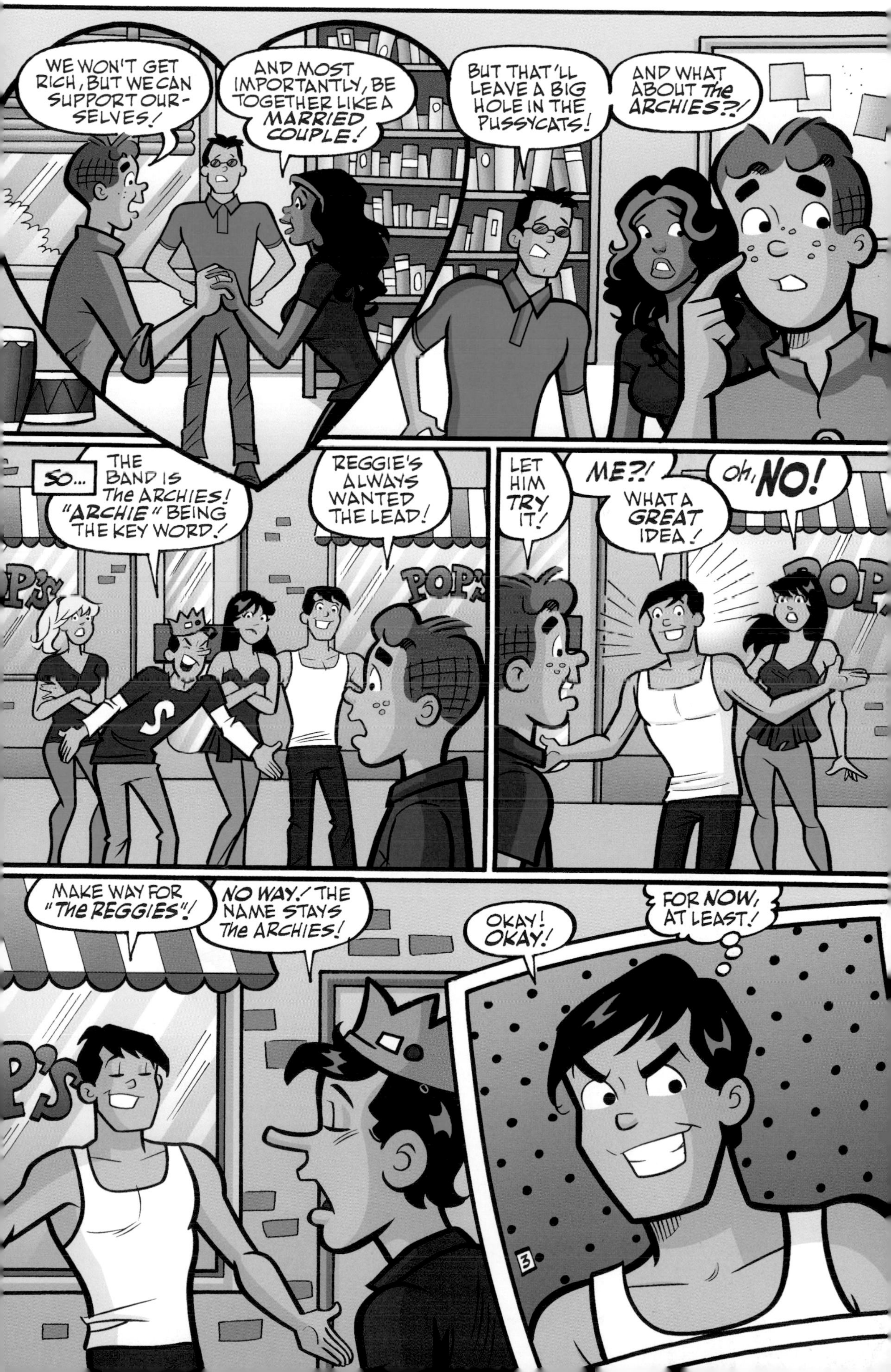
WE WON'T GET RICH, BUT WE CAN SUPPORT OUR-SELVES!
AND MOST IMPORTANTLY, BE TOGETHER LIKE A MARRIED COUPLE!
BUT THAT'LL LEAVE A BIG HOLE IN THE PUSSYCATS!
AND WHAT ABOUT The ARCHIES?!
SO...
THE BAND IS The ARCHIES! "ARCHIE" BEING THE KEY WORD!
REGGIE'S ALWAYS WANTED THE LEAD!
POP'S
LET HIM TRY IT!
ME?!
WHAT A GREAT IDEA!
Oh, NO!
MAKE WAY FOR "The REGGIES"!
NO WAY! THE NAME STAYS The ARCHIES!
OKAY! OKAY!
FOR NOW, AT LEAST!
3

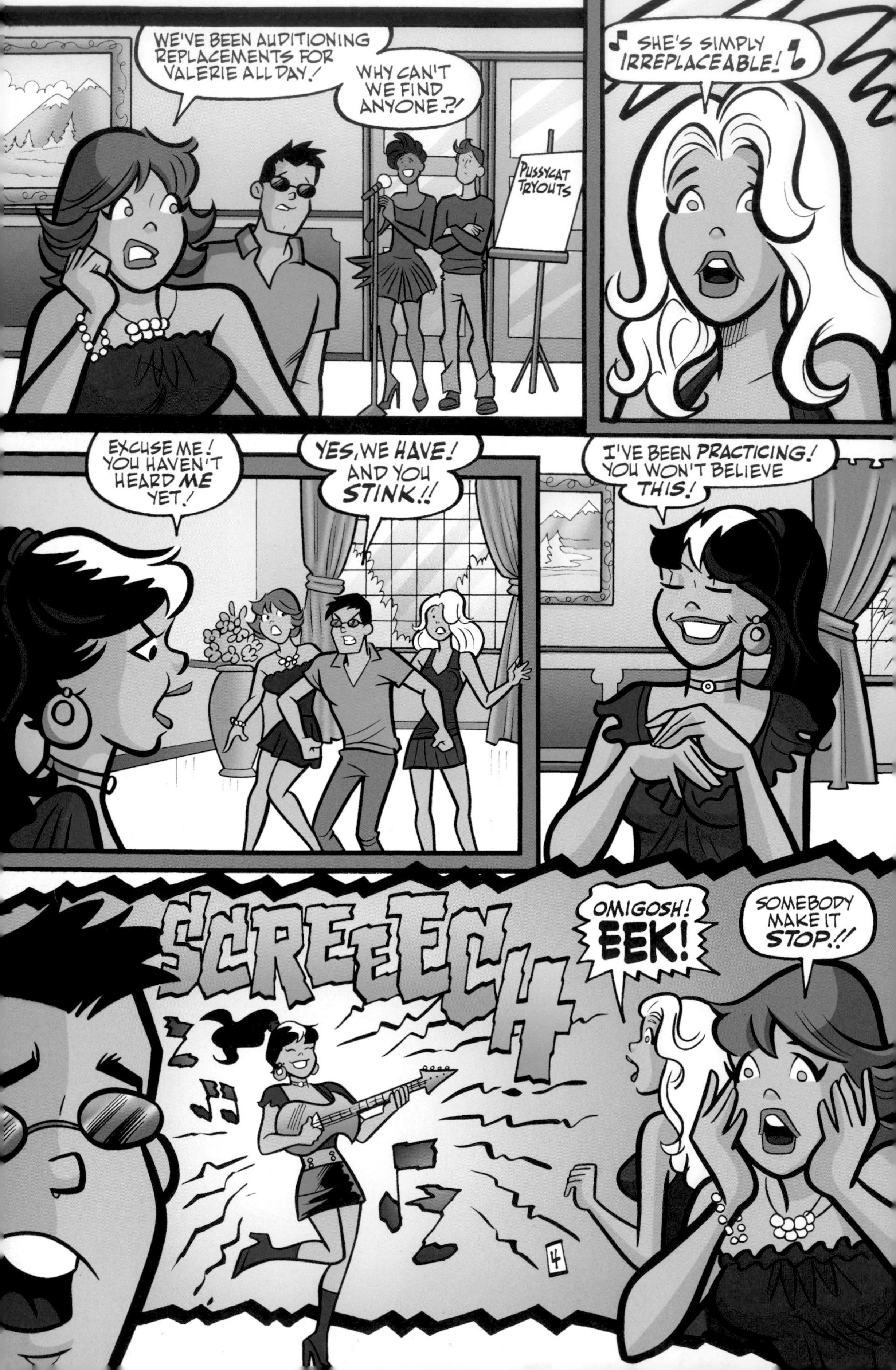
WE'VE BEEN AUDITIONING REPLACEMENTS FOR VALERIE ALL DAY!
WHY CAN'T WE FIND ANYONE?!
PUSSYCAT TRYOUTS
SHE'S SIMPLY IRREPLACEABLE!
EXCUSE ME! YOU HAVEN'T HEARD ME YET!
YES, WE HAVE! AND YOU STINK!!
I'VE BEEN PRACTICING! YOU WON'T BELIEVE THIS!
SCREEECH
OMIGOSH! EEK!
SOMEBODY MAKE IT STOP!!
4

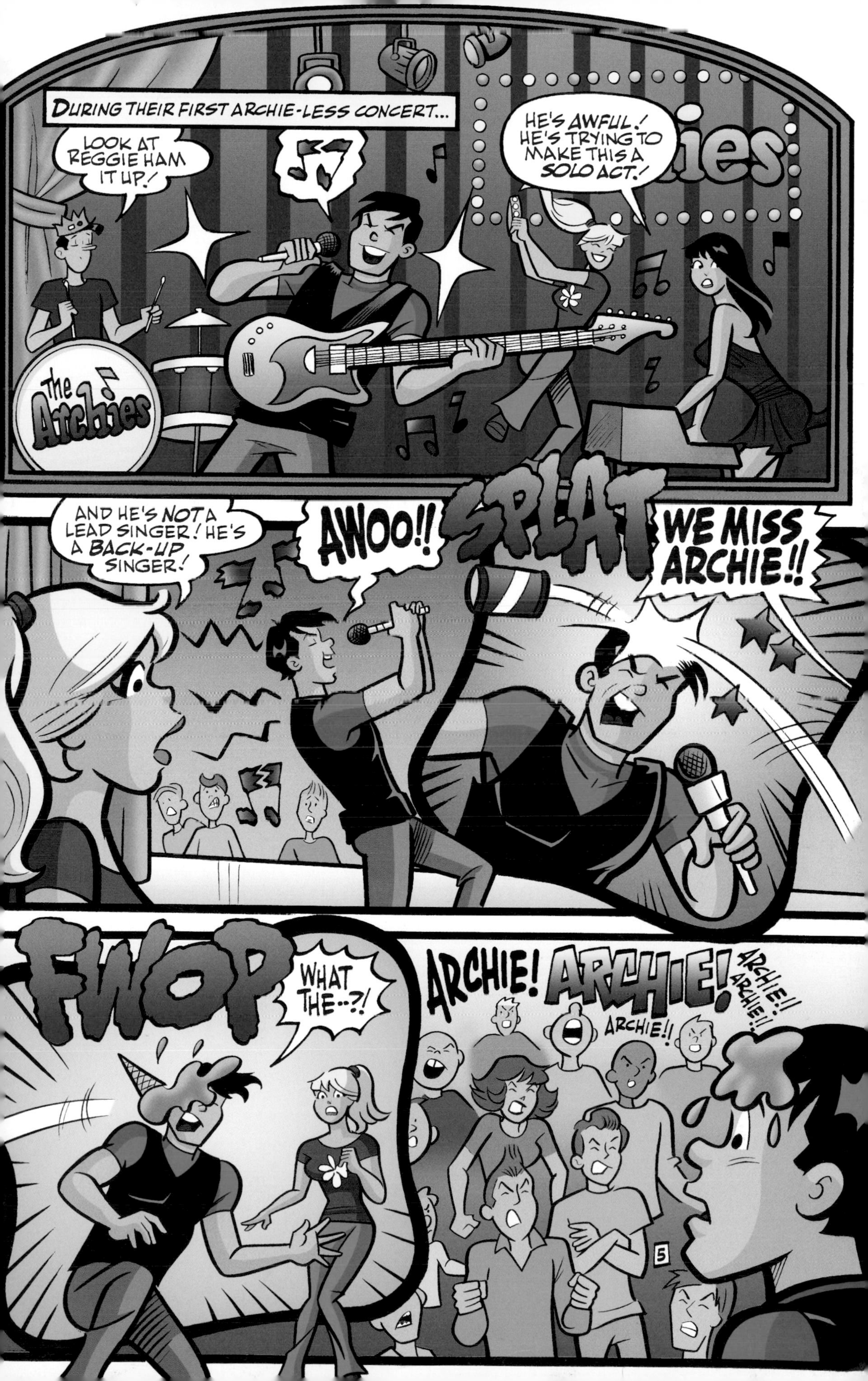

DURING THEIR FIRST ARCHIE-LESS CONCERT...
LOOK AT REGGIE HAM IT UP!
HE'S AWFUL! HE'S TRYING TO MAKE THIS A SOLO ACT!
The Archies
AND HE'S NOT A LEAD SINGER! HE'S A BACK-UP SINGER!
AWOO!!
SPLAT
WE MISS ARCHIE!!
FWOP
WHAT THE--?!
ARCHIE! ARCHIE!
ARCHIE!! ARCHIE!!
ARCHIE!!
5

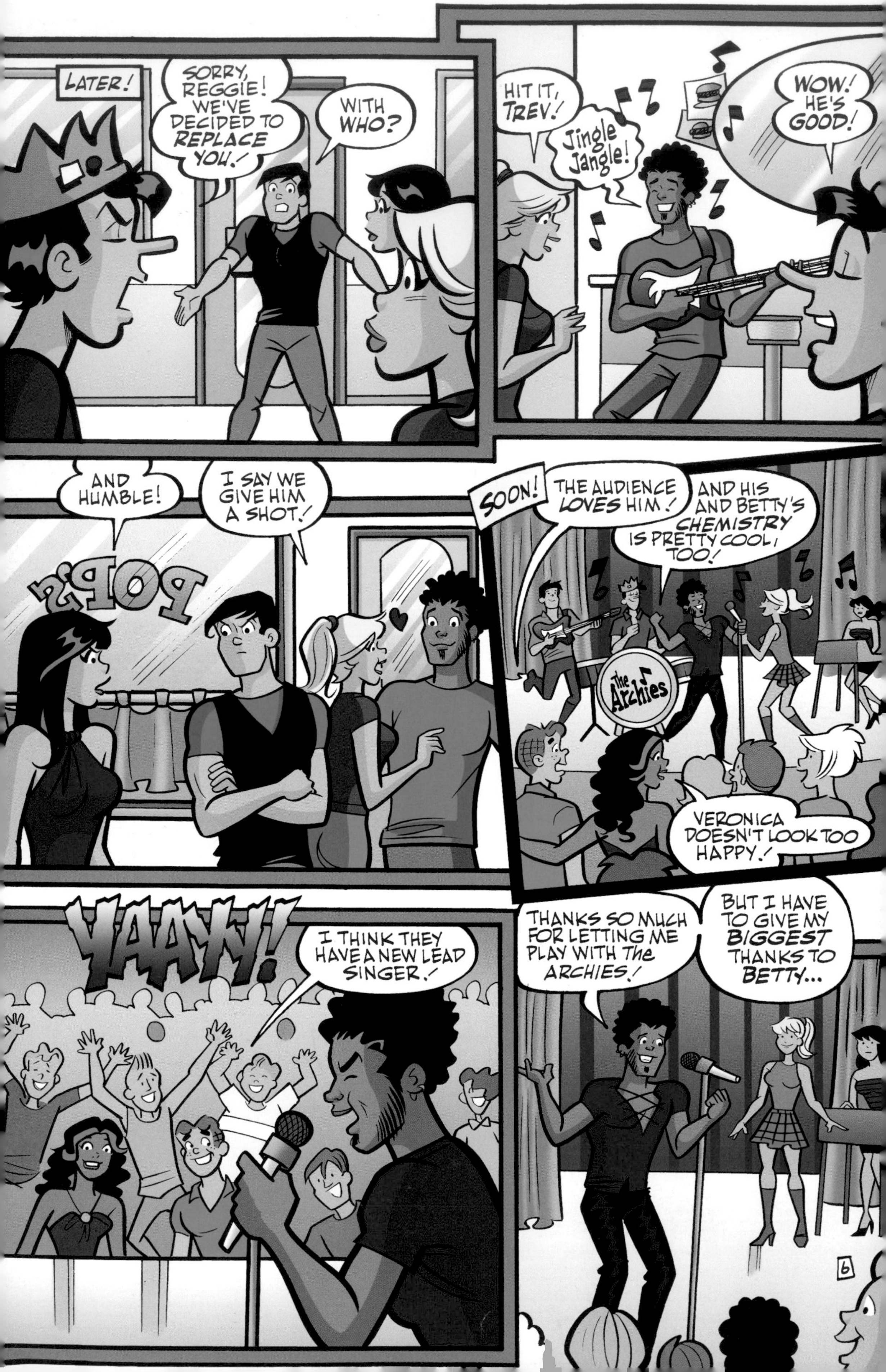
LATER!
SORRY, REGGIE! WE'VE DECIDED TO REPLACE YOU!
WITH WHO?
HIT IT, TREV!
Jingle Jangle!
WOW! HE'S GOOD!
AND HUMBLE!
I SAY WE GIVE HIM A SHOT!
POP'S
SOON!
THE AUDIENCE LOVES HIM!
AND HIS AND BETTY'S CHEMISTRY IS PRETTY COOL, TOO!
The Archies
VERONICA DOESN'T LOOK TOO HAPPY!
YAAY!
I THINK THEY HAVE A NEW LEAD SINGER!
THANKS SO MUCH FOR LETTING ME PLAY WITH The ARCHIES!
BUT I HAVE TO GIVE MY BIGGEST THANKS TO BETTY...
6

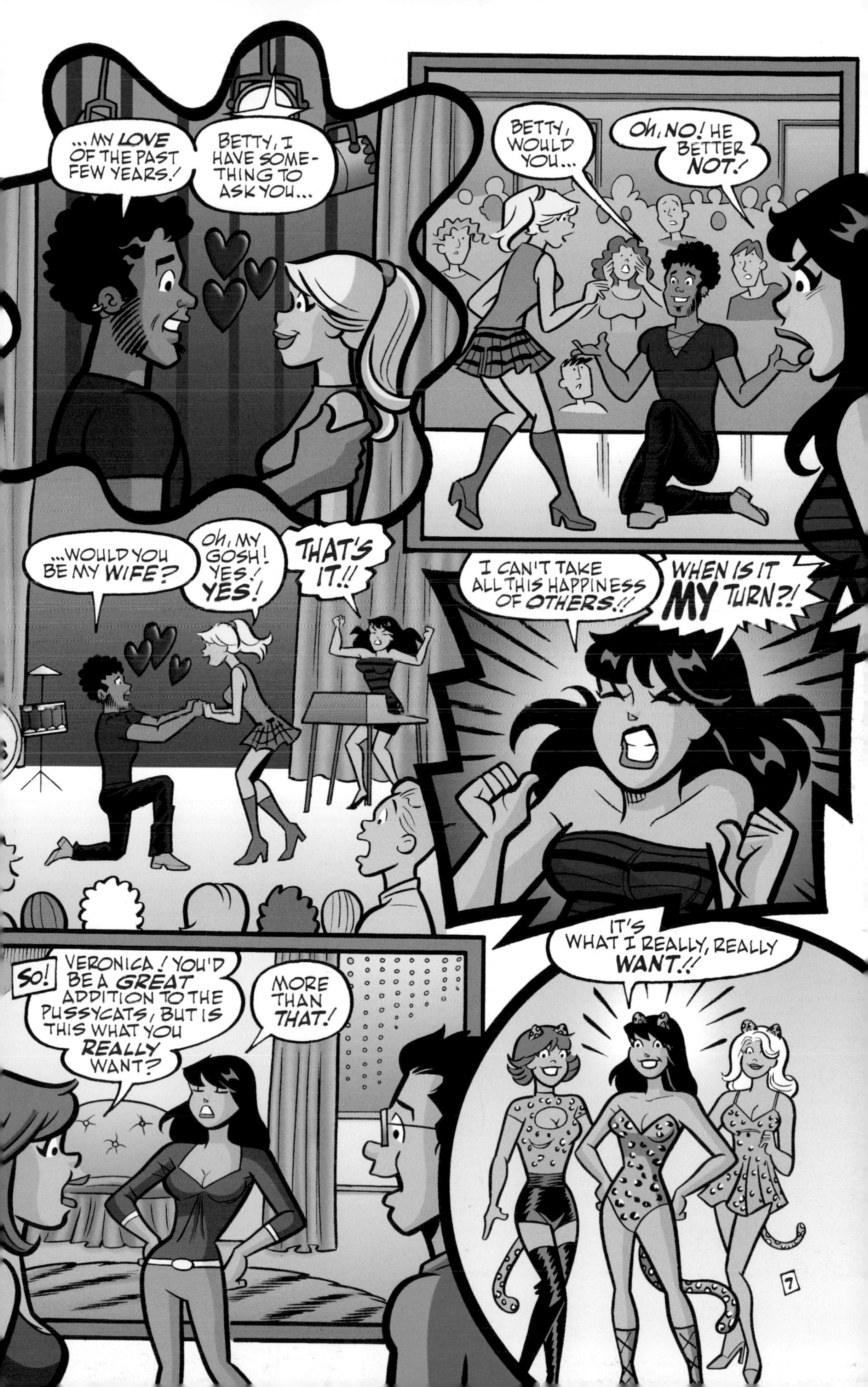
...MY LOVE OF THE PAST FEW YEARS!
BETTY, I HAVE SOME-THING TO ASK YOU...
BETTY, WOULD YOU...
Oh, NO! HE BETTER NOT!
...WOULD YOU BE MY WIFE?
Oh, MY GOSH! YES! YES!
THAT'S IT!!
I CAN'T TAKE ALL THIS HAPPINESS OF OTHERS!!
WHEN IS IT MY TURN?!
SO!
VERONICA! YOU'D BE A GREAT ADDITION TO THE PUSSYCATS, BUT IS THIS WHAT YOU REALLY WANT?
MORE THAN THAT!
IT'S WHAT I REALLY, REALLY WANT!!

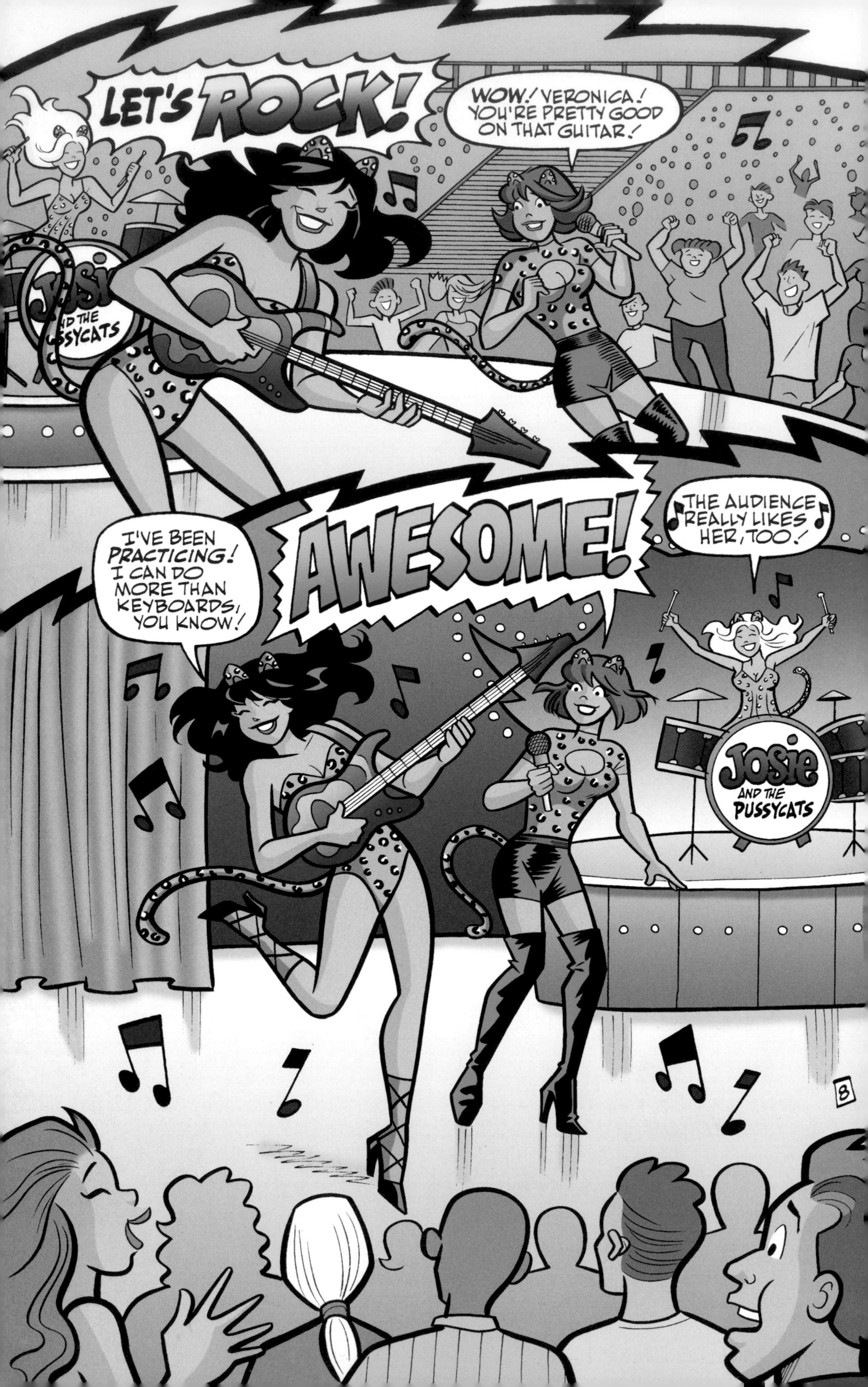
LET'S ROCK!
WOW! VERONICA! YOU'RE PRETTY GOOD ON THAT GUITAR!
JOSIE AND THE PUSSYCATS
AWESOME!
I'VE BEEN PRACTICING! I CAN DO MORE THAN KEYBOARDS, YOU KNOW!
THE AUDIENCE REALLY LIKES HER, TOO!
JOSIE AND THE PUSSYCATS

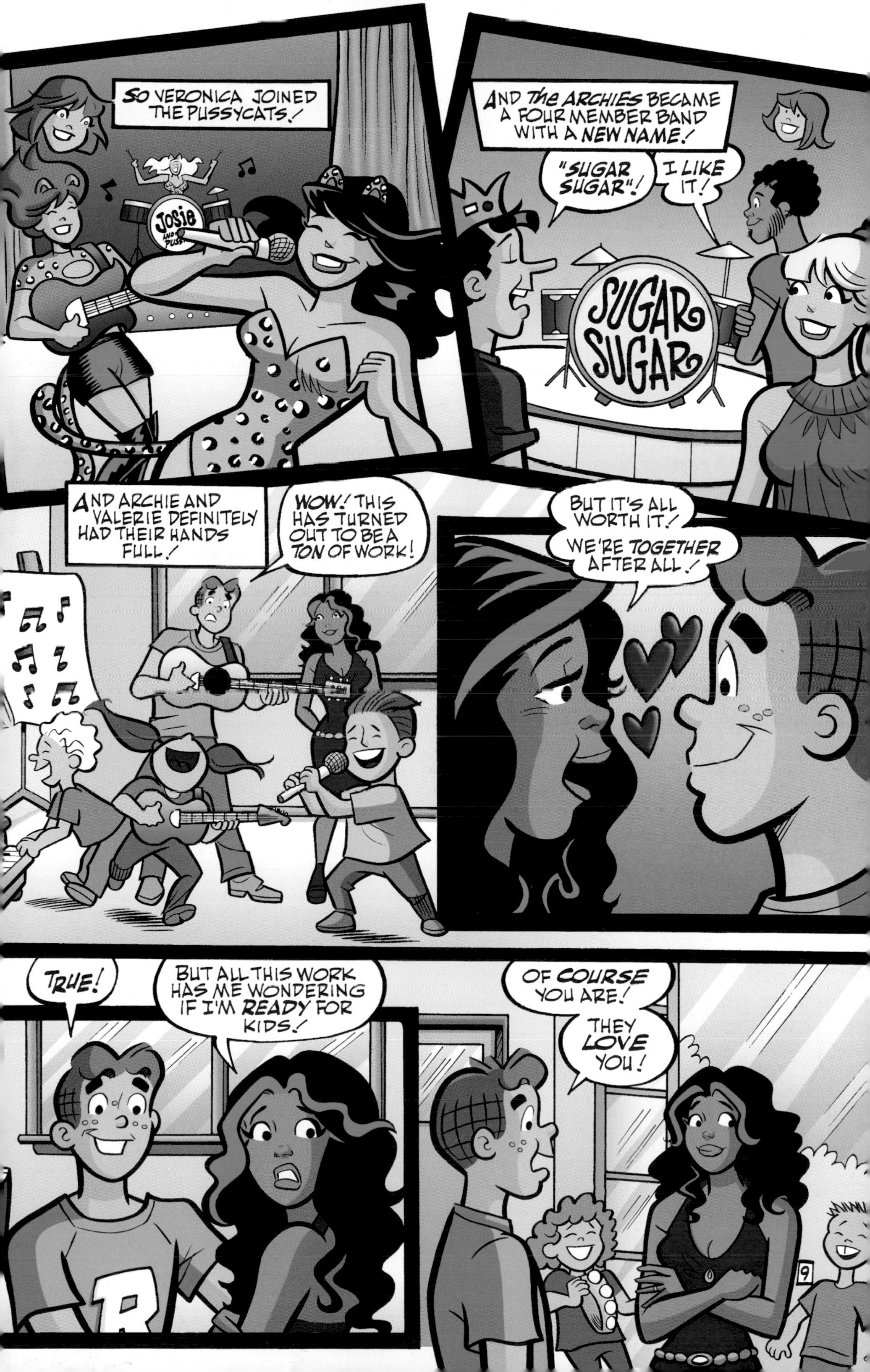
SO VERONICA JOINED THE PUSSYCATS!
JOSIE AND THE PUSSY
AND THE ARCHIES BECAME A FOUR MEMBER BAND WITH A NEW NAME!
"SUGAR SUGAR"!
I LIKE IT!
SUGAR SUGAR
AND ARCHIE AND VALERIE DEFINITELY HAD THEIR HANDS FULL!
WOW! THIS HAS TURNED OUT TO BE A TON OF WORK!
BUT IT'S ALL WORTH IT!
WE'RE TOGETHER AFTER ALL!
TRUE!
BUT ALL THIS WORK HAS ME WONDERING IF I'M READY FOR KIDS!
OF COURSE YOU ARE!
THEY LOVE YOU!

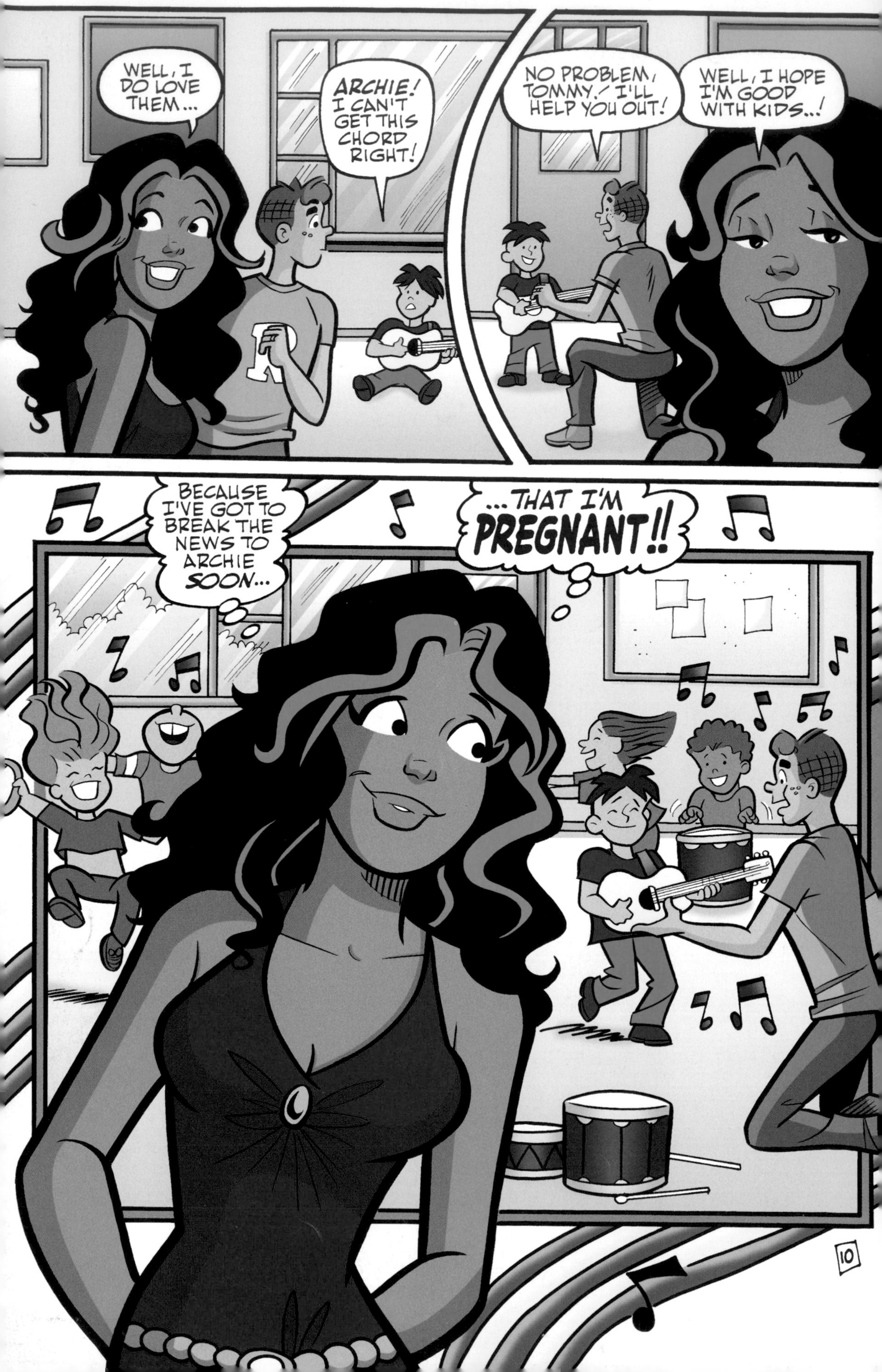
WELL, I DO LOVE THEM...
ARCHIE! I CAN'T GET THIS CHORD RIGHT!
NO PROBLEM, TOMMY! I'LL HELP YOU OUT!
WELL, I HOPE I'M GOOD WITH KIDS...!
BECAUSE I'VE GOT TO BREAK THE NEWS TO ARCHIE SOON...
...THAT I'M PREGNANT!!

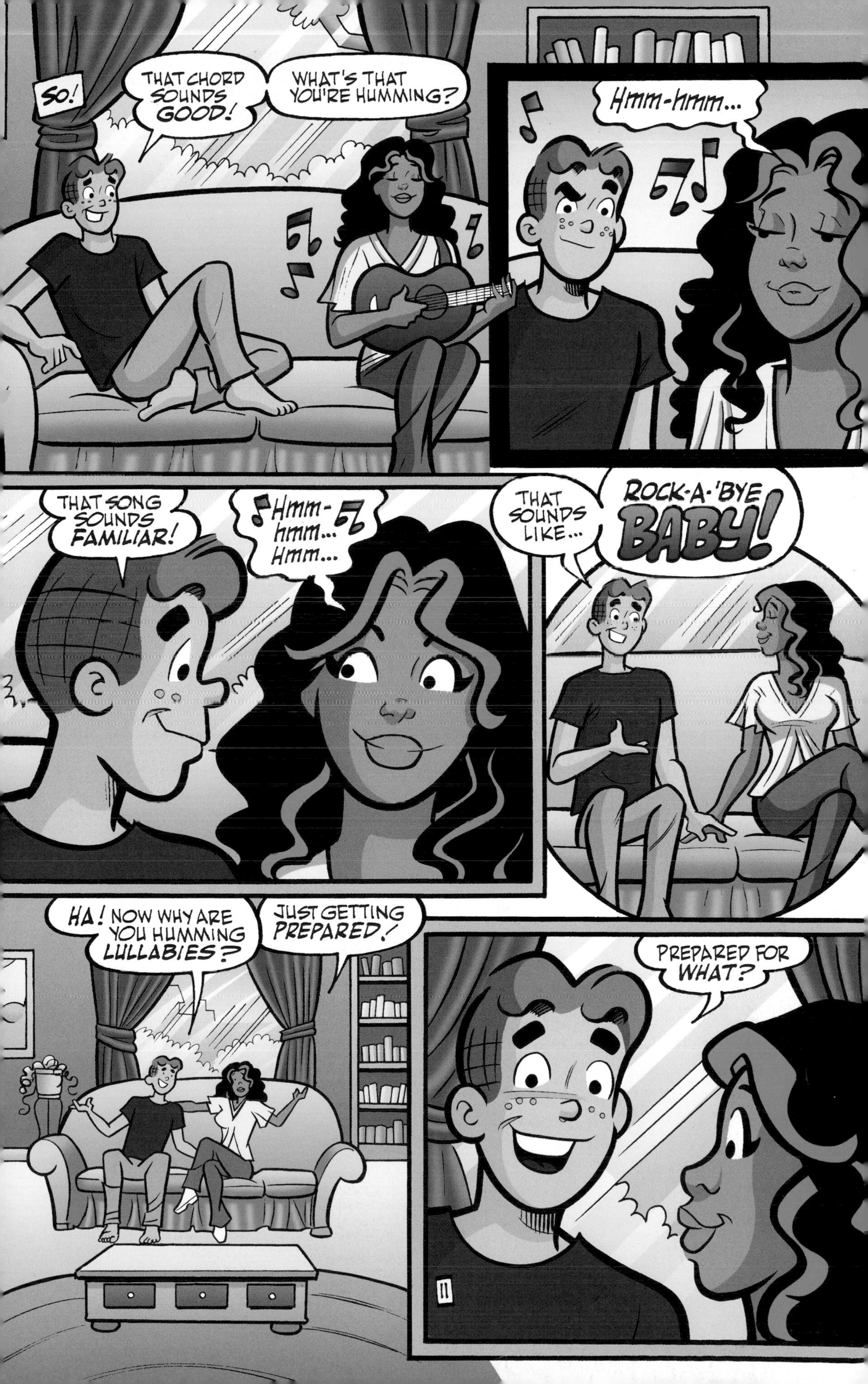
SO!
THAT CHORD SOUNDS GOOD!
WHAT'S THAT YOU'RE HUMMING?
Hmm-hmm...
THAT SONG SOUNDS FAMILIAR!
Hmm-hmm... Hmm...
THAT SOUNDS LIKE...
ROCK-A-'BYE BABY!
HA! NOW WHY ARE YOU HUMMING LULLABIES?
JUST GETTING PREPARED!
PREPARED FOR WHAT?
11

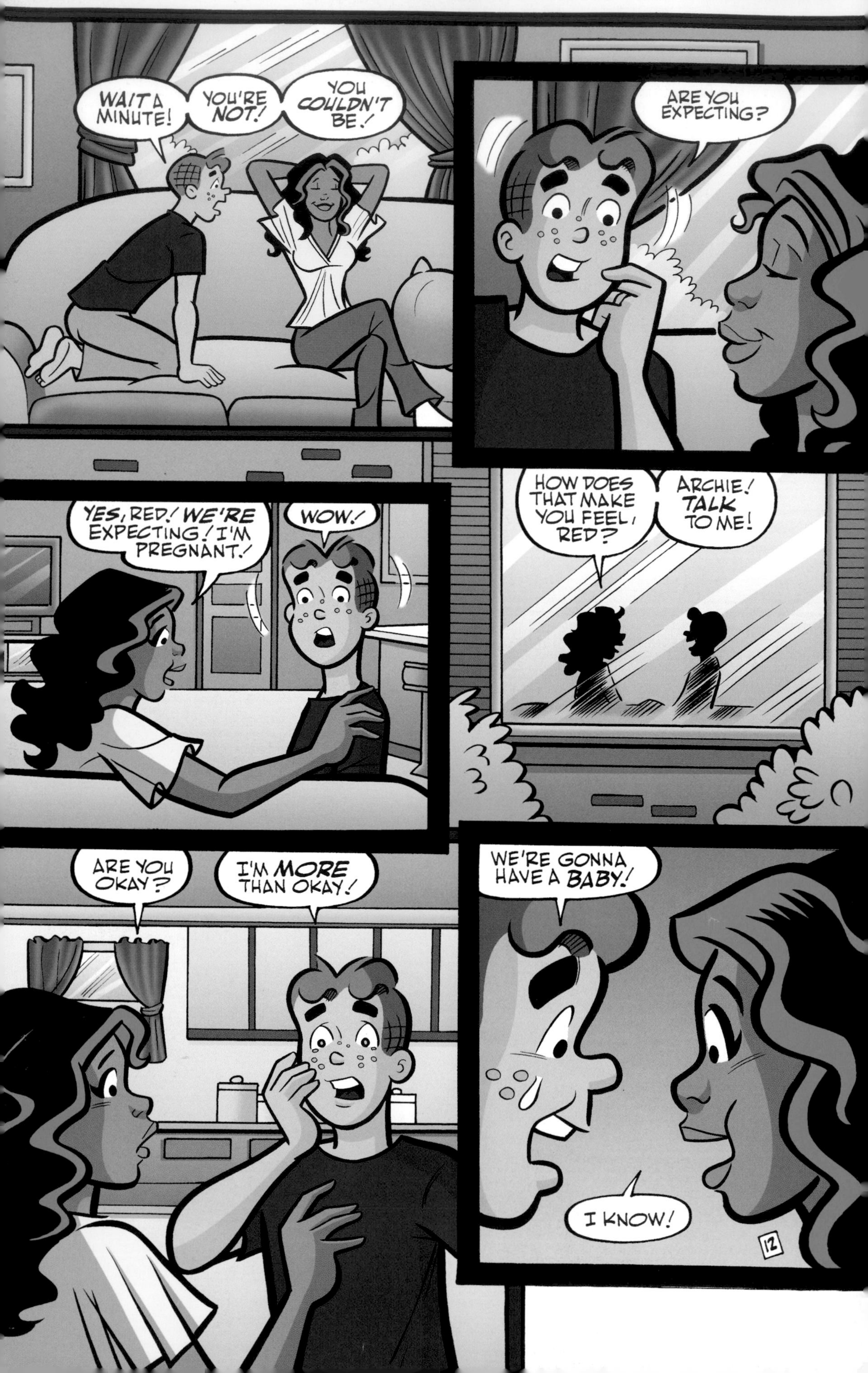
WAIT A MINUTE!
YOU'RE NOT!
YOU COULDN'T BE!
ARE YOU EXPECTING?
YES, RED! WE'RE EXPECTING! I'M PREGNANT!
WOW!
HOW DOES THAT MAKE YOU FEEL, RED?
ARCHIE! TALK TO ME!
ARE YOU OKAY?
I'M MORE THAN OKAY!
WE'RE GONNA HAVE A BABY!
I KNOW!
12

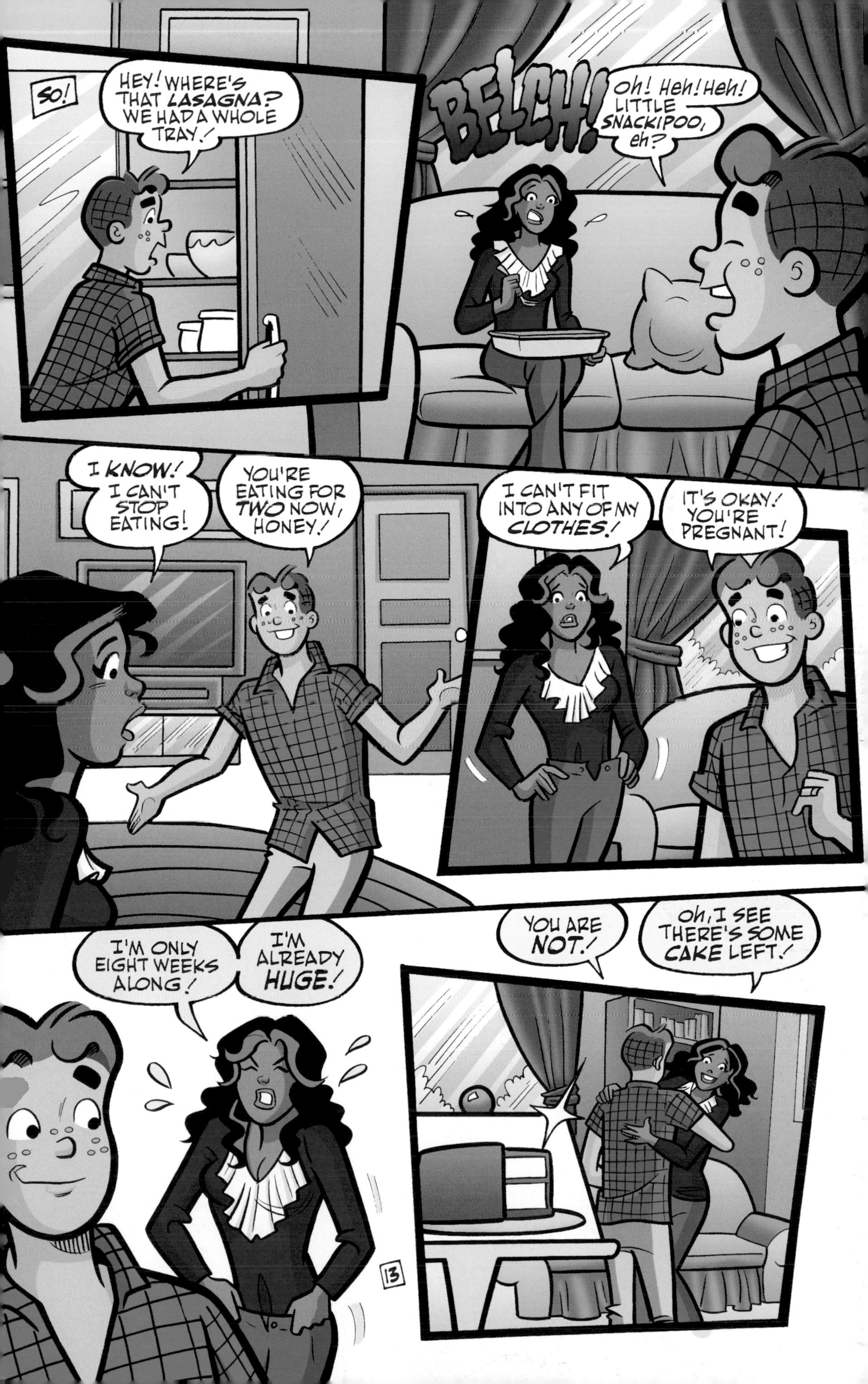
SO!
HEY! WHERE'S THAT LASAGNA? WE HAD A WHOLE TRAY!
BELCH!
Oh! Heh! Heh! LITTLE SNACKIPOO, eh?
I KNOW! I CAN'T STOP EATING!
YOU'RE EATING FOR TWO NOW, HONEY!
I CAN'T FIT INTO ANY OF MY CLOTHES!
IT'S OKAY! YOU'RE PREGNANT!
I'M ONLY EIGHT WEEKS ALONG!
I'M ALREADY HUGE!
YOU ARE NOT!
Oh, I SEE THERE'S SOME CAKE LEFT!
13

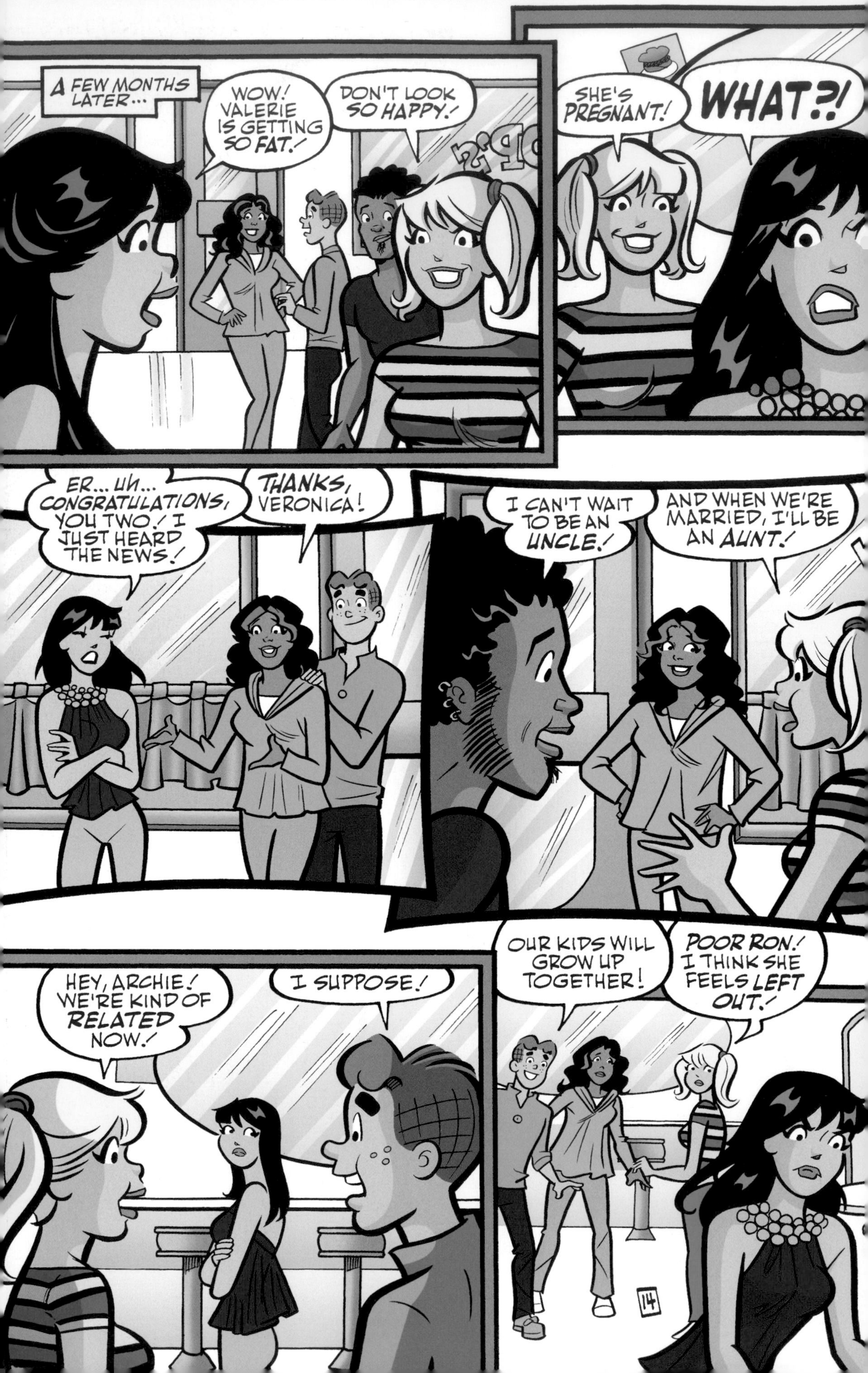

A FEW MONTHS LATER...
WOW! VALERIE IS GETTING SO FAT!
DON'T LOOK SO HAPPY!
SHE'S PREGNANT!
WHAT?!
ER... UH... CONGRATULATIONS, YOU TWO! I JUST HEARD THE NEWS!
THANKS, VERONICA!
I CAN'T WAIT TO BE AN UNCLE!
AND WHEN WE'RE MARRIED, I'LL BE AN AUNT!
HEY, ARCHIE! WE'RE KIND OF RELATED NOW!
I SUPPOSE!
OUR KIDS WILL GROW UP TOGETHER!
POOR RON! I THINK SHE FEELS LEFT OUT!
14

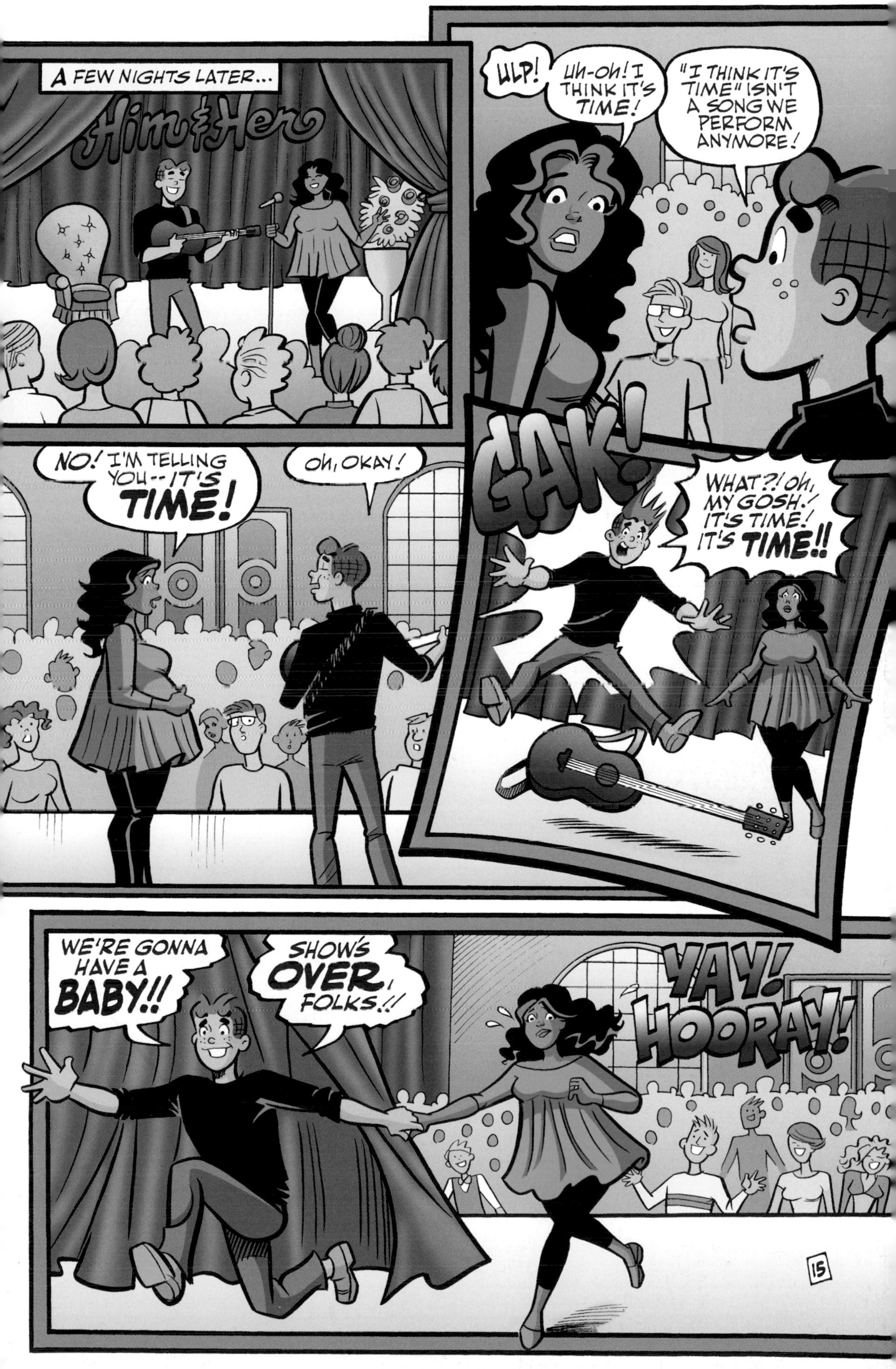
A FEW NIGHTS LATER...
Him & Her
ULP!
UH-OH! I THINK IT'S TIME!
"I THINK IT'S TIME" ISN'T A SONG WE PERFORM ANYMORE!
NO! I'M TELLING YOU-- IT'S TIME!
OH, OKAY!
GAK!
WHAT?! OH, MY GOSH! IT'S TIME! IT'S TIME!!
WE'RE GONNA HAVE A BABY!!
SHOW'S OVER, FOLKS!!
YAY! HOORAY!

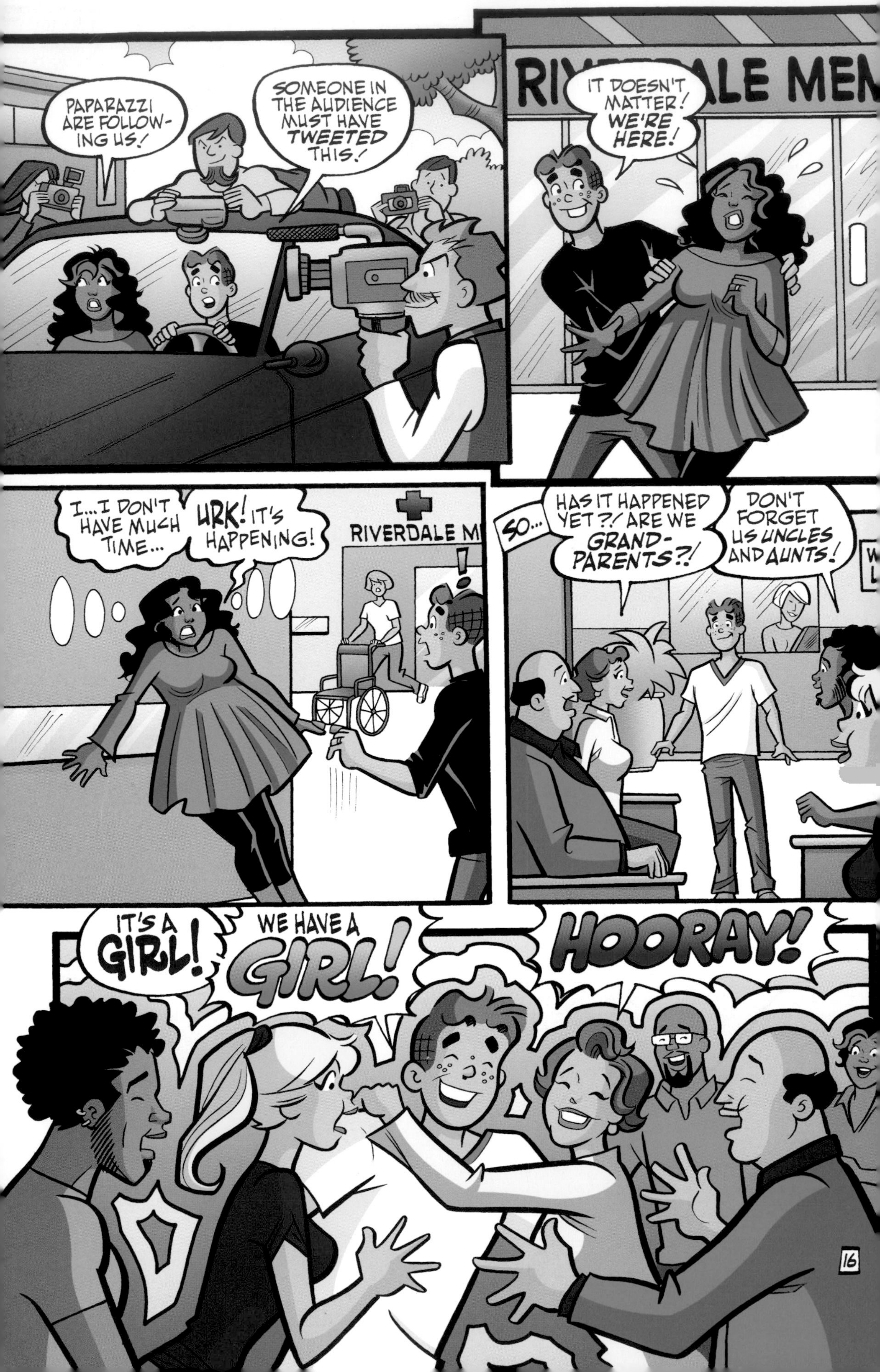
PAPARAZZI ARE FOLLOWING US!
SOMEONE IN THE AUDIENCE MUST HAVE TWEETED THIS!
RIVERDALE MEM
IT DOESN'T MATTER! WE'RE HERE!
I...I DON'T HAVE MUCH TIME...
URK! IT'S HAPPENING!
RIVERDALE M
SO...
HAS IT HAPPENED YET?! ARE WE GRAND-PARENTS?!
DON'T FORGET US UNCLES AND AUNTS!
IT'S A GIRL!
WE HAVE A GIRL!
HOORAY!
16

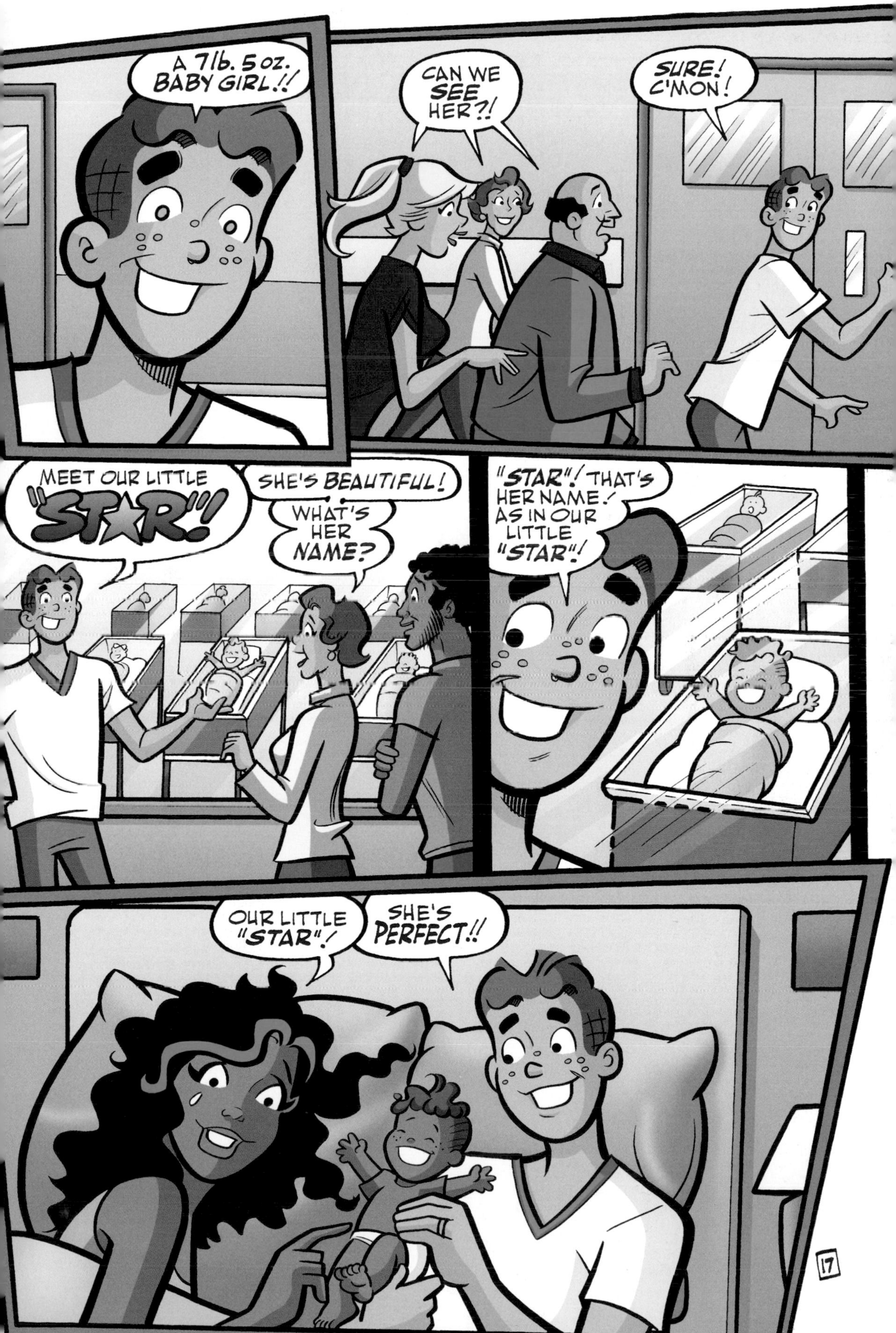

A 7lb. 5 oz. BABY GIRL!!
CAN WE SEE HER?!
SURE! C'MON!
MEET OUR LITTLE "STAR"!
SHE'S BEAUTIFUL!
WHAT'S HER NAME?
"STAR"! THAT'S HER NAME! AS IN OUR LITTLE "STAR"!
OUR LITTLE "STAR"!
SHE'S PERFECT!!

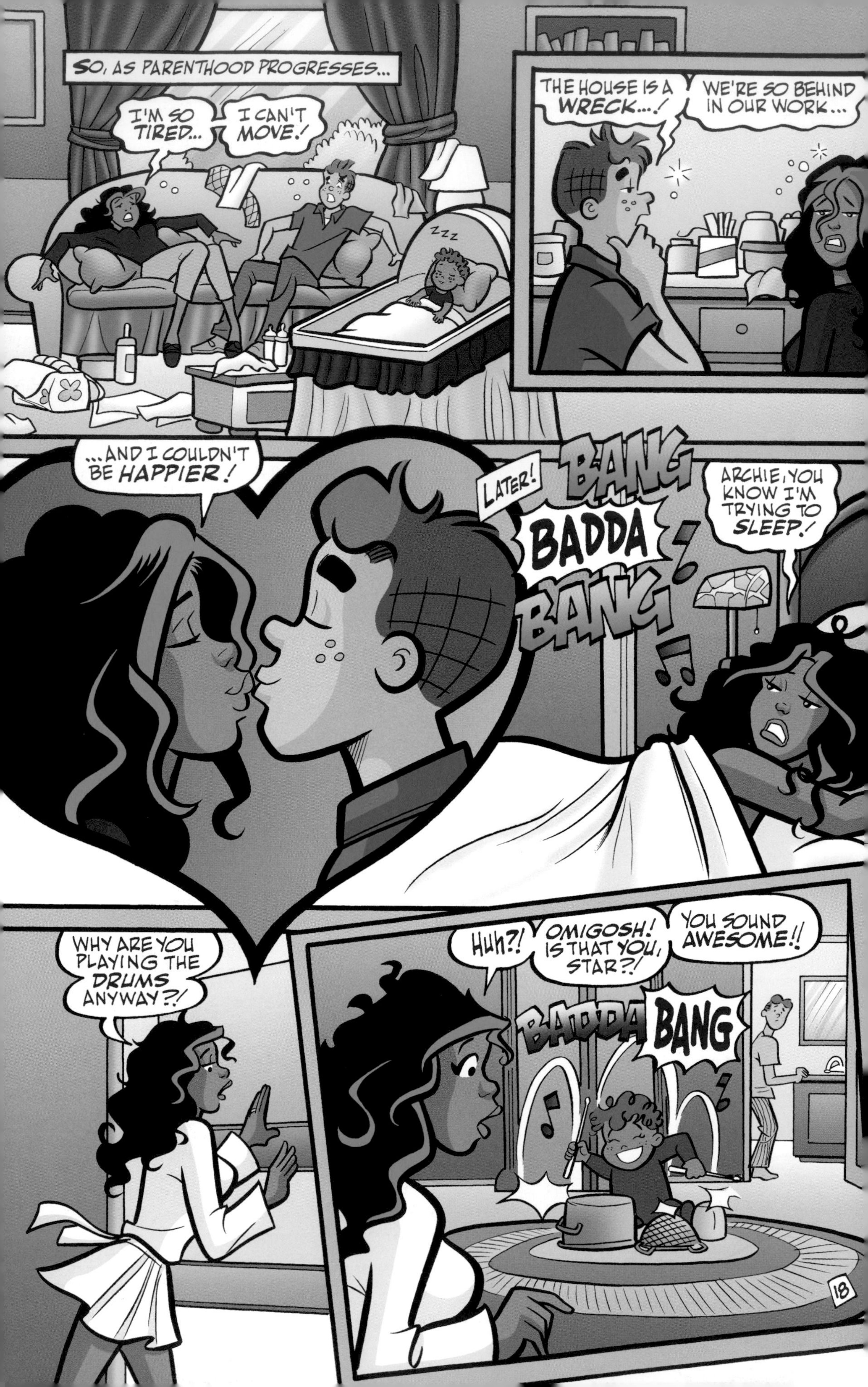
SO, AS PARENTHOOD PROGRESSES...
I'M SO TIRED...
I CAN'T MOVE.!
Z Z Z
THE HOUSE IS A WRECK...!
WE'RE SO BEHIND IN OUR WORK...
...AND I COULDN'T BE HAPPIER!
LATER!
BANG
BADDA
BANG
ARCHIE, YOU KNOW I'M TRYING TO SLEEP!
WHY ARE YOU PLAYING THE DRUMS ANYWAY?!
Huh?!
OMIGOSH! IS THAT YOU, STAR?!
YOU SOUND AWESOME!!
BADDA BANG
18

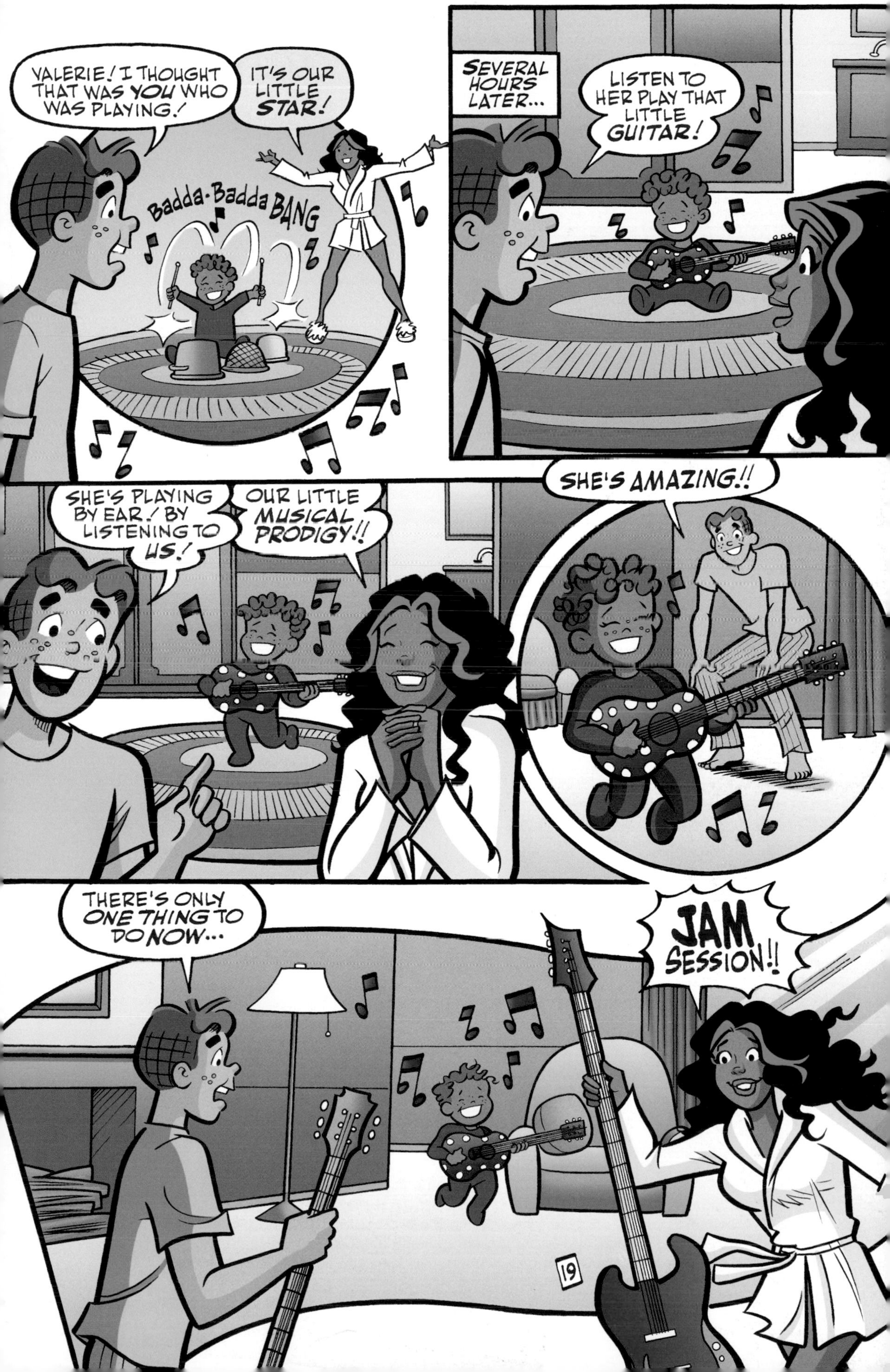
VALERIE! I THOUGHT THAT WAS YOU WHO WAS PLAYING!
IT'S OUR LITTLE STAR!
Badda-Badda BANG
SEVERAL HOURS LATER...
LISTEN TO HER PLAY THAT LITTLE GUITAR!
SHE'S PLAYING BY EAR! BY LISTENING TO US!
OUR LITTLE MUSICAL PRODIGY!!
SHE'S AMAZING!!
THERE'S ONLY ONE THING TO DO NOW...
JAM SESSION!!
19

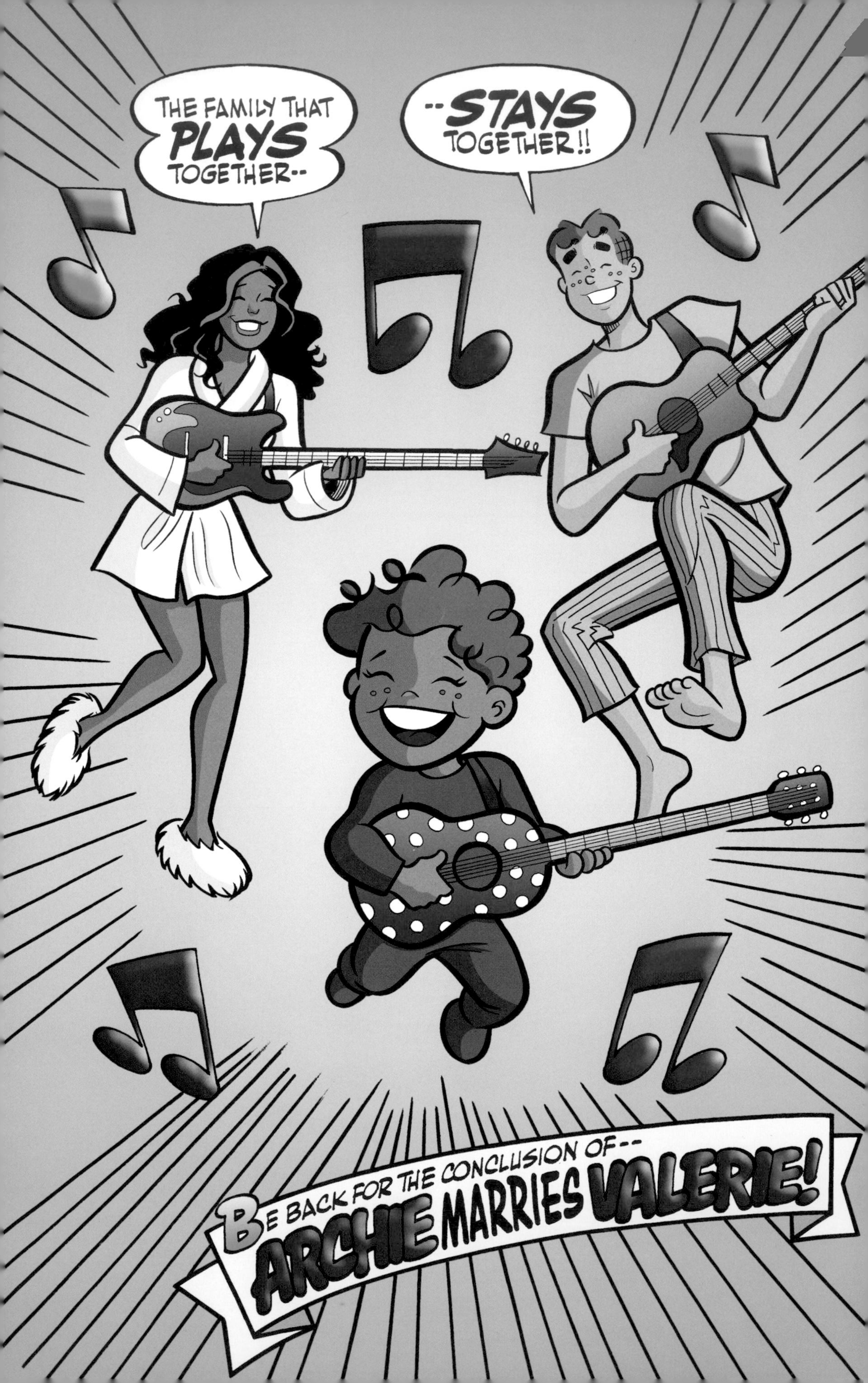
THE FAMILY THAT PLAYS TOGETHER--
--STAYS TOGETHER!!
BE BACK FOR THE CONCLUSION OF--
ARCHIE MARRIES VALERIE!

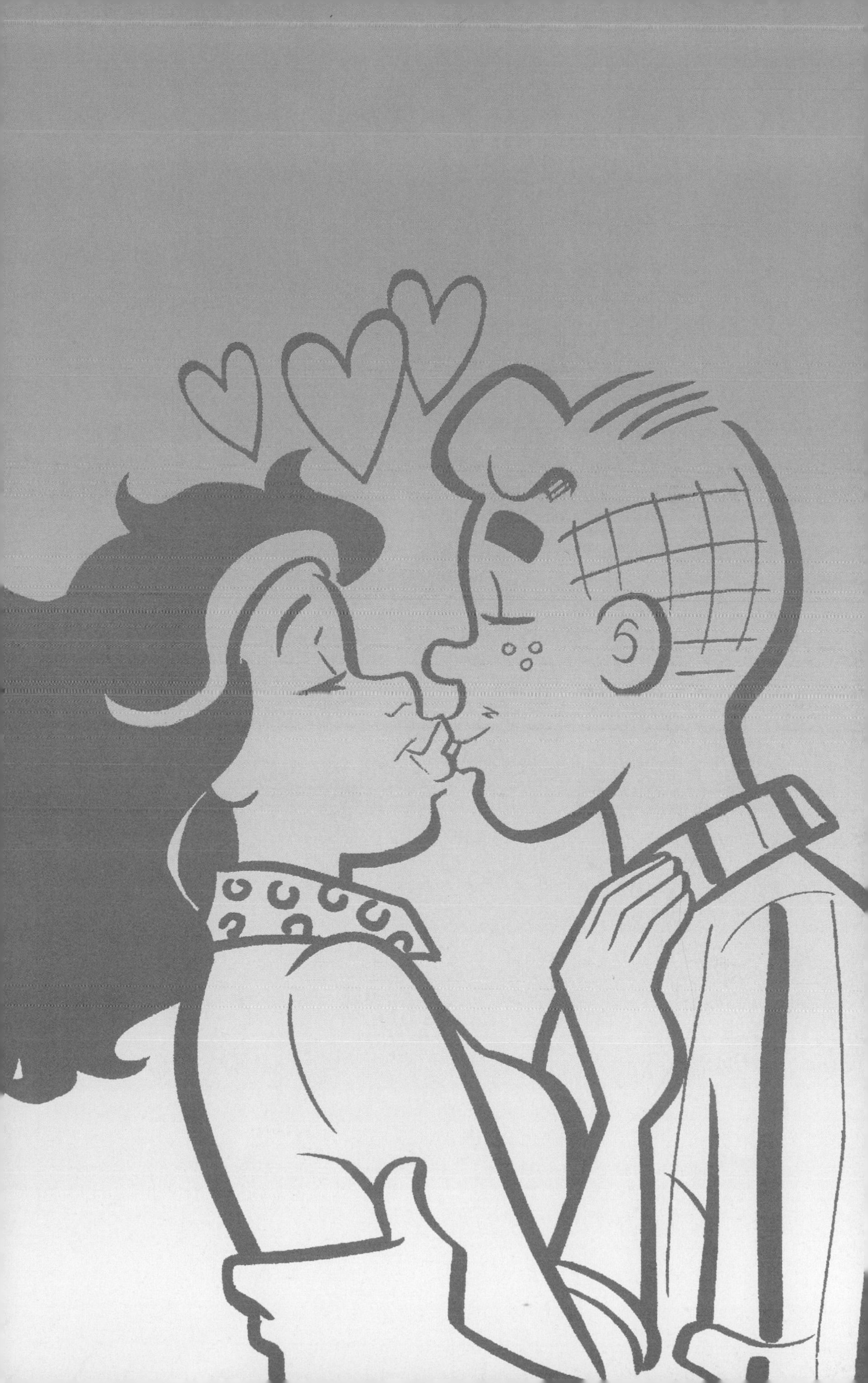

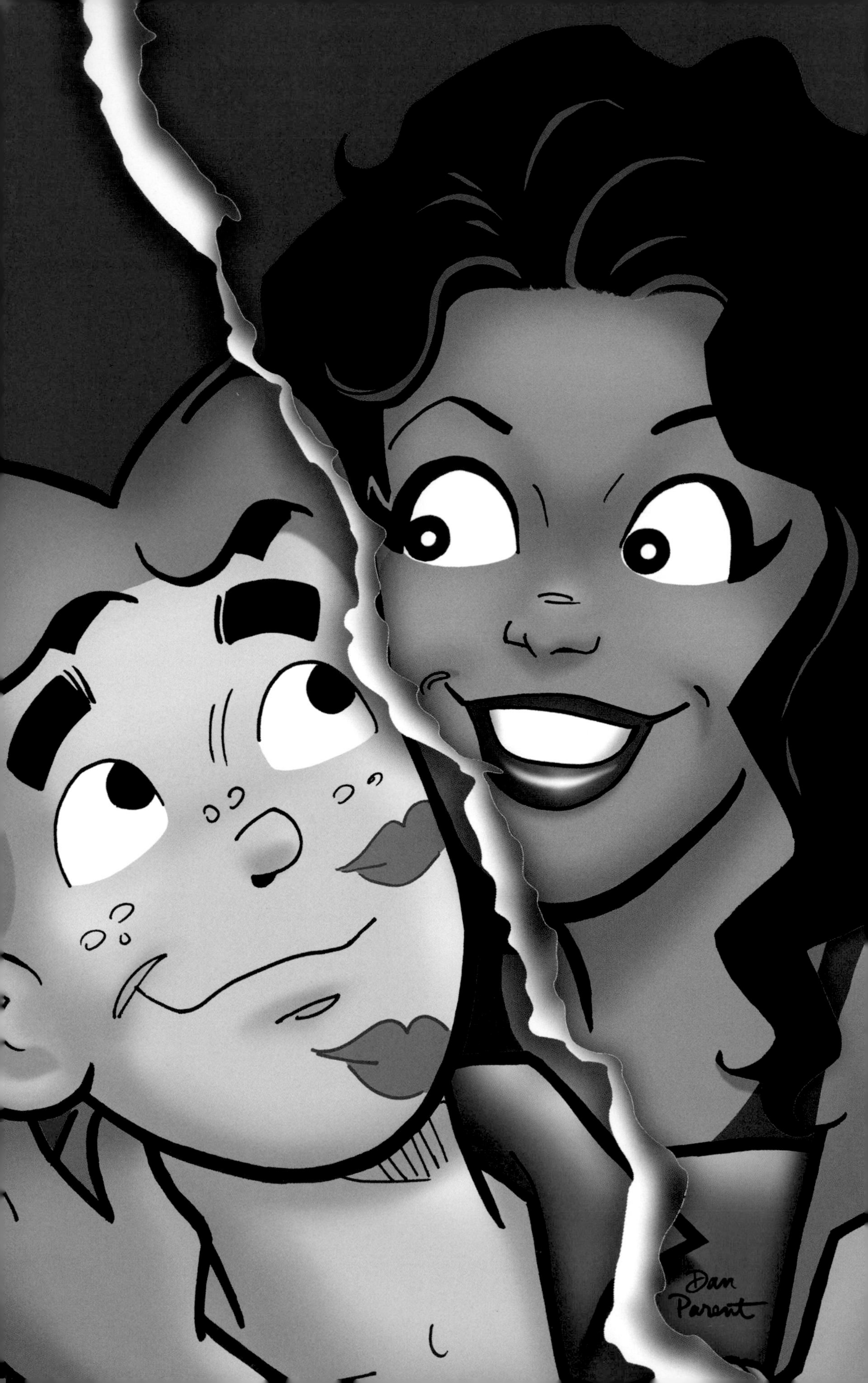
Dan Parent

Chapter Four:

Here and Now

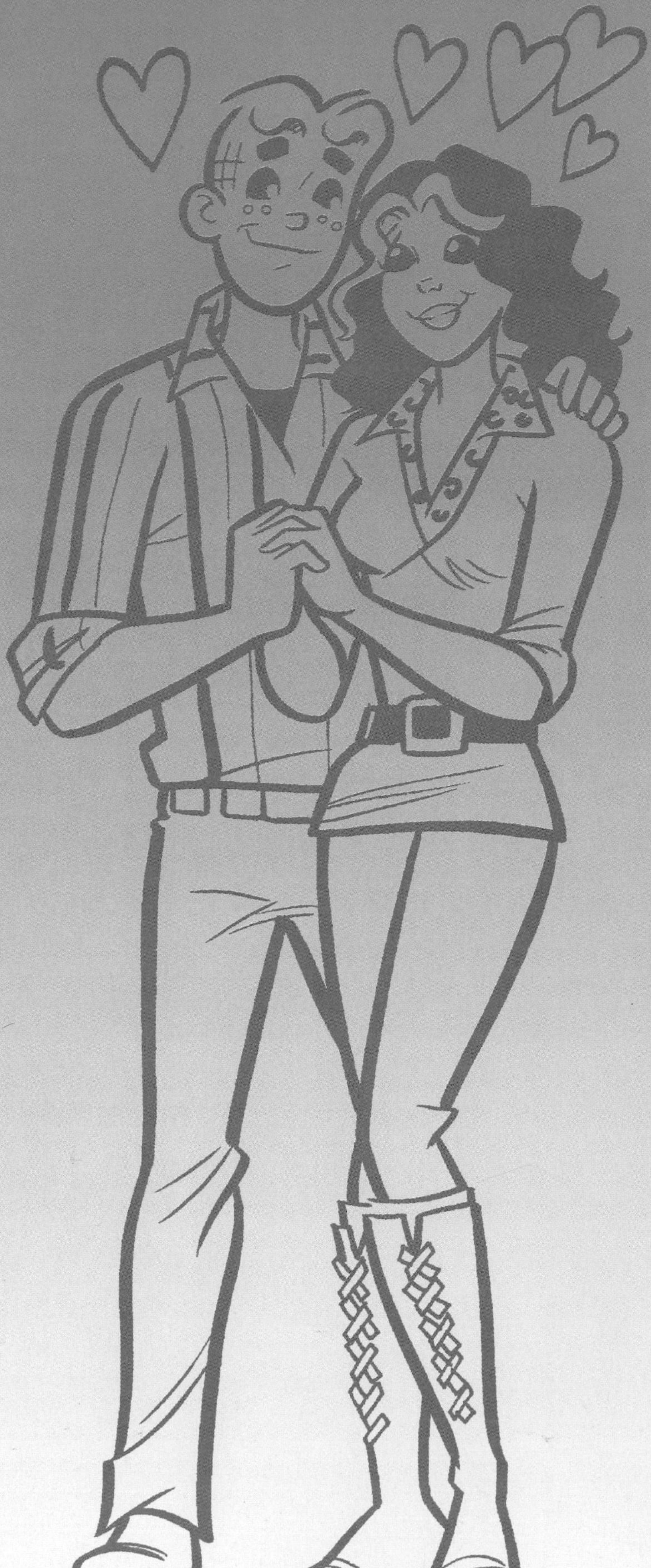

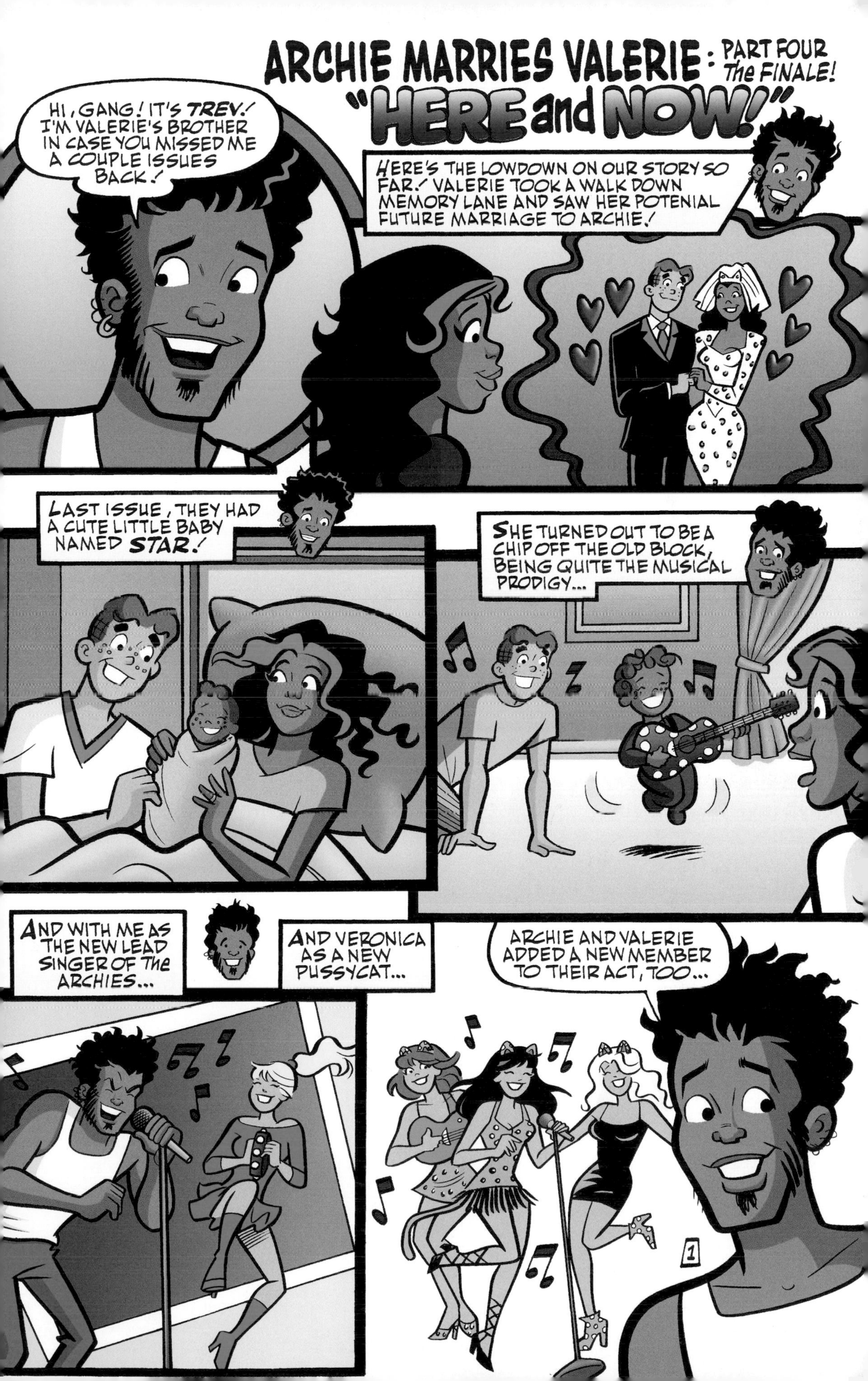

ARCHIE MARRIES VALERIE: PART FOUR The FINALE!
"HERE and NOW!"
HI, GANG! IT'S TREV! I'M VALERIE'S BROTHER IN CASE YOU MISSED ME A COUPLE ISSUES BACK!
HERE'S THE LOWDOWN ON OUR STORY SO FAR! VALERIE TOOK A WALK DOWN MEMORY LANE AND SAW HER POTENIAL FUTURE MARRIAGE TO ARCHIE!
LAST ISSUE, THEY HAD A CUTE LITTLE BABY NAMED STAR!
SHE TURNED OUT TO BE A CHIP OFF THE OLD BLOCK, BEING QUITE THE MUSICAL PRODIGY...
AND WITH ME AS THE NEW LEAD SINGER OF THE ARCHIES...
AND VERONICA AS A NEW PUSSYCAT...
ARCHIE AND VALERIE ADDED A NEW MEMBER TO THEIR ACT, TOO...
1

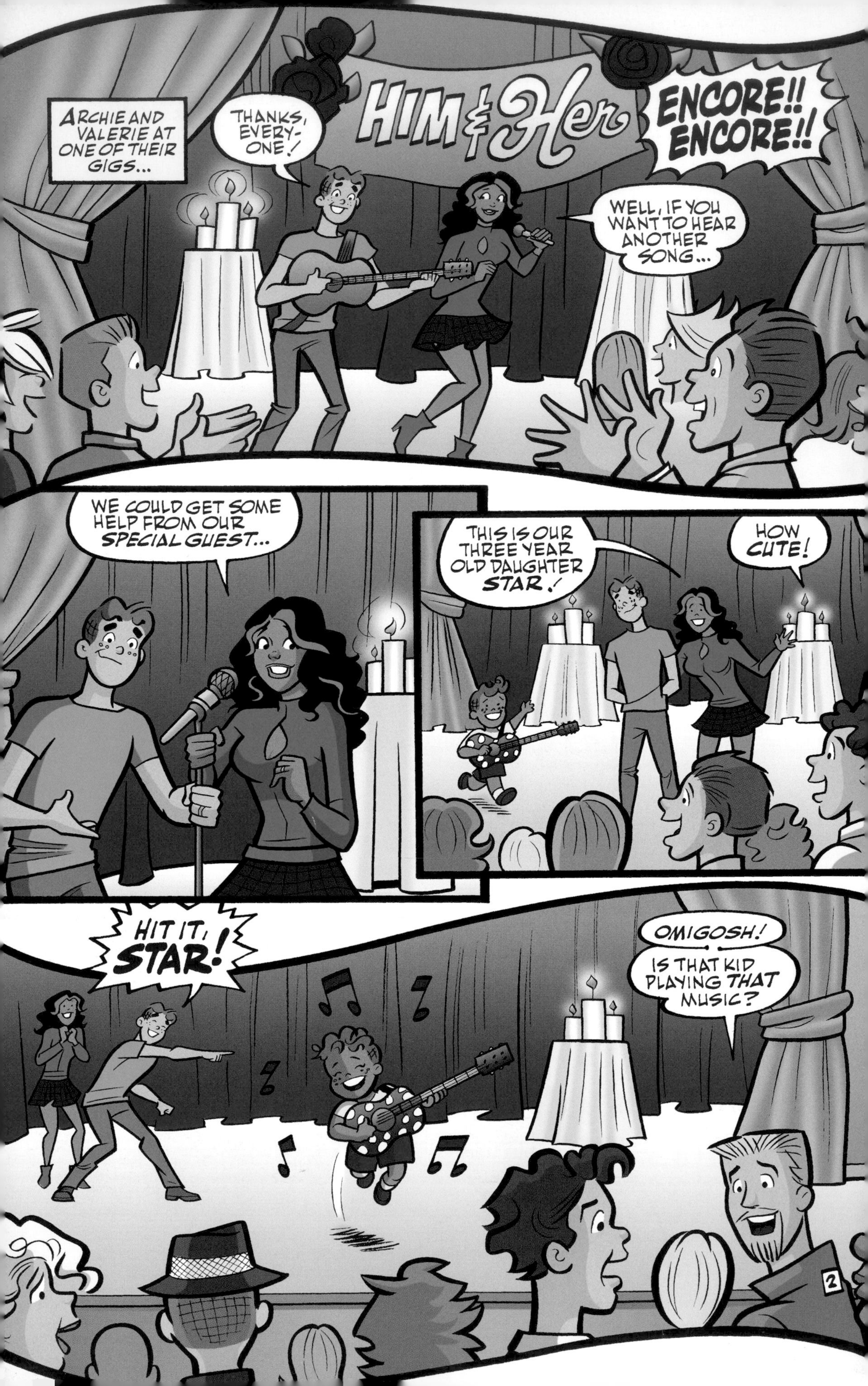
ARCHIE AND VALERIE AT ONE OF THEIR GIGS...
THANKS, EVERY-ONE!
HIM & HER
ENCORE!! ENCORE!!
WELL, IF YOU WANT TO HEAR ANOTHER SONG...
WE COULD GET SOME HELP FROM OUR SPECIAL GUEST...
THIS IS OUR THREE YEAR OLD DAUGHTER STAR!
HOW CUTE!
HIT IT, STAR!
OMIGOSH!
IS THAT KID PLAYING THAT MUSIC?
2

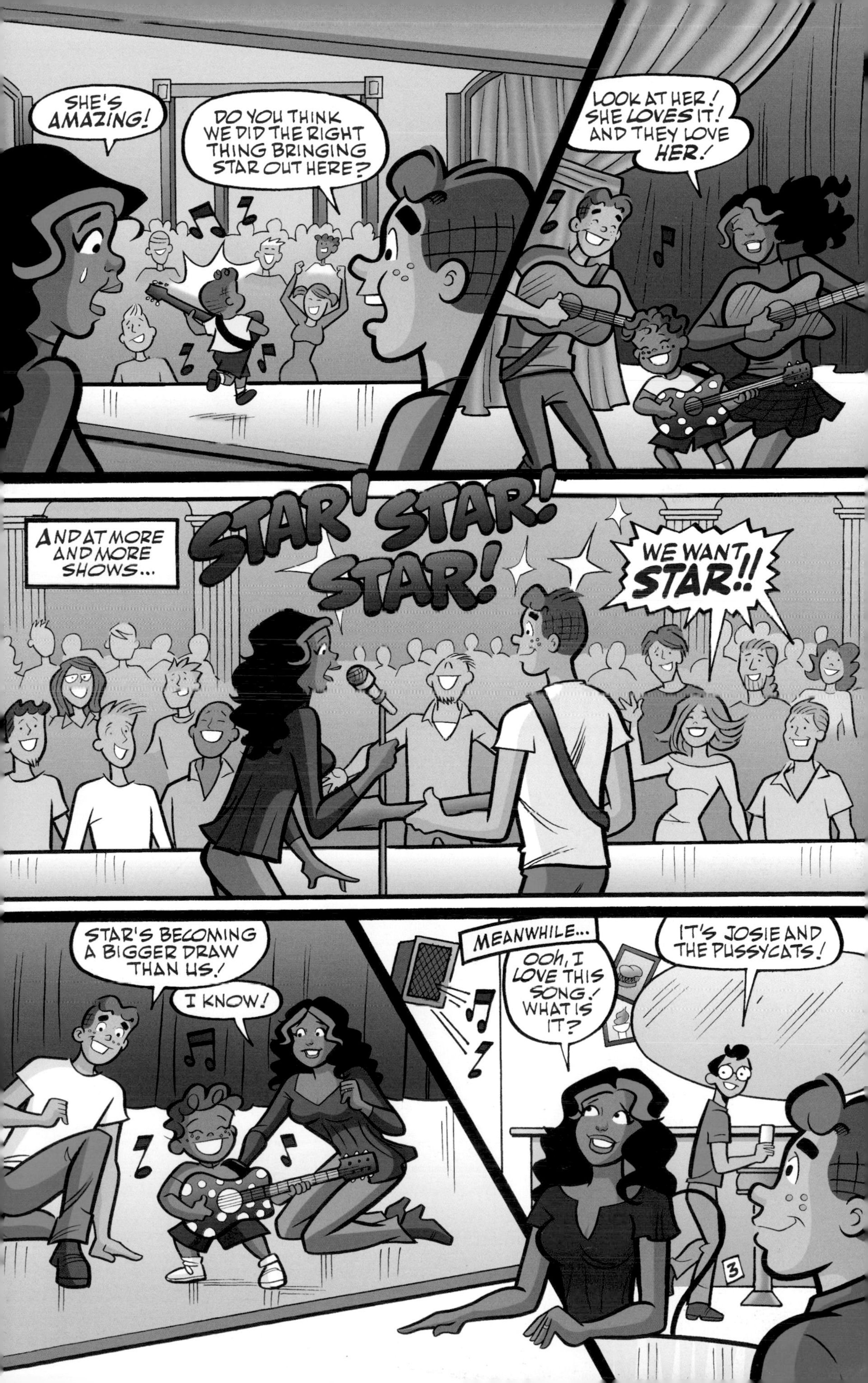
SHE'S AMAZING!
DO YOU THINK WE DID THE RIGHT THING BRINGING STAR OUT HERE?
LOOK AT HER! SHE LOVES IT! AND THEY LOVE HER!
AND AT MORE AND MORE SHOWS...
STAR! STAR! STAR!
WE WANT STAR!!
STAR'S BECOMING A BIGGER DRAW THAN US!
I KNOW!
MEANWHILE...
OOH, I LOVE THIS SONG! WHAT IS IT?
IT'S JOSIE AND THE PUSSYCATS!
3

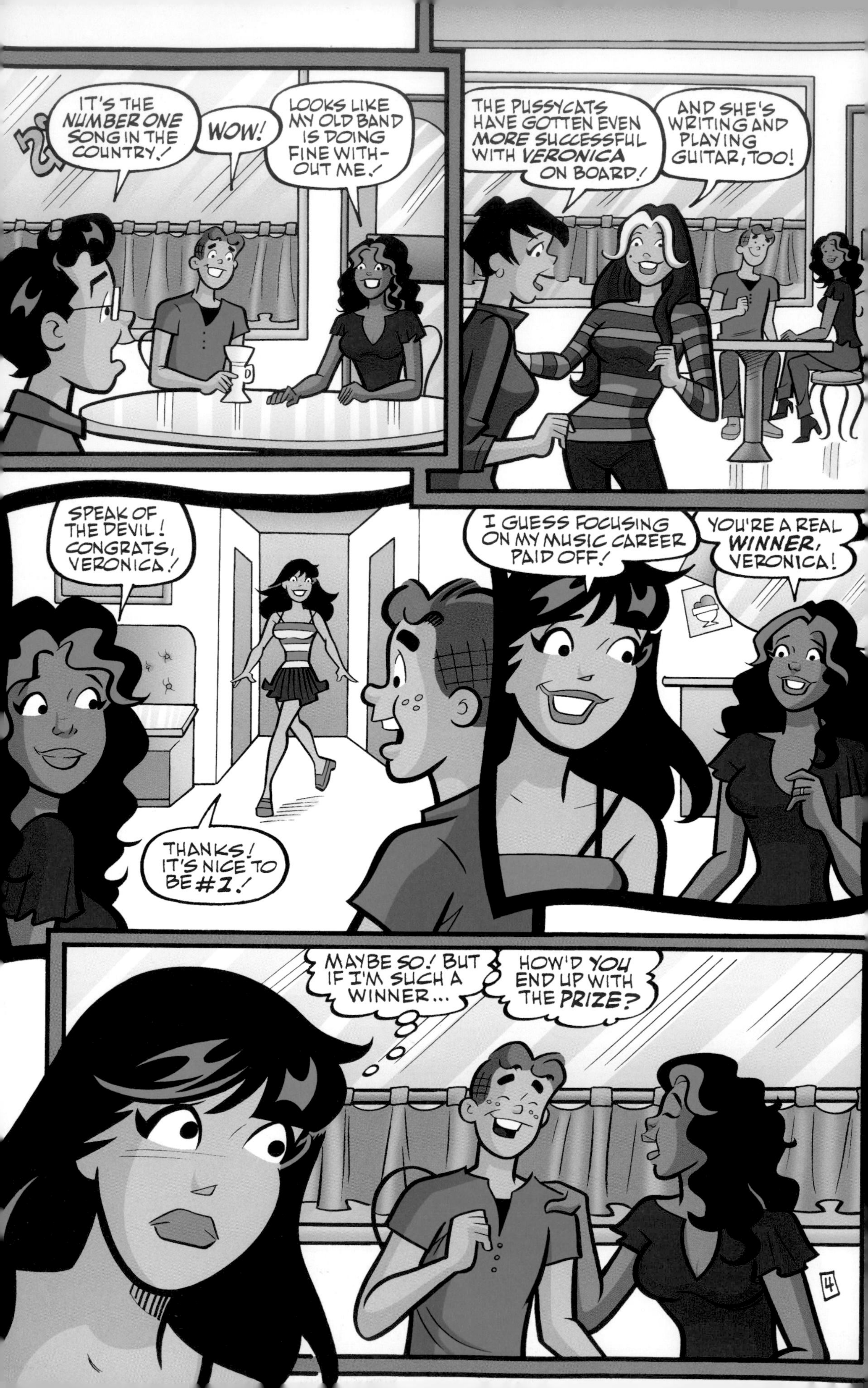
IT'S THE NUMBER ONE SONG IN THE COUNTRY!
WOW!
LOOKS LIKE MY OLD BAND IS DOING FINE WITH-OUT ME!
THE PUSSYCATS HAVE GOTTEN EVEN MORE SUCCESSFUL WITH VERONICA ON BOARD!
AND SHE'S WRITING AND PLAYING GUITAR, TOO!
SPEAK OF THE DEVIL! CONGRATS, VERONICA!
THANKS! IT'S NICE TO BE #1!
I GUESS FOCUSING ON MY MUSIC CAREER PAID OFF!
YOU'RE A REAL WINNER, VERONICA!
MAYBE SO! BUT IF I'M SUCH A WINNER...
HOW'D YOU END UP WITH THE PRIZE?
4

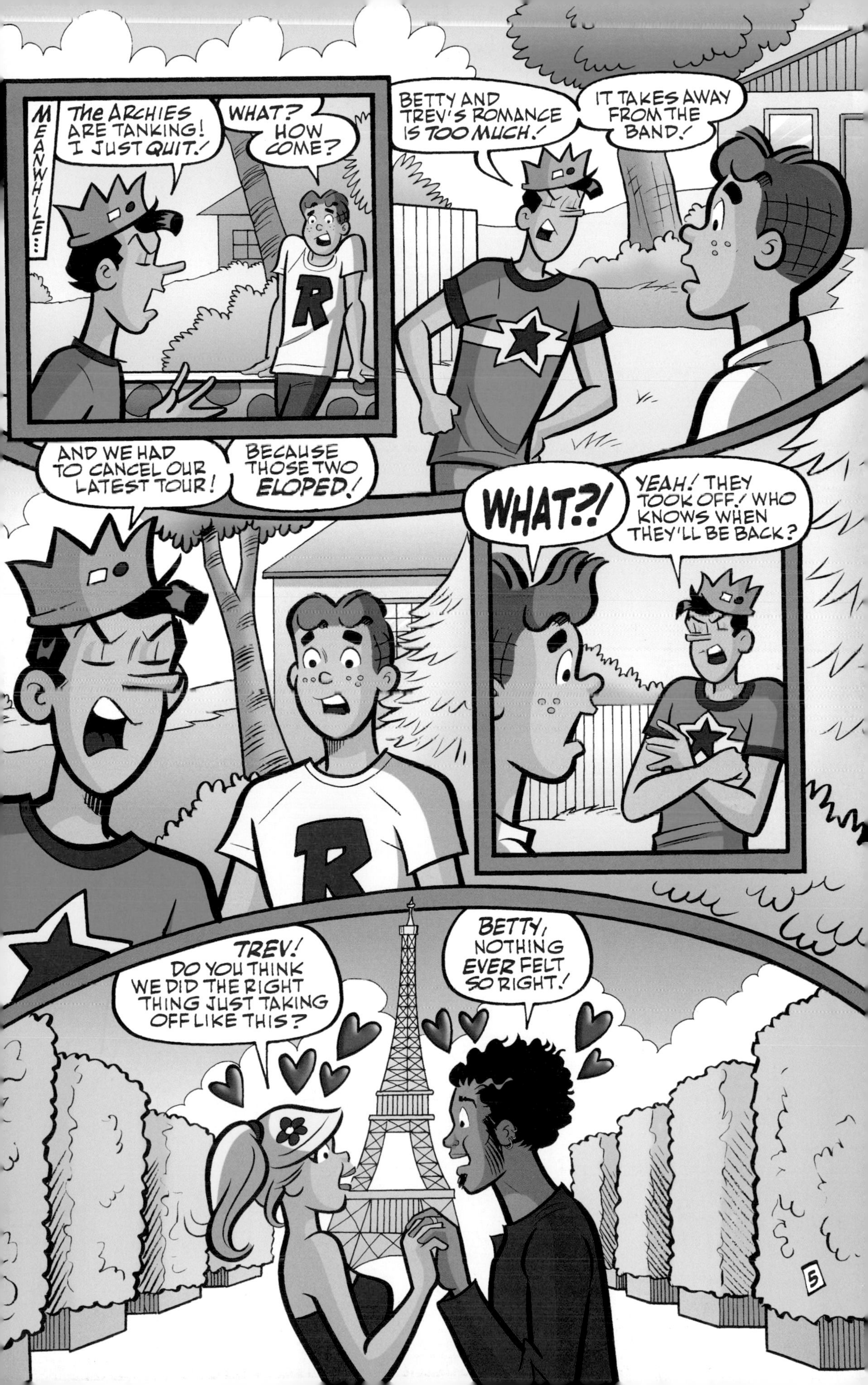
MEANWHILE...
The ARCHIES ARE TANKING! I JUST QUIT!
WHAT? HOW COME?
BETTY AND TREV'S ROMANCE IS TOO MUCH!
IT TAKES AWAY FROM THE BAND!
AND WE HAD TO CANCEL OUR LATEST TOUR!
BECAUSE THOSE TWO ELOPED!
WHAT?!
YEAH! THEY TOOK OFF! WHO KNOWS WHEN THEY'LL BE BACK?
TREV! DO YOU THINK WE DID THE RIGHT THING JUST TAKING OFF LIKE THIS?
BETTY, NOTHING EVER FELT SO RIGHT!
5

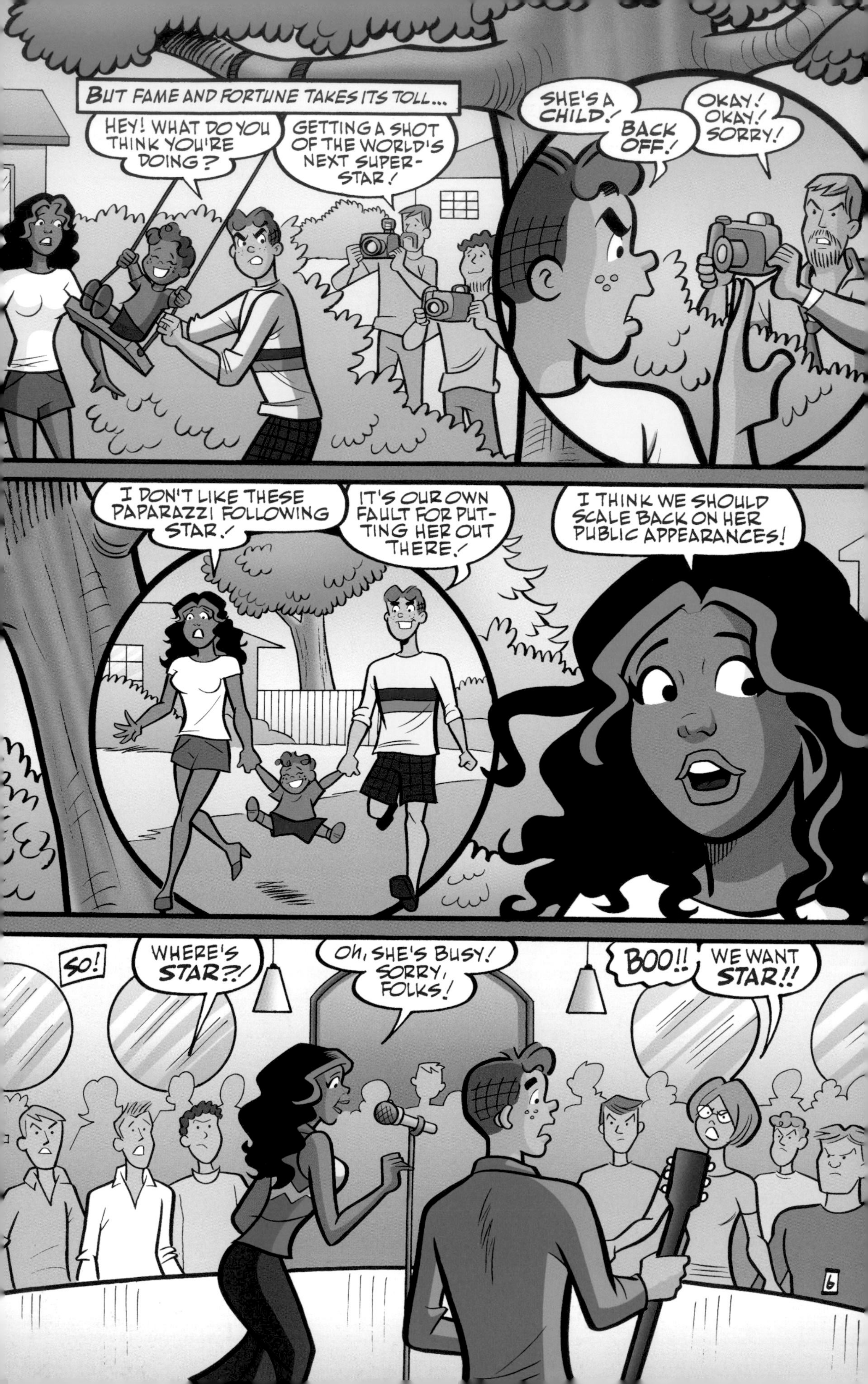
BUT FAME AND FORTUNE TAKES ITS TOLL...
HEY! WHAT DO YOU THINK YOU'RE DOING?
GETTING A SHOT OF THE WORLD'S NEXT SUPER-STAR!
SHE'S A CHILD!
BACK OFF!
OKAY! OKAY! SORRY!
I DON'T LIKE THESE PAPARAZZI FOLLOWING STAR!
IT'S OUR OWN FAULT FOR PUTTING HER OUT THERE!
I THINK WE SHOULD SCALE BACK ON HER PUBLIC APPEARANCES!
SO!
WHERE'S STAR?!
OH, SHE'S BUSY! SORRY, FOLKS!
BOO!!
WE WANT STAR!!
6

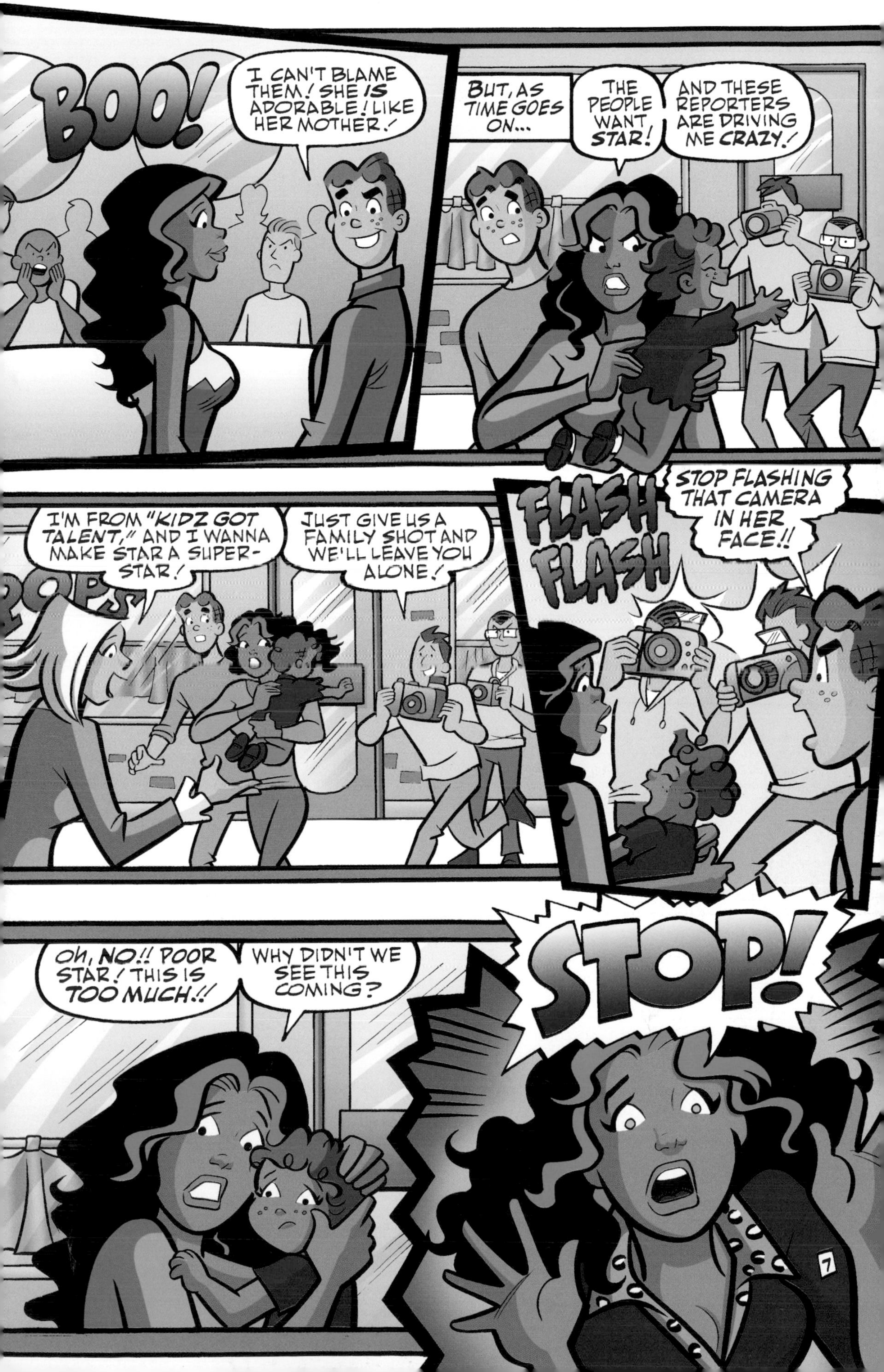
BOO!
I CAN'T BLAME THEM! SHE IS ADORABLE! LIKE HER MOTHER!
BUT, AS TIME GOES ON...
THE PEOPLE WANT STAR!
AND THESE REPORTERS ARE DRIVING ME CRAZY!
I'M FROM "KIDZ GOT TALENT," AND I WANNA MAKE STAR A SUPER-STAR!
JUST GIVE US A FAMILY SHOT AND WE'LL LEAVE YOU ALONE!
FLASH FLASH
STOP FLASHING THAT CAMERA IN HER FACE!!
OH, NO!! POOR STAR! THIS IS TOO MUCH!!
WHY DIDN'T WE SEE THIS COMING?
STOP!
7

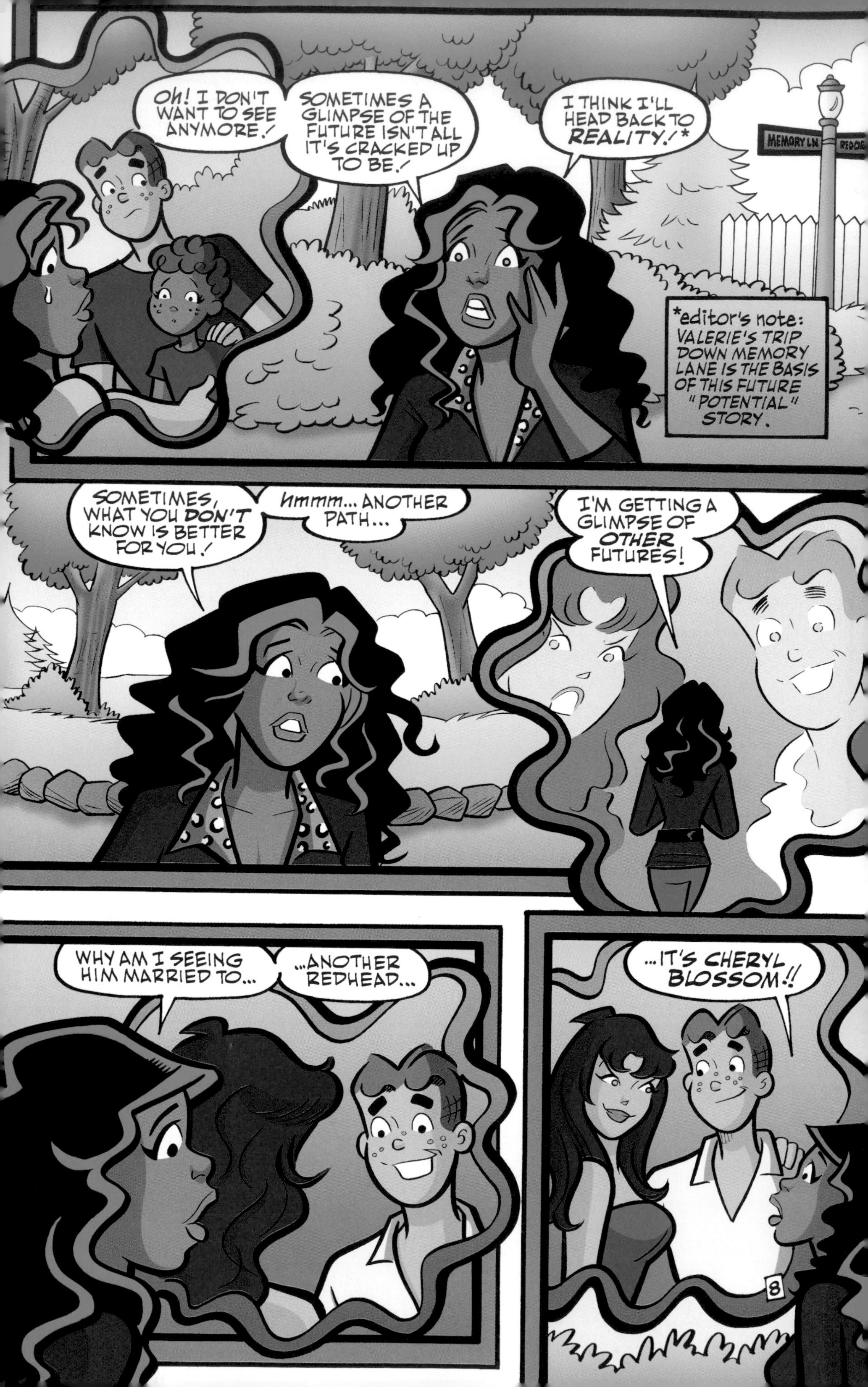

Oh! I DON'T WANT TO SEE ANYMORE.!
SOMETIMES A GLIMPSE OF THE FUTURE ISN'T ALL IT'S CRACKED UP TO BE.!
I THINK I'LL HEAD BACK TO REALITY.! *
MEMORY LN
*editor's note: VALERIE'S TRIP DOWN MEMORY LANE IS THE BASIS OF THIS FUTURE "POTENTIAL" STORY.
SOMETIMES, WHAT YOU DON'T KNOW IS BETTER FOR YOU.!
Hmmm... ANOTHER PATH...
I'M GETTING A GLIMPSE OF OTHER FUTURES!
WHY AM I SEEING HIM MARRIED TO...
...ANOTHER REDHEAD...
...IT'S CHERYL BLOSSOM!!
8

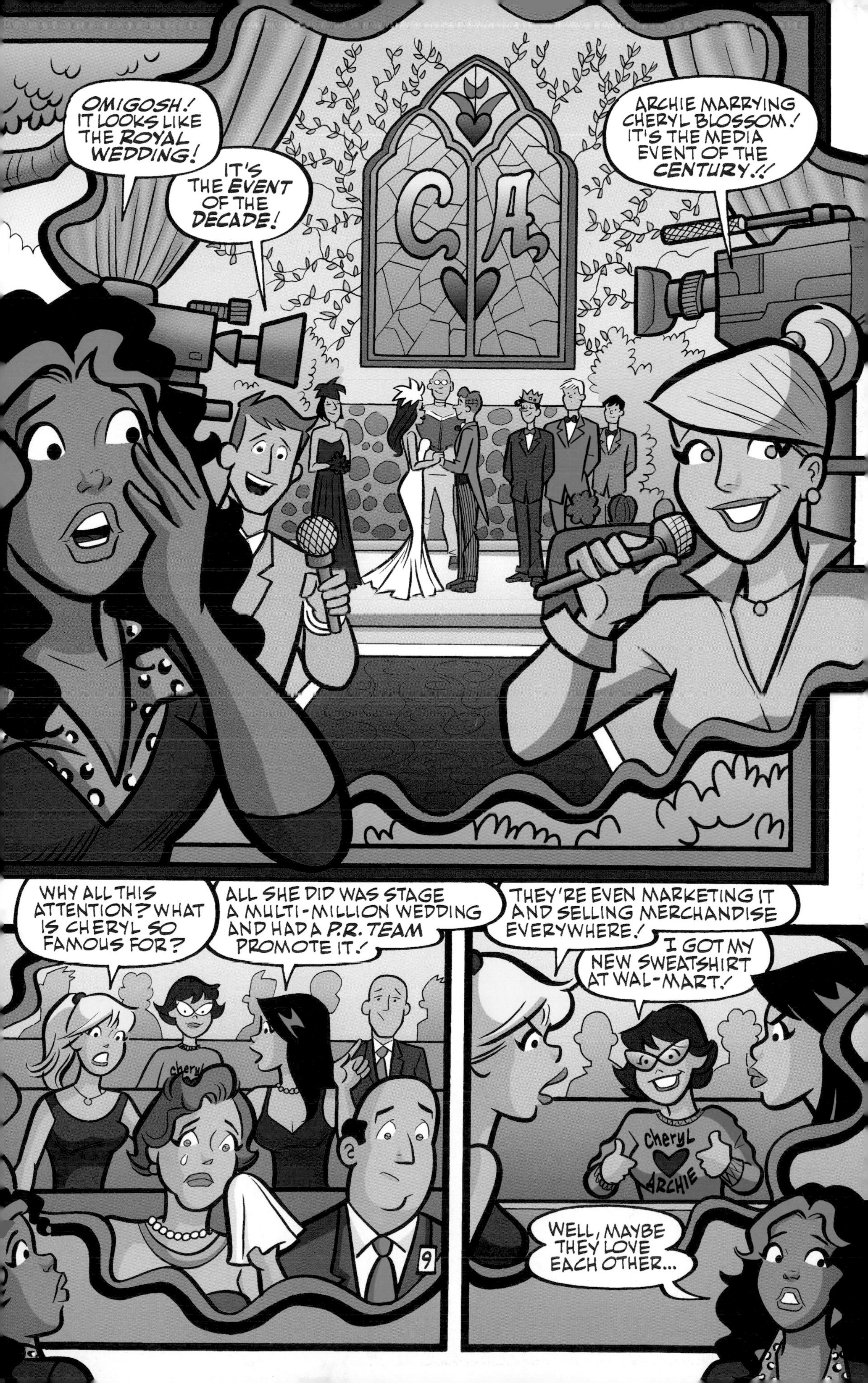
OMIGOSH! IT LOOKS LIKE THE ROYAL WEDDING!
IT'S THE EVENT OF THE DECADE!
ARCHIE MARRYING CHERYL BLOSSOM! IT'S THE MEDIA EVENT OF THE CENTURY!!
WHY ALL THIS ATTENTION? WHAT IS CHERYL SO FAMOUS FOR?
ALL SHE DID WAS STAGE A MULTI-MILLION WEDDING AND HAD A P.R. TEAM PROMOTE IT!
cheryl
9
THEY'RE EVEN MARKETING IT AND SELLING MERCHANDISE EVERYWHERE!
I GOT MY NEW SWEATSHIRT AT WAL-MART!
Cheryl ARCHIE
WELL, MAYBE THEY LOVE EACH OTHER...

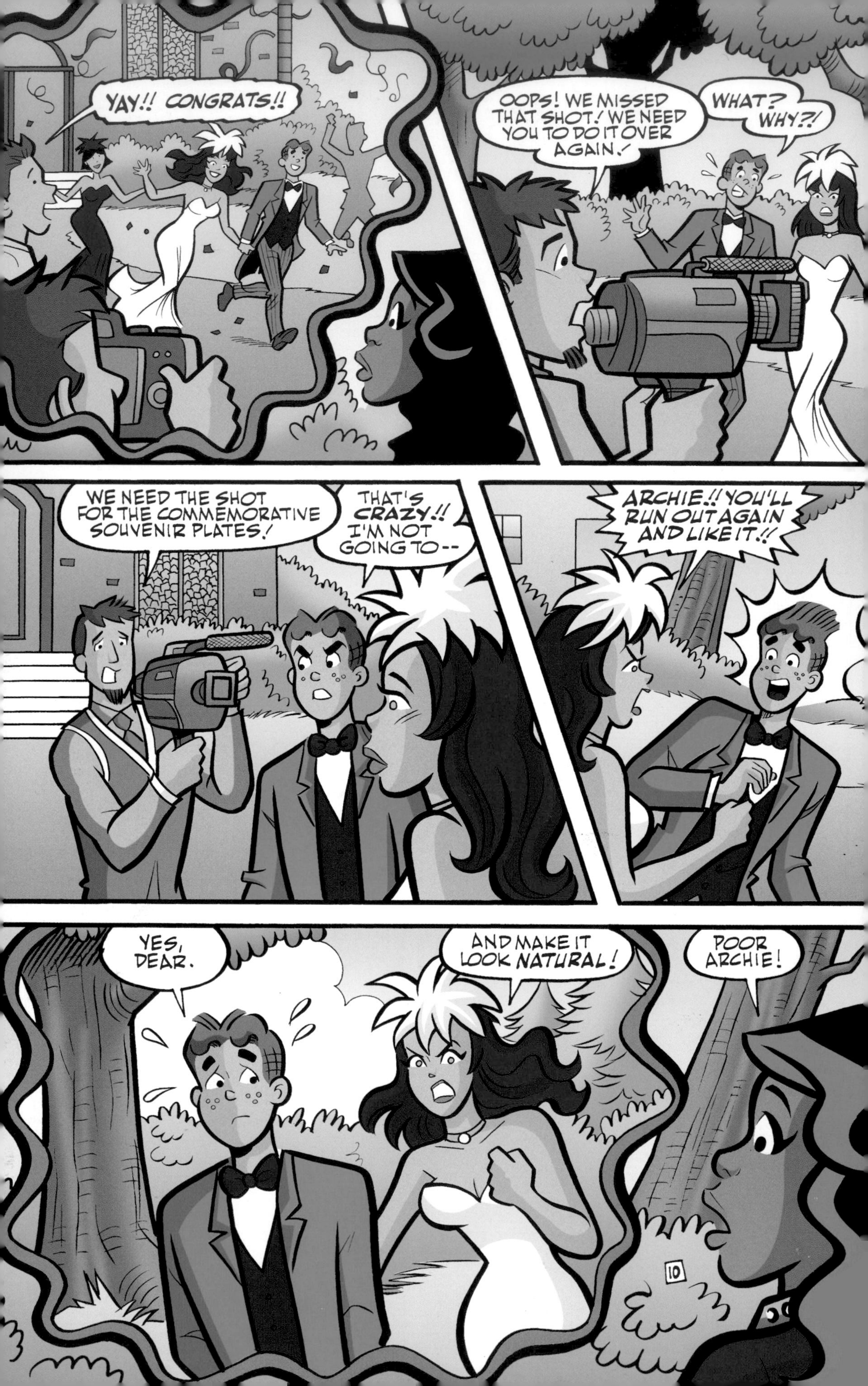
YAY!! CONGRATS!!
OOPS! WE MISSED THAT SHOT! WE NEED YOU TO DO IT OVER AGAIN!
WHAT? WHY?!
WE NEED THE SHOT FOR THE COMMEMORATIVE SOUVENIR PLATES!
THAT'S CRAZY!! I'M NOT GOING TO --
ARCHIE!! YOU'LL RUN OUT AGAIN AND LIKE IT!!
YES, DEAR.
AND MAKE IT LOOK NATURAL!
POOR ARCHIE!
10

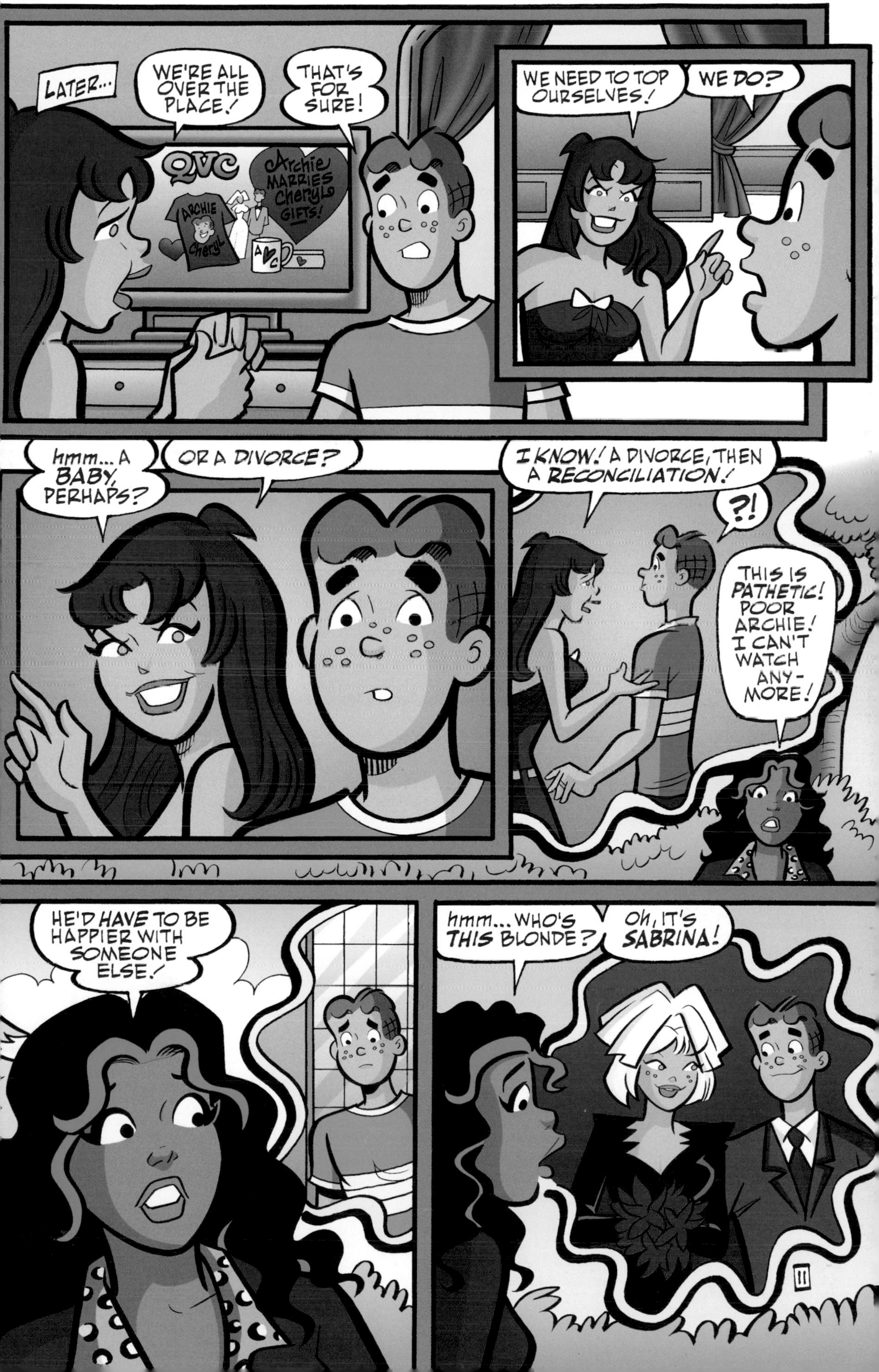
LATER...
WE'RE ALL OVER THE PLACE!
THAT'S FOR SURE!
QVC
Archie MARRIES Cheryl GIFTS!
ARCHIE Cheryl
A C
WE NEED TO TOP OURSELVES!
WE DO?
hmm... A BABY, PERHAPS?
OR A DIVORCE?
I KNOW! A DIVORCE, THEN A RECONCILIATION!
?!
THIS IS PATHETIC! POOR ARCHIE! I CAN'T WATCH ANY-MORE!
HE'D HAVE TO BE HAPPIER WITH SOMEONE ELSE!
hmm... WHO'S THIS BLONDE?
Oh, IT'S SABRINA!
11

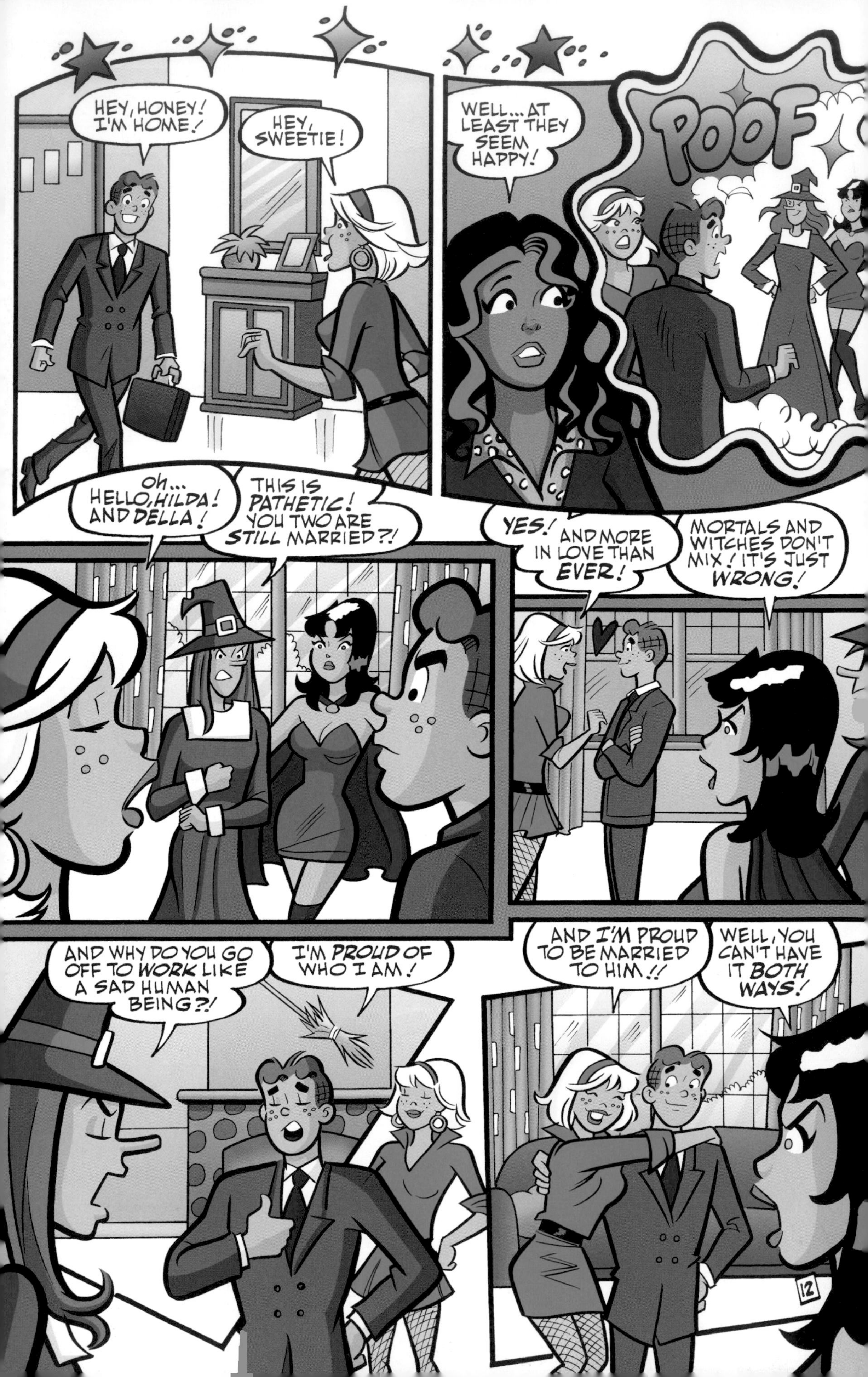
HEY, HONEY! I'M HOME!
HEY, SWEETIE!
WELL... AT LEAST THEY SEEM HAPPY!
POOF
oh... HELLO, HILDA! AND DELLA!
THIS IS PATHETIC! YOU TWO ARE STILL MARRIED?!
YES! AND MORE IN LOVE THAN EVER!
MORTALS AND WITCHES DON'T MIX! IT'S JUST WRONG!
AND WHY DO YOU GO OFF TO WORK LIKE A SAD HUMAN BEING?!
I'M PROUD OF WHO I AM!
AND I'M PROUD TO BE MARRIED TO HIM!!
WELL, YOU CAN'T HAVE IT BOTH WAYS!
12

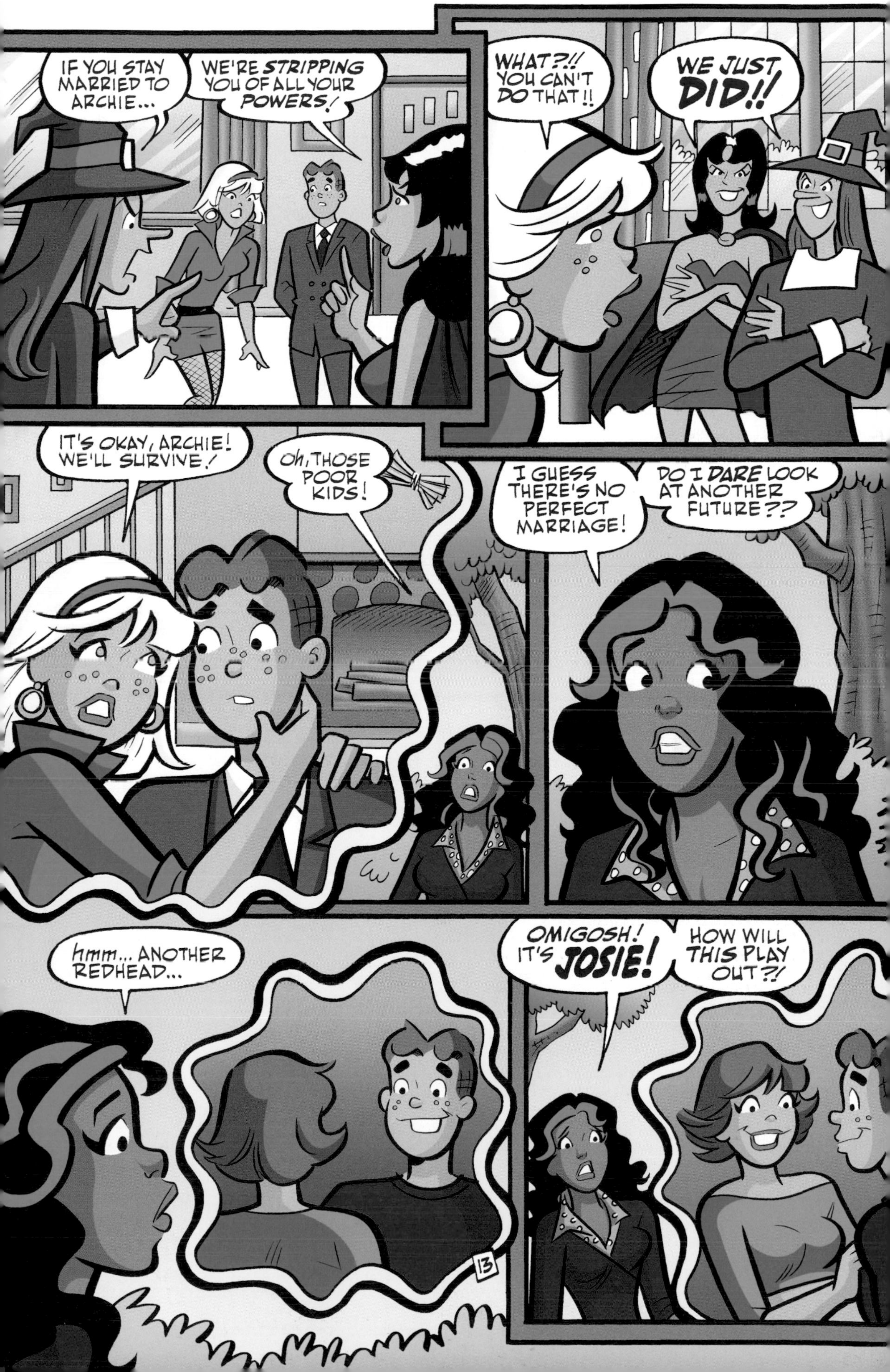
IF YOU STAY MARRIED TO ARCHIE...
WE'RE STRIPPING YOU OF ALL YOUR POWERS!
WHAT?!! YOU CAN'T DO THAT!!
WE JUST DID!!
IT'S OKAY, ARCHIE! WE'LL SURVIVE!
Oh, THOSE POOR KIDS!
I GUESS THERE'S NO PERFECT MARRIAGE!
DO I DARE LOOK AT ANOTHER FUTURE??
hmm... ANOTHER REDHEAD...
OMIGOSH! IT'S JOSIE!
HOW WILL THIS PLAY OUT?!
13

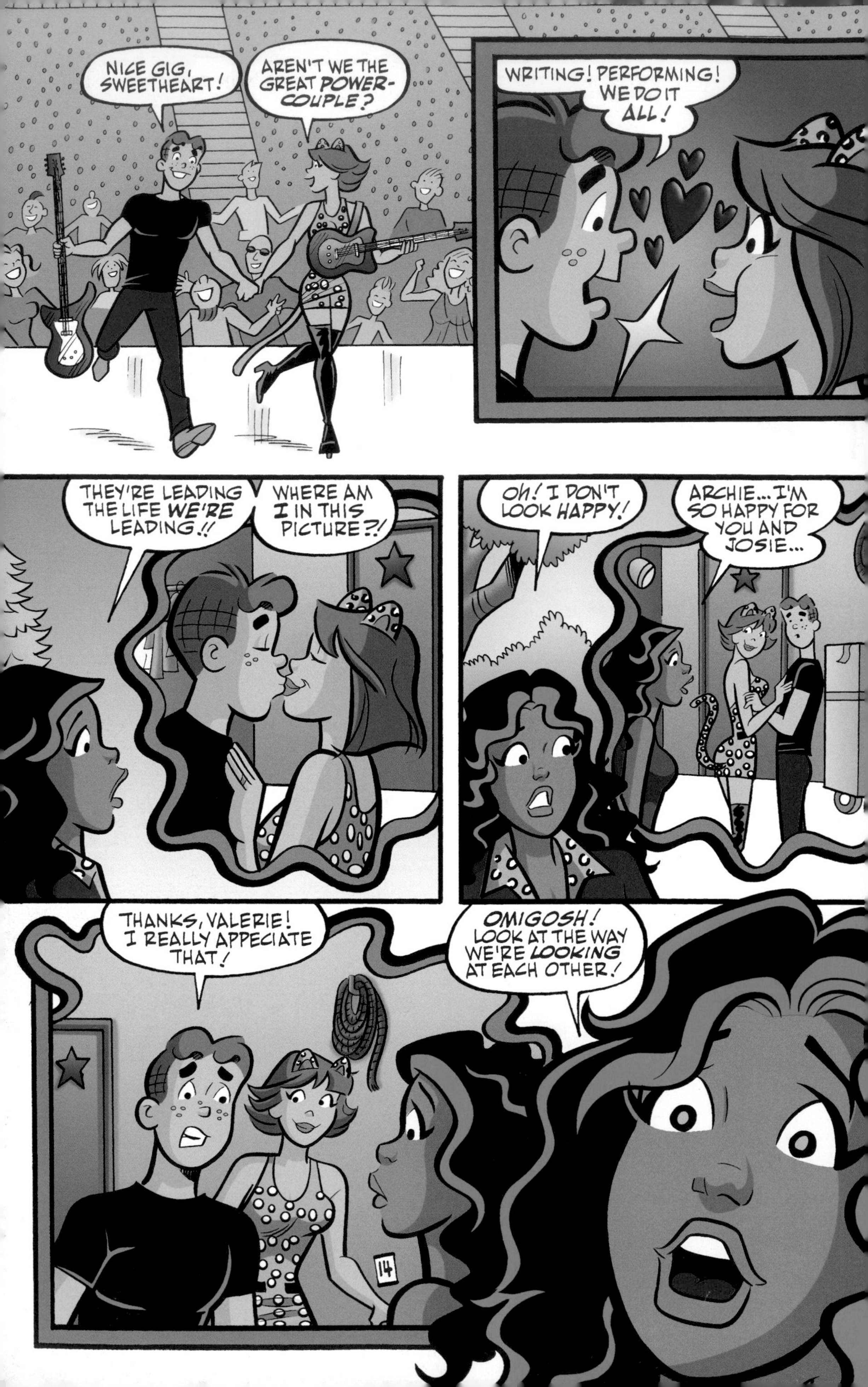

NICE GIG, SWEETHEART!
AREN'T WE THE GREAT POWER-COUPLE?
WRITING! PERFORMING! WE DO IT ALL!
THEY'RE LEADING THE LIFE WE'RE LEADING!!
WHERE AM I IN THIS PICTURE?!
OH! I DON'T LOOK HAPPY!
ARCHIE...I'M SO HAPPY FOR YOU AND JOSIE...
THANKS, VALERIE! I REALLY APPECIATE THAT!
OMIGOSH! LOOK AT THE WAY WE'RE LOOKING AT EACH OTHER!
14

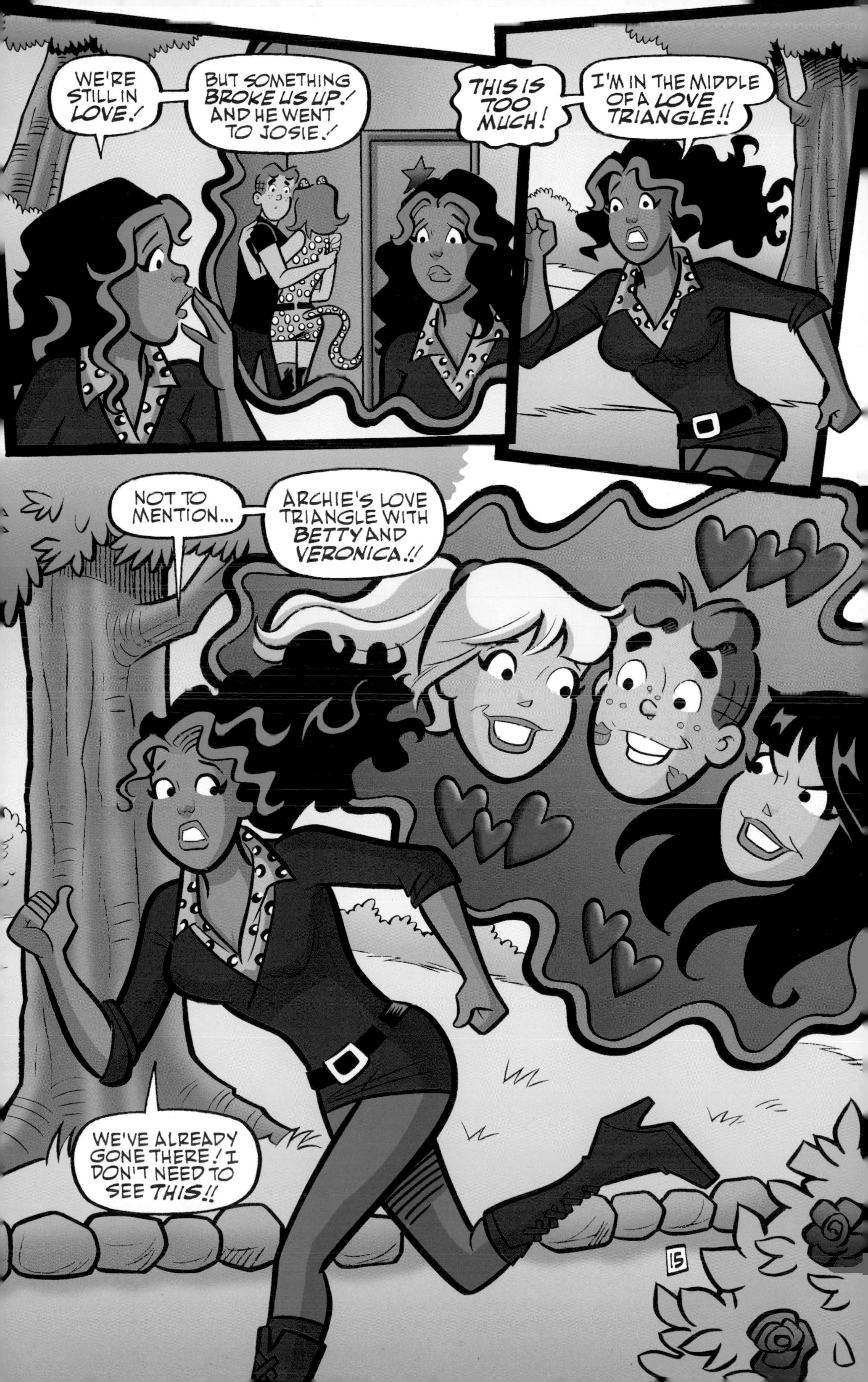
WE'RE STILL IN LOVE.!
BUT SOMETHING BROKE US UP.! AND HE WENT TO JOSIE.!
THIS IS TOO MUCH!
I'M IN THE MIDDLE OF A LOVE TRIANGLE!!
NOT TO MENTION...
ARCHIE'S LOVE TRIANGLE WITH BETTY AND VERONICA.!!
WE'VE ALREADY GONE THERE! I DON'T NEED TO SEE THIS!!
15

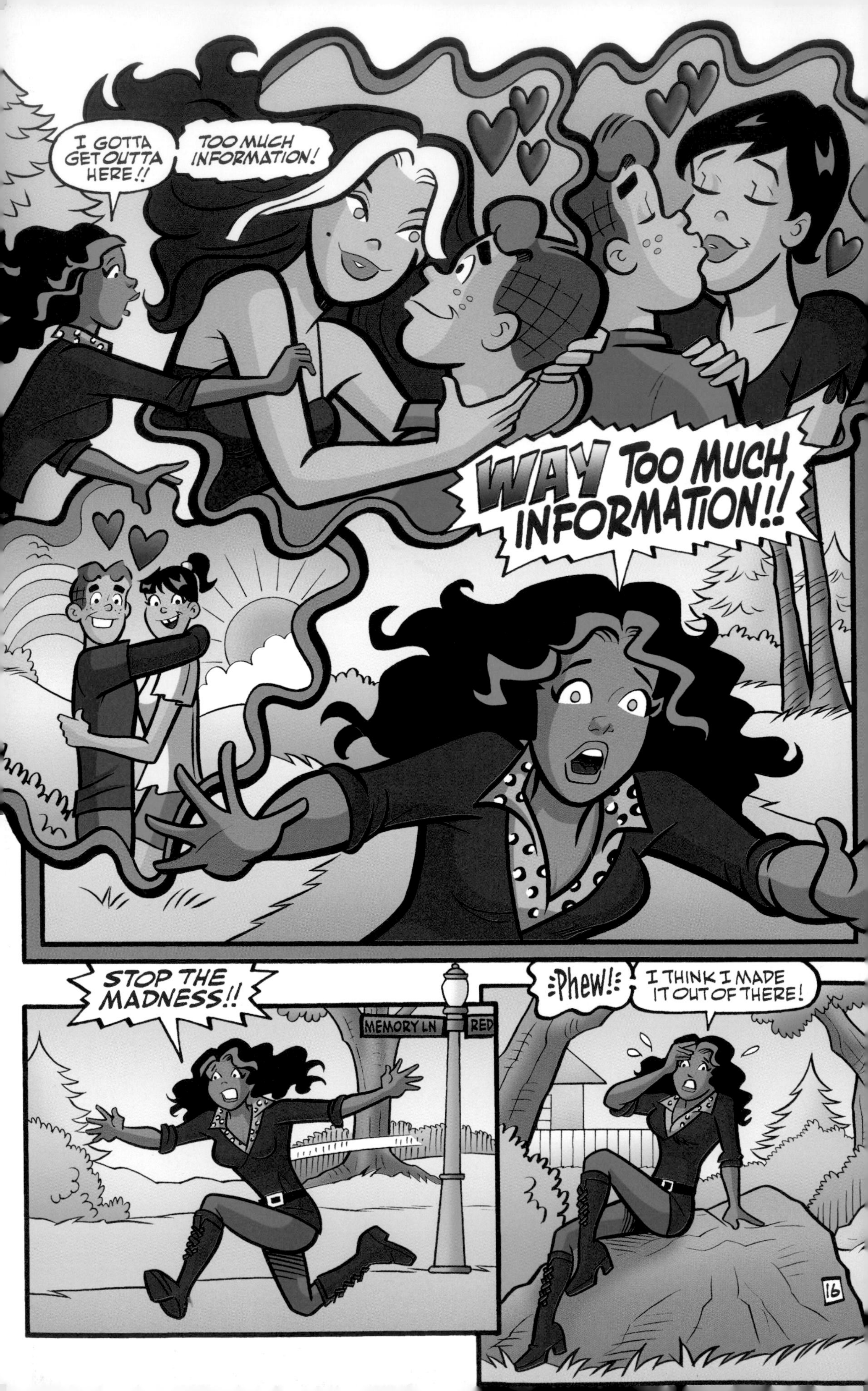

I GOTTA GET OUTTA HERE!!
TOO MUCH INFORMATION!
WAY TOO MUCH INFORMATION!!
STOP THE MADNESS!!
MEMORY LN
RED
Phew!
I THINK I MADE IT OUT OF THERE!
16

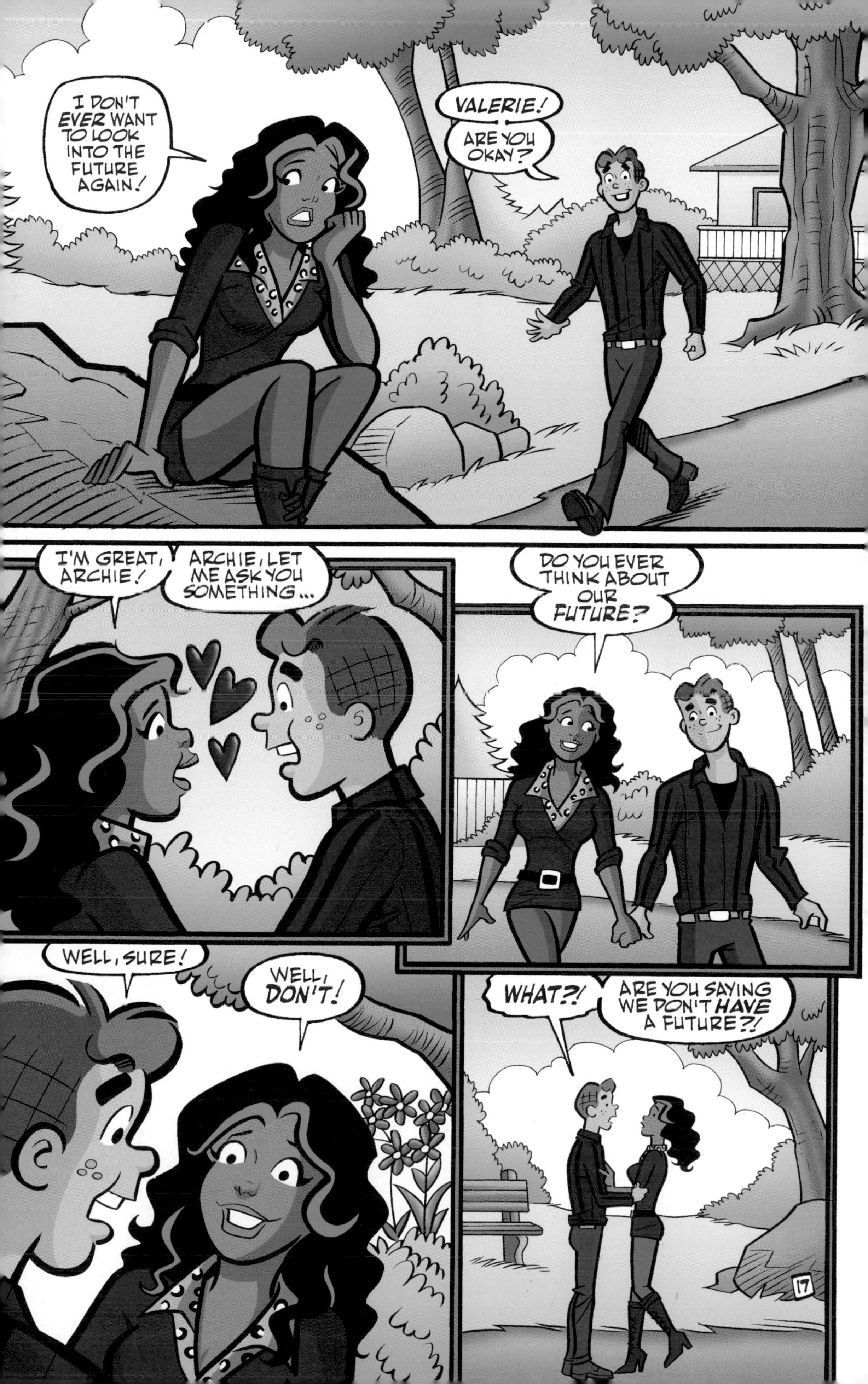
I DON'T EVER WANT TO LOOK INTO THE FUTURE AGAIN!
VALERIE!
ARE YOU OKAY?
I'M GREAT, ARCHIE!
ARCHIE, LET ME ASK YOU SOMETHING...
DO YOU EVER THINK ABOUT OUR FUTURE?
WELL, SURE!
WELL, DON'T!
WHAT?!
ARE YOU SAYING WE DON'T HAVE A FUTURE?!
17

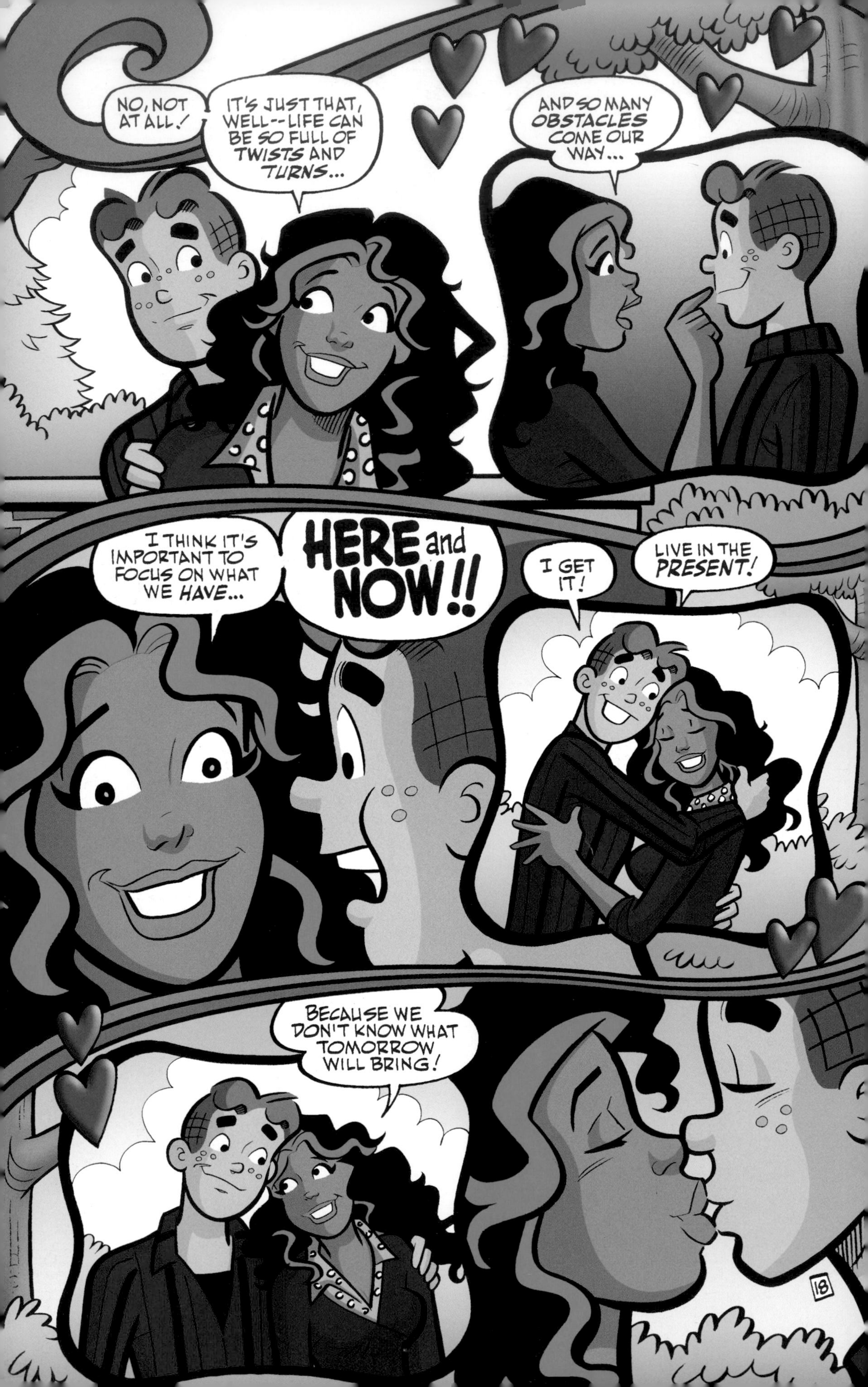
NO, NOT AT ALL!
IT'S JUST THAT, WELL--LIFE CAN BE SO FULL OF TWISTS AND TURNS...
AND SO MANY OBSTACLES COME OUR WAY...
I THINK IT'S IMPORTANT TO FOCUS ON WHAT WE HAVE...
HERE and NOW!!
I GET IT!
LIVE IN THE PRESENT!
BECAUSE WE DON'T KNOW WHAT TOMORROW WILL BRING!
18

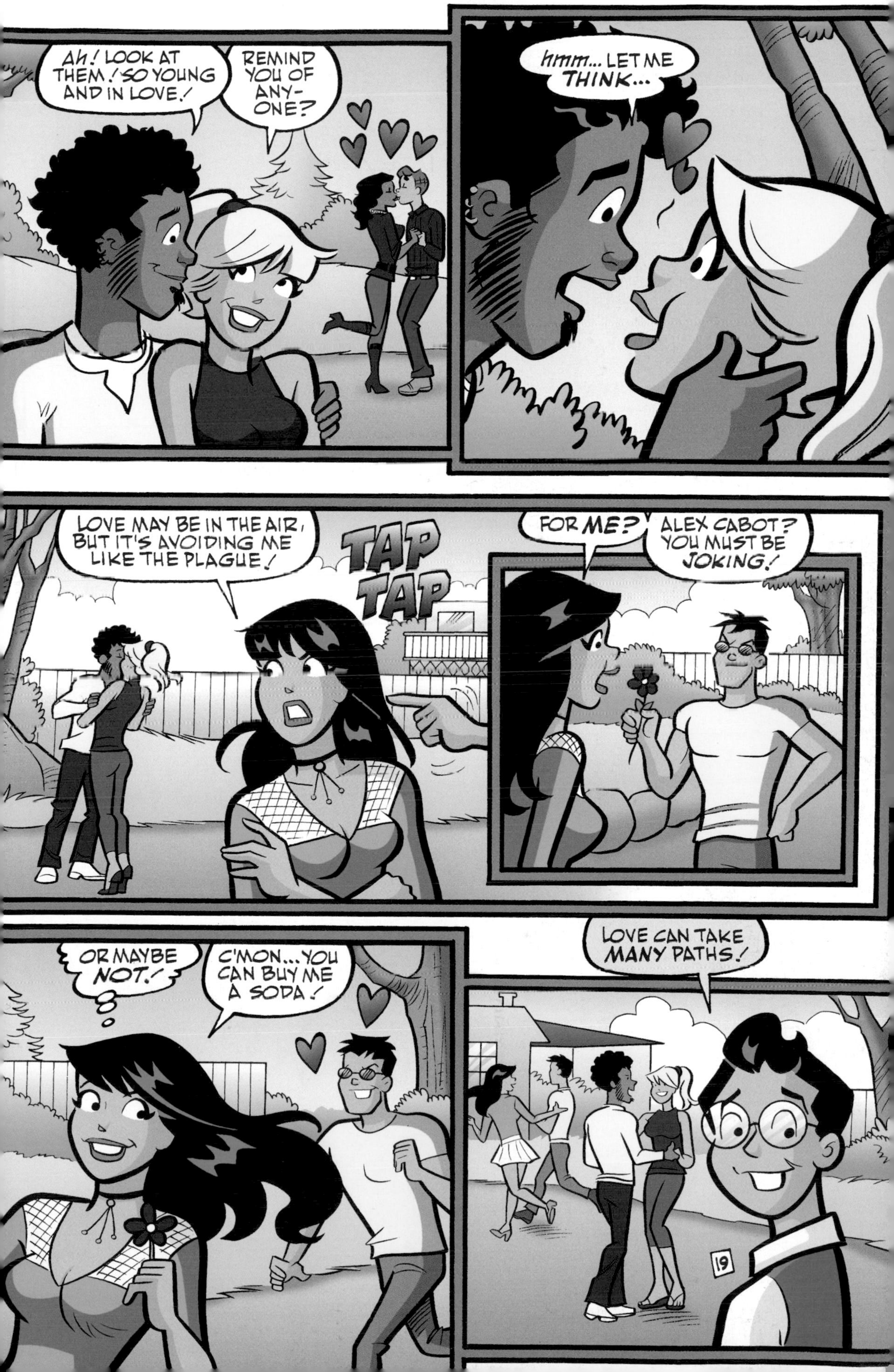

AH! LOOK AT THEM! SO YOUNG AND IN LOVE!
REMIND YOU OF ANY-ONE?
hmm... LET ME THINK...
LOVE MAY BE IN THE AIR, BUT IT'S AVOIDING ME LIKE THE PLAGUE!
TAP TAP
FOR ME?
ALEX CABOT? YOU MUST BE JOKING!
OR MAYBE NOT!
C'MON... YOU CAN BUY ME A SODA!
LOVE CAN TAKE MANY PATHS!
19

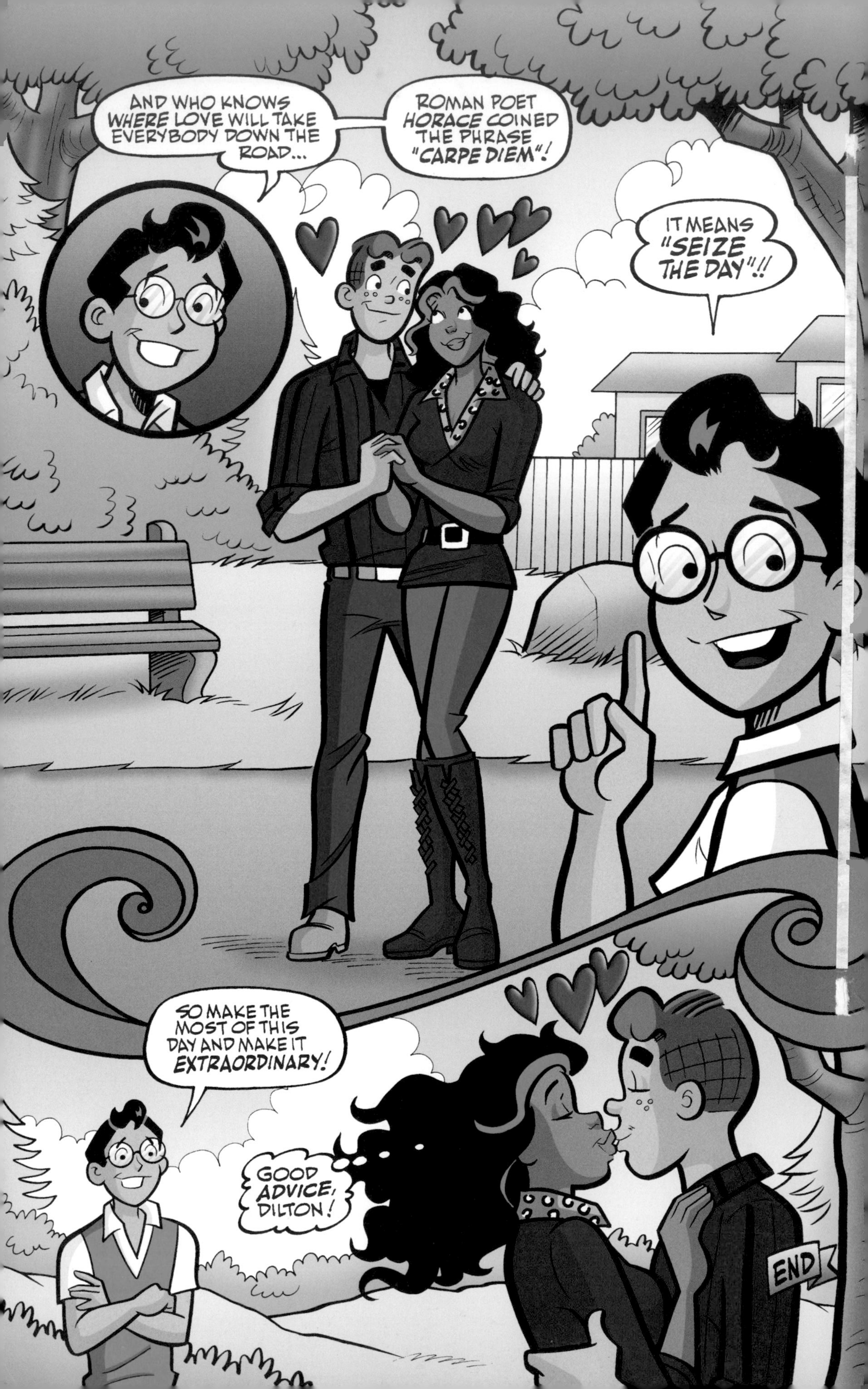
AND WHO KNOWS WHERE LOVE WILL TAKE EVERYBODY DOWN THE ROAD...
ROMAN POET HORACE COINED THE PHRASE "CARPE DIEM"!
IT MEANS "SEIZE THE DAY"!!
SO MAKE THE MOST OF THIS DAY AND MAKE IT EXTRAORDINARY!
GOOD ADVICE, DILTON!
END

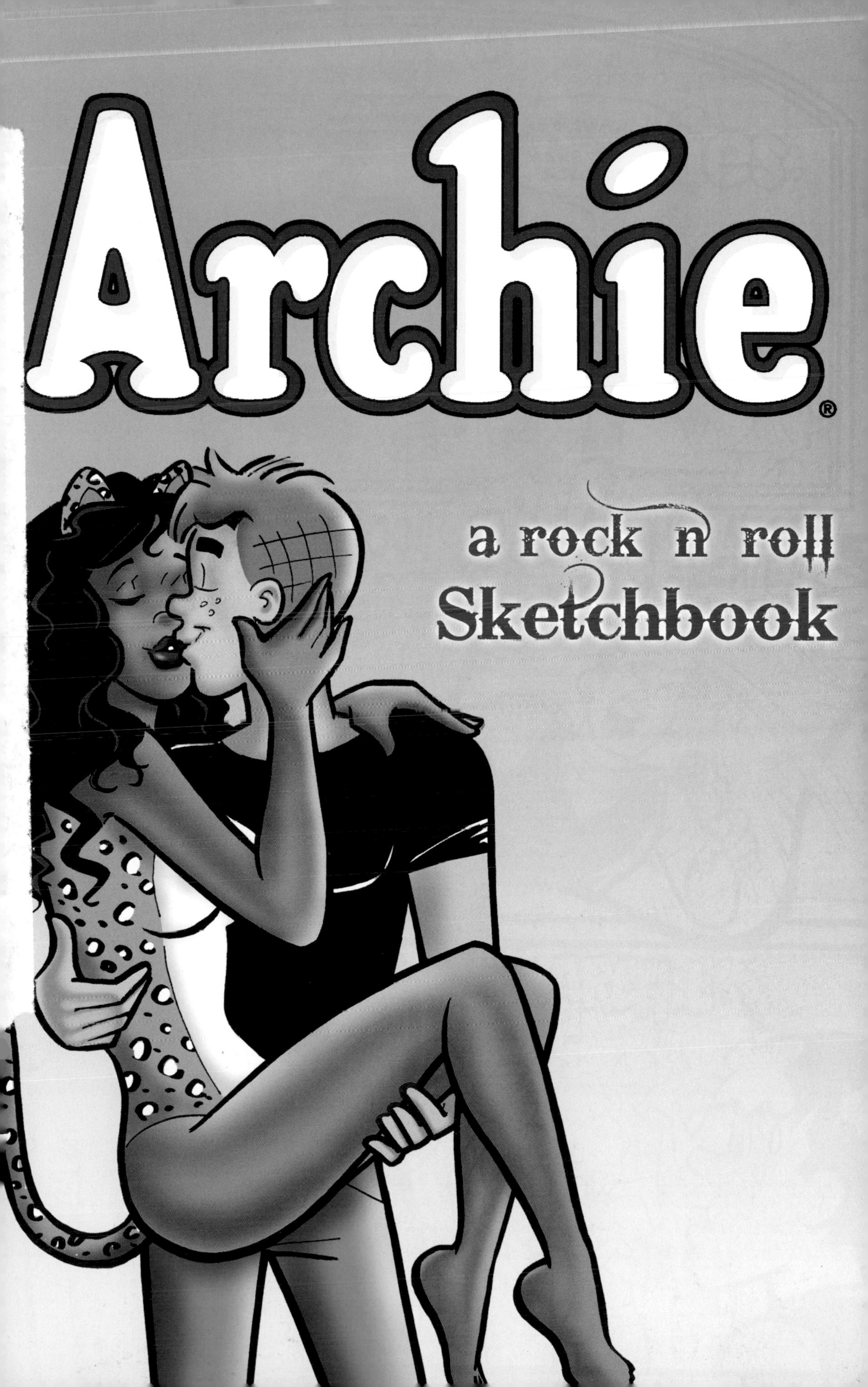
Archie®
a rock n roll Sketchbook

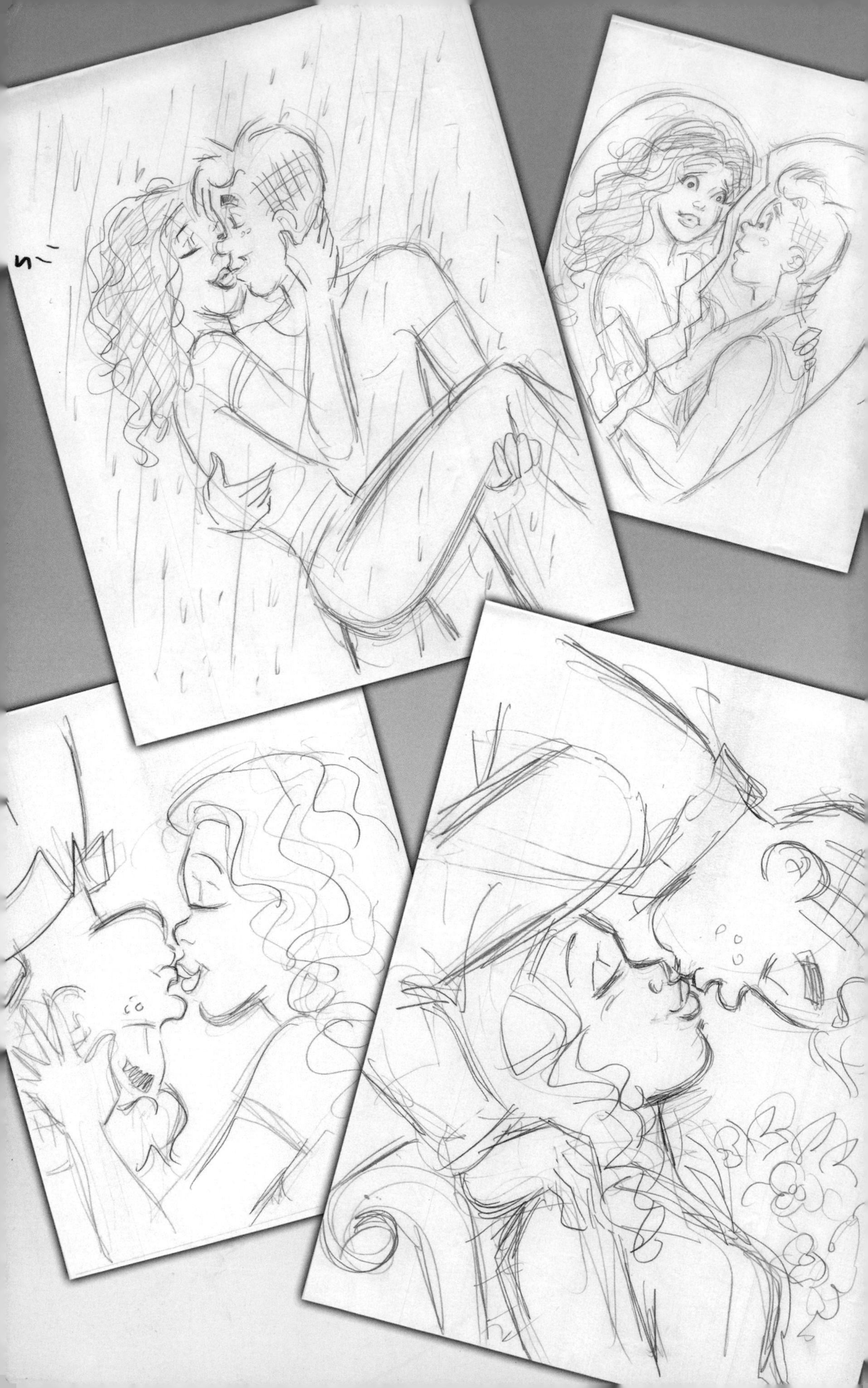

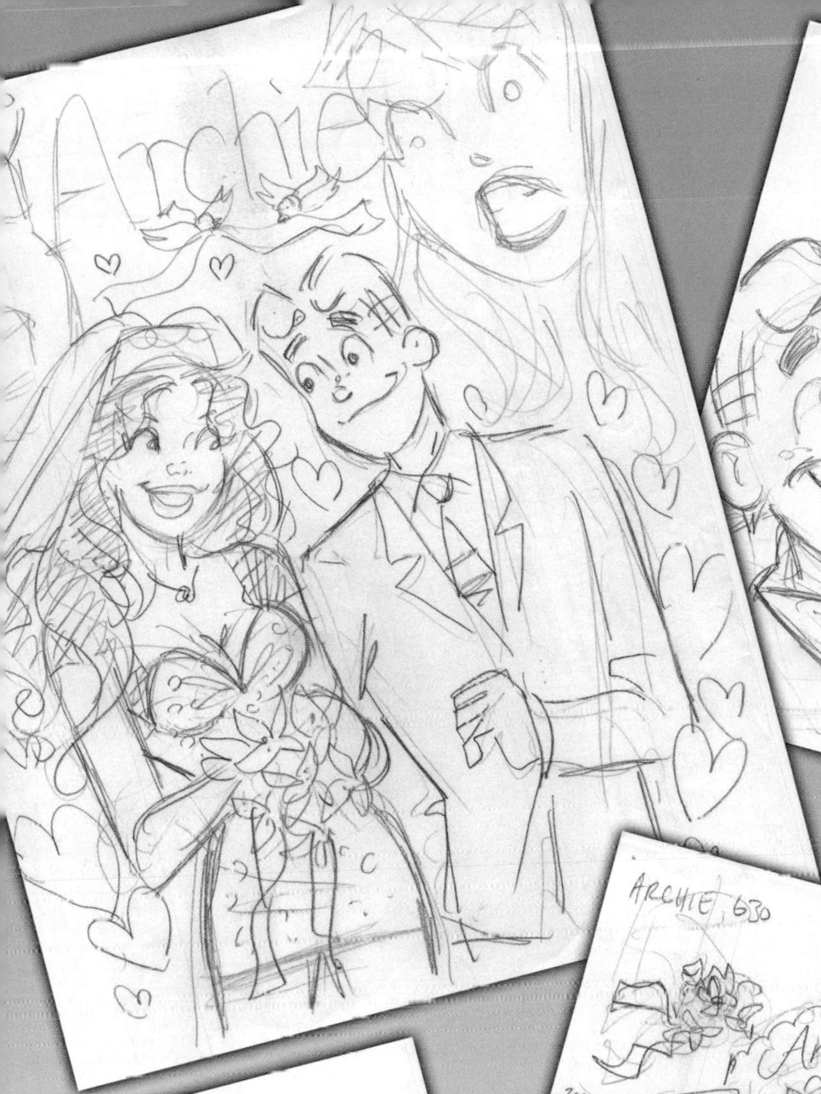
Archie

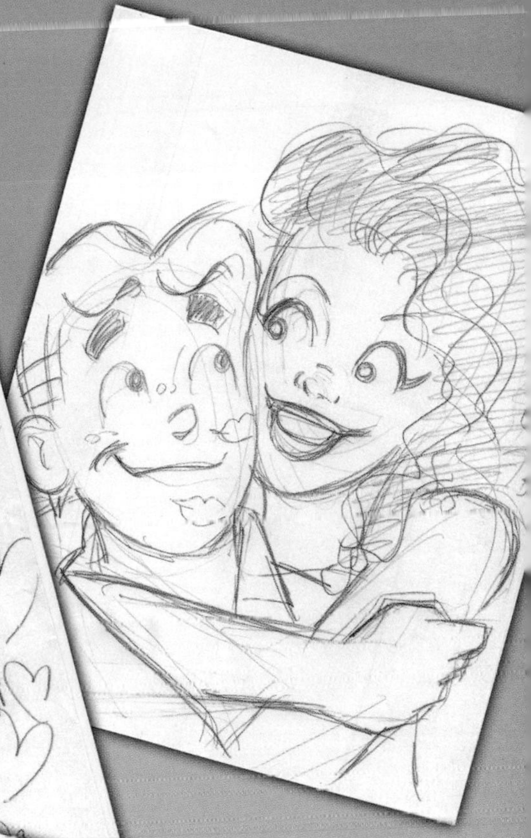

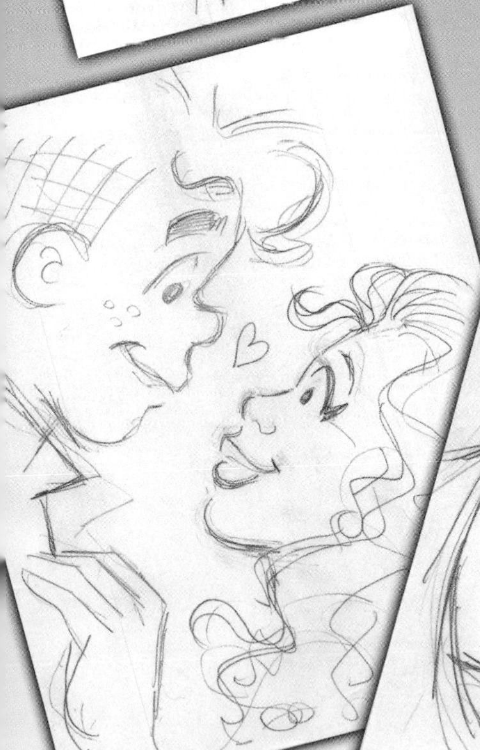

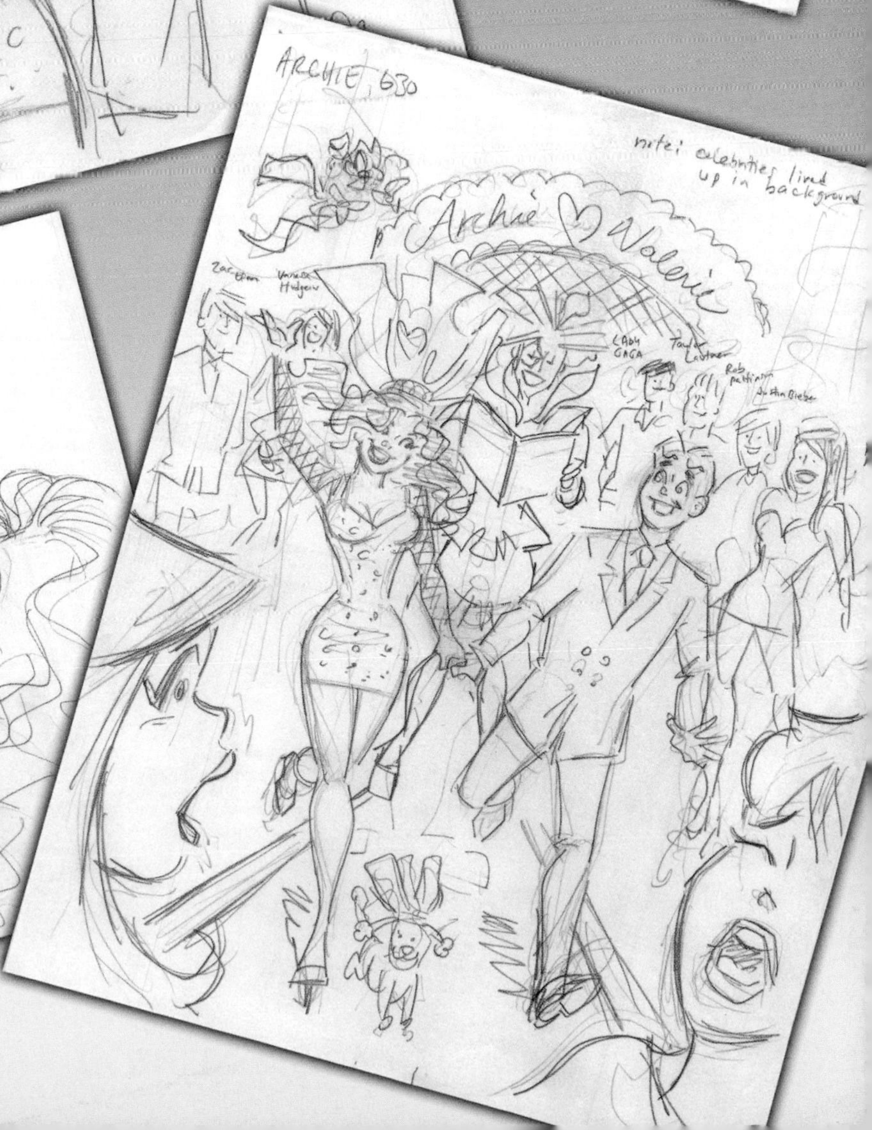
ARCHIE 630
note: celebrities lined up in background
Archie Valerie
Zac Efron
Vanessa Hudgens
LADY GAGA
Taylor Lautner
Rob pattinson
Justin Bieber

Archie: The Married Life Book One

Collecting the first 6 parts of the critically acclaimed Archie Marries... story.

ISBN: 978-1-936975-01-3

Archie: The Married Life Book Two

Collecting parts 7-12 of the critically acclaimed Archie Marries... story.

ISBN: 978-1-879794-99-3

Archie: The Married Life Book Three

Collecting parts 13-18 of the critically acclaimed Archie Marries Betty and Archie Marries Veronica storylines.

ISBN: 978-1-936975-35-8

Archie: The Married Life Book Four

Collecting parts 19-24 of the critically acclaimed Archie Marries Betty and Archie Marries Veronica storylines.

ISBN: 978-1-936975-69-3

Archie: Love Showdown

The epic love triangle is challenged when a rival returns for Archie!

ISBN: 978-1-936975-21-1

The Archie Wedding: Will You Marry Me?

Archie has finally chosen! The winner is... BOTH OF THEM!

ISBN: 978-1-879794-51-1

The Best of Archie Comics

Collecting some of the very best stories from the past 70 years!

ISBN: 978-1-879794-84-9

The Best of Archie Comics: Book Two

Collecting some of the very best stories from the past 70 years!

ISBN: 978-1-936975-20-4